What Christian Authors are Saying about Grace Livingston Hill:

Grace Livingston Hill, oftestian Romance,"
has given millions of reader inspiration,
romance, and adventure. Th ks reminds us
that God has the answer to

—Wand ork Times bestselling author

I've long been a fan of Grace Livingston Hill. Her romance and attention to detail has always captivated me—even as a young girl. I'm excited to see these books will continue to be available to new generations and highly recommend them to readers who haven't yet tried them. And for those of you like me who have read the books, I hope you'll revisit the stories and fall in love with them all over again.

—Tracie Peterson, award-winning, bestselling author of the Song of Alaska and Striking a Match series

Grace Livingston Hill's books are a treasured part of my young adult years. There was such bedrock faith to them along with the fun. Her heroines were intrepid yet vulnerable. Her heroes were pure of heart and noble (unless they needed to be reformed of course). And the books were often adventures. Just writing this makes me want to hunt down and read again a few of my favorites.

—Mary Connealy, Carol Award-winning author of Cowboy Christmas and the Lassoed in Texas series

Grace Livingston Hill books were a big part of my life, from the time I was a teenager and onward. My mother loved her books and shared them with me and my sisters. We always knew we could find an engaging, uplifting story between the covers. And her stories are still enjoyable and encouraging. It's hard to pick a favorite, but The Girl from Montana and Marcia Schuyler are two of my favorites. Terrific stories!

—Susan Page Davis, author of The Ladies' Shooting Club and Prairie Dreams series

The hero, in Grace Livingston Hill's timeless romantic novels, is always a hero. The heroine is always a strong woman who stands up for her beliefs. He is always handsome; she is always beautiful. And an inviting message of faith is woven throughout each story without preaching. These enduring stories will continue to delight a new generation of readers—just as they did for our great-grandmothers.

—Suzanne Woods Fisher, bestselling author of the Lancaster County Secret series

As a young reader just beginning to know what romance was all about, I was introduced to Grace Livingston Hill's books. She created great characters with interesting backgrounds and then plopped them down into fascinating settings where they managed to get into romantic pickles that kept me reading until the love-conquers-all endings. Her romance-filled stories showed this young aspiring writer that yes, love can make the fictional world go round.

—Ann H. Gabhart, award-winning author

My grandmother was an avid reader, and Grace Livingston Hill's books lined her shelves for the years of my childhood and adolescence. Once I dipped into one of them, I was hooked. Years of reading Hill's stories without a doubt influenced my own desire to become a storyteller, and it's with great fondness that I remember many of her titles.

—Tracy L. Higley, author of *Garden of Madness*

If you've enjoyed the classic works of writers like Jane Austen and Georgette Heyer, it is way past time for you to discover the inspirational stories of Grace Livingston Hill!

—Anna Schmidt, award-winning author of
the Women of Pinecraft series

Ah, Grace Livingstone Hill! Can any other writer compare? Her lyrical, majestic tone, her vivid descriptions. . .they melt the heart of readers from every generation. Some of my fondest memories from years gone by involve curling up in my mother's chair and reading her Grace Livington Hill romances. They swept me away to places unknown and reminded me that writers—especially writers of faith—could truly impact their world.

—Janice Hanna Thompson, author of the
Weddings by Bella series

Grace Livingston Hill's stories are like taking a stroll through a garden in the spring: refreshing, fragrant, and delightful—a place you'll never want to leave.

—MaryLu Tyndall, Christy nominee and
author of the Surrender to Destiny series

Enduring stories of hope, triumph over adversity, and true sacrificial love await every time you pick up a Grace Livingston Hill romance.

—Erica Vetsch, author of *A Bride's Portrait of Dodge City, Kansas*

Grace Livingston Hill

*America's Best-Loved
Storyteller*

A NEW NAME

BARBOUR
PUBLISHING

Print ISBN 978-1-61626-653-0

eBook Editions:
Adobe Digital Edition (.epub) 978-1-60742-798-8
Kindle and MobiPocket Edition (.prc) 978-1-60742-799-5

Cover design: Faceout Studio, www.faceoutstudio.com

Published by Barbour Publishing, Inc., P.O. Box 719, Uhrichsville, Ohio 44683, www.barbourbooks.com

Our mission is to publish and distribute inspirational products offering exceptional value and biblical encouragement to the masses.

Member of the
Evangelical Christian
Publishers Association

Printed in the United States of America.

Chapter 1

1920s,
Eastern United States

Murray Van Rensselaer had been waiting for an hour and a quarter in the reception room of the Blakeley Hospital.

He was not good at waiting. Things usually came at his call, or sometimes even anticipated his desires. It was incredible that he should suddenly find himself in such a maddening set of circumstances!

He still wore the great fur-lined overcoat in which he had arrived after the accident, but he seemed to be unaware of it as he paced excitedly up and down the stark leather-upholstered room.

Across the marble corridor he could just see the tip of white, starched linen that was the cap of the uniformed person with bifocals who sat at the rolltop desk and presided over this fiend-ish place.

Three times he had pranced pompously across the tessellated floor and demanded to know what had become of the patient he had brought in. She had only looked him over coldly, im-personally, and reiterated that word would be sent to him as soon as the examination was completed. Even his name, which he had condescendingly mentioned, had failed to make the slightest impression upon her. She had merely filed his immaculate calling card and ordered him back to the reception room.

The tall clock in the corner, the only live thing in the room, seemed to tick in eons, not seconds. He regarded it belligerently. Why should a clock seem to have eyes that searched to your soul? What was a clock doing there anyway, in a place where they regarded not time, and were absorbed in their own terrible affairs? The clock seemed to be the only connecting link with the out-side world.

He strode nearer and read the silver plate of the donor, inscribed in memory of "Elizabeth," and turned sharply back to the door again with a haunting vision of the white-faced girl he had brought in awhile before. Bessie! Little Bessie Chapparelle! She was "Elizabeth" too.

What a cute kid she had been when he first knew her! Strange that on this day of all days he should have come upon her standing at that corner after all these years, suddenly grown up and stunningly beautiful!

And now she lay crumpled, somewhere up in those distant marble halls!

He shuddered in his heavy coat and mopped the cold perspiration from his brows. If anything should happen to Bessie! And his fault! Everybody would of course say it was his fault! He knew he was a reckless driver. He knew he took chances, but he had always gotten by before! If she hadn't been so darned pretty, so surprisingly sweet and unusual, and like the child she used to be—and that truck coming around the corner at thirty-five miles an hour!

The air was full of antiseptics. It seemed to him that he had been breathing it in until his head was swimming, that cold, pungent, penetrating smell that dwelt within those white marble walls like a living spirit of the dead!

Gosh! What a place! Why did he stay? He could go home and telephone later. Nobody was compelling him to stay. Bessie was a poor girl with nobody to take her side. Nobody but her mother!

He halted in his excited walk. *Her mother!* If anything happened to Bessie, somebody would have to tell her mother!

A door opened far away in the upper marble regions, and the echo of a delirious cry shivered down through the corridors. Rubber wheels somewhere rolled a heavy object down a space and out of hearing; voices rose in a subdued murmur as if they passed a certain point and drifted away from the main speech, drifted down the stairs, vague, detached words. Then all was still again.

Something dragged at his heart. He had thought they were

coming, and now suddenly he was afraid to have them come. What a relief! Just a little longer respite till he could get ahold of himself. He wasn't at all fit, or things wouldn't get ahold of him this way. He had been going pretty hard since he left college. Too many highballs! Too late at night!—Too many cigarettes! The old man was right! If he hadn't been so infernally offensive in the way he put it! But one couldn't of course go that pace forever and not feel it.

What was it he had been thinking about when those voices passed that point above the stairs? Oh! Yes! Her mother! Someone would have to tell her mother! She was a woman with a kind twinkle in her eyes. One would find it terrible to quench that twinkle in her eyes! He remembered how she had bandaged his cut finger one day and given him a cookie. Those were happy days!—Ah! *There!* There was that sound of an opening door again!—Voices!—Footsteps! Listen! They were coming! Yes—they were coming! Rubber heels on marble treads! And now he was in a frenzy of fear.

Bessie, little blue-eyed Bessie with the gold hair all about her white face!—

The steps came on down the hall, and he held his breath in the shelter of a heavy tan-colored velvet curtain. He must get himself in hand before he faced anyone. If he only hadn't left his flask in the car! Oh, but of course! The car was wrecked! What was he thinking about? But there would be other flasks! If only he could get out of this!

The nurse came on down the hall. He could see her reflection in the plate glass of the front door that was within his vision as he stood with his back toward the desk. She was going straight to the desk with a message!

The front doorknob rattled.

He glared impatiently at the blurred interruption to his vision of the nurse. A sallow man with a bandaged head was fumbling with the doorknob, and the white uniform of the nurse was no longer plain. He held his breath and listened:

"Well, is there any change?" asked the voice behind the rolltop desk, impassively.

"Yes, she's dead!" answered the nurse.

"Well, you'd better go down to that man in the reception room. He's been pestering the life out of me. He thinks he's the only one—

"I can't!" said the nurse sharply. "I've got to call up the police station first. The doctor said—" She lowered her voice inaudibly. The man with the bandaged head had managed the doorknob at last.

The door swung wide, noiselessly, on its well-oiled hinges, letting in the bandaged man; and as he limped heavily in, a shadow slipped from the folds of the heavy curtain and passed behind him into the night.

Chapter 2

In the big white marble house on the avenue that Murray Van Rensselaer called home, the servants were lighting costly lamps and drawing silken shades. A little Pekingese pet came tiptoeing out with one man to see what was the matter with the light over the front entrance, stood for a brief second glancing up and down haughtily, barked sharply at a passerby, and retreated plumily into the dark of the entrance hall with an air of ownership, clicking off to find his mistress. Sweet perfumes drifted out from shadowy rooms where masses of hothouse flowers glowed in costly jardinières, and a wood fire flickered softly over deep-toned rugs and fine old polished woods, reflected from illuminated covers of many rare books behind leaded panes of glass. It flickered and lighted the dreary face of the haughty master of the house as he sat in a deep chair and watched the flames, and seemed to be watching the burning out of his own life in bitter disappointment.

The great dining room glittered with crystal and silver, and abounded in exquisite table linen, hand-wrought, beautiful and fine as a spider's web or a tracery of frost. The table was set for a large dinner, and a profusion of roses graced its center.

Ancestral portraits looked down from the walls.

At one end of the room, in a screened balcony behind great fronds of mammoth ferns, musicians were preparing to play, arranging music, speaking in low tones.

The footsteps of the servants were inaudible as they came and went over the deep pile of ancient rugs.

A deep-throated chime from a tall old clock in the hall called out the hour, and a bell somewhere in the distance rang sharply, imperatively.

A maid came noiselessly down the stairs and paused beside the library door, tapping gently.

"Mr. Van Rensselaer, Mrs. Van Rensselaer would like to see you at once if you're not busy."

The wistful look in the master's eyes changed at the summons into his habitual belligerence, and he rose with a sigh of impatience. He mounted the stairs like one going to a familiar stake.

Mrs. Van Rensselaer sat at her dressing table fresh from the hands of her maid, a perfectly groomed woman in the prime of her life. Not a wrinkle marred the loveliness of her complexion, not a line of tenderness, or suffering, or self-abnegation gave character to her exquisite features. She had been considered the most beautiful woman of the day when Charles Van Rensselaer married her, and she still retained her beauty. No one, not even her bitterest enemy, could say that she had aged or faded. Her face and her figure were her first concern. She never let anything come between her and her ambition to remain young and lovely.

If her meaningless beauty had long since palled upon the man who had worked hard in his younger days to win her hand, he nevertheless yielded her the pomp which she demanded; and if there was sometimes a note of mock ceremony in his voice, it was well guarded.

He stood in the violet shadow of her silken-shrouded lamp and watched her with a bitter sadness in his eyes. It was a moment when they might have met on common ground and drawn nearer to one another if she had but sensed it. But she was busy trying the effect of different earrings against her pearly tinted neck. Should it be the new rock crystals or the jade, or should she wear the Van Rensselaer emeralds after all?

She turned at last, as if just aware that he had come in, and spoke in an annoyed tone: "Charles, you really will have to speak to Murray again."

She turned to get the effect of the jewel and tilted her chin haughtily.

"He is simply *unspeakable!*"

She held up her hand mirror and turned her head the other way to get a look at the other ear.

Her husband drew a deep, fortifying breath, wet his lips nervously with the tip of his tongue the way a dog does when he is expecting a whipping, and braced himself for action.

"What's Murray been doing now?" he asked crisply, belligerently. There was fight in his eye and a set to his jaw, although the lean cheekbones just below the eyes seemed to wince as at a blow.

"Why, he's making himself conspicuous again with that lowdown De Flora woman. Marian Stewart has been telling me that he took her to the Assembly last night and danced every dance with her. And it's got to stop! I'm not going to have our name dragged in the dust by my own son."

"But I don't understand," said her husband dryly. "You didn't object when he did the same thing with the Countess Lenowski, and she was twice divorced. I spoke of it then, for it seemed to me morals were more in your line than mine, but you thought it was all right. I'm sure I don't see what you can expect of him now when you sanctioned that two years ago."

"Now, Charles! Don't be tiresome! The Countess Lenowski was a very different person. Rich as Croesus, and titled, and beautiful and young. You can't blame the poor child for being divorced from men who were seeking her merely for her money!"

"The Countess Lenowski is neither so young nor so innocent as she would have everybody believe, and I told you at the time that her beauty wasn't even skin deep. I don't get your fine distinctions. What's the matter with this De Flora woman? Isn't she rich? Doesn't your son think she's beautiful? And she's young enough. They say she's never been married at all, let alone divorced. I made a point to look into that."

"Now, Charles, you're being difficult! That's all there is to it. You're just trying to be difficult! And there's no use talking to you when you get difficult. You know as well as I do what that De Flora woman is. Some little insignificant movie actress, not even a star! With all Murray's money and family, of course, every little upstart is simply flinging herself at him, and you must speak to him! You really must. Let him know his allowance will stop and he can't have any more cars unless he behaves himself!"

"And why must I be the one to speak? I left all questions of social and moral obligations to you when he was young. I am sure it is late in the day for me to meddle now."

"Now, Charles, you are being difficult again. You are quibbling. I called you up to let you know that Murray needs advice, and you're to give it! That's all! It's time you were dressing. We have a dinner, you remember. The Arlingtons and the Schuylers. Do be ready. It's so tiresome to have to wait for you."

Thus dismissed, the head of the house looked at his wife's slim young back and well-cut coiffure with an expression of mingled scorn and despair, which she might have seen in her mirror if she had not been too much absorbed with her own image, but it is doubtful she would have understood if she had seen it. It was because he had long ago recognized her obtuseness in these fine points that Charles Van Rensselaer had been able to maintain his habitual air of studied mock politeness. Her name was Violet, and she knew she could count always on courtesy from him, no matter how his eyes mocked. With that she was content.

He watched her a full minute, noting the grace of movement as she turned her head from side to side perfecting the details of her contour, marked the luster of her amber hair, the sweep of lovely white shoulder against the low severe line of her dinner gown, looked almost wistfully, like a child, for something more, something tender, something gentler than her last words, less cold and formal; yet he knew he would not get it. He had always been watching for something more from her than he knew he could ever get; something more than he knew she possessed. Just because she was outwardly lovely, it seemed as if there must be something beautiful hidden within her somewhere that some miracle would sometime bring forth. The love of his early youth believed that, would always cling to it, thinking that sometime it would be revealed—yet knowing it was an impossibility for which he hoped.

With a sigh almost inaudible he turned and went down the heavily carpeted hall, followed by the trail of her impatient cold words: "Oh, are you there yet? Why won't you hurry? I know you'll be late!"

He shut the great mahogany door behind him with a dull thud. He would have liked to have slammed it, but the doors in that house could not slam. They were too heavy and too well hung on their oiled hinges. It shut him in like a vault to a costly room where everything had been done for his comfort, yet comfort was not. He did not hasten even yet. He went and stood at the window looking out, looking down to the area below, to the paved alleyway that ran between the blocks and gave access to the back door and the garage. A row of brick houses on the side street ended at that alleyway, and a light twinkled in a kitchen window where a woman's figure moved to and fro between a table and the stove—a pleasant, cheery scene reminding one of homecoming and sweet domesticity, a thing he had always yearned for yet never found since he was a little child in his father's home at the farm, with a gentle mother living and a house full of boisterous, loving brothers and sisters. He watched the woman wistfully. What if Violet had been a woman like that, who would set the table for supper and go about the stove preparing little dishes? He laughed aloud bitterly at the thought. Violet in her slim dinner gown, her dangling earrings, and her french bob, risking her lily-and-rose complexion over a fire!

He turned sharply back to his room, snapped on the electric light, and went and stood before the two great silver frames that adorned his dressing table. One held the picture of the lovely delicate woman, almost a girl in appearance, smart, artistic, perfect as the world counts perfection. It was a part of her pride that placed her picture in his room for others to see his devotion, and had it changed each time a new picture that pleased her was taken. His pleasure in her picture had long ago vanished, but he studied her face now with that yearning look in his own, as if again he searched for the thing that was not there, as if his eyes would force from the photograph a quality that the soul must be hiding.

Then with a long sigh he turned to the other frame—the young, careless, handsome face of his son, Murray Montgomery

Van Rensselaer. That honored name! How proud he had been when they gave it to his child! What dreams he had had that his son would add still more honor to that name!

He studied the handsome face intently, searching there for the thing he could not find in the mother's face. How alike they were, those two, who belonged to him, yet were to him almost as strangers—one might almost say as enemies sometimes, when they combined to break his will or his request.

Yet of the two the boy was nearest to him. There had been times when Murray was very young that they had grown almost close—fishing excursions, and a hike or two, a camping trip—rare times, broken up always by Violet, who demanded their attention and resented rough things for her son.

The boy's face was too slender, too girlish, almost effeminate, yet behind it there was a daredevil in his eyes that suggested something more rugged, more manly, perhaps, when he would settle down. The father kept wishing, hoping, that the thing he had not found to satisfy his longing in his wife would someday develop in his son, and then they might be all in all to one another.

With another deep sigh he turned away and began mechanically to dress for the evening, his mind not on what he was doing. But then why should it be when everything was laid out for him? It required no thought. He was thinking about Murray. How they had spoiled him between them! Violet indulging him and repressing all his natural bent toward simple, natural things, molding him into a young fop, insisting on alternately coddling and scolding him, never loving to him even in her indulgence, always cold and unsympathetic toward all that did not go the way she chose.

For himself, he had been so bitterly disappointed in the lad that the years had brought about an attitude of habitual disapproval, as high and as wide and as separating as any stone wall that was ever built. Yet the father's heart ached for his son, and the years were growing bleak with his denial. Why did the boy choose only folly? Scrapes in school and worse in college. Clubs and sports and drinking affairs. Speeding and women and idleness! What a life! What would the grandsire who had founded the ancient and honorable house and had given them the honored name think of such an heir? Yet what could one expect with a mother such as he had given his son?

He gave a last comprehensive survey of his well-groomed self and turned out the light. With deliberate intent he walked across to the window again and looked out to that bright little kitchen window across the alley.

Darkness had dropped down upon the city since he had lighted his room, evening complete, and the little bright window with its aproned figure moving steadily back and forth with brisk step between stove and table stood out clearly in the crisp night. He could see the knife in her hand as she stirred something in a pan on the stove. He could see the foaming pitcher of milk she put in the center of the white-draped table. He could see a griddle over the flame, with blue smoke rising from it. Pancakes. They were going to have pancakes for supper! His mother used to have pancakes for supper when he was a little lad out at the old farm, pancakes with maple syrup! How he wished he could go over there to the little two-story redbrick house and sit down at that white table and eat some. There would be syrup like amber perhaps in a glass pitcher, and how good they would taste! What would they say if he were to go over and ask if he might eat supper with them? What would Violet say if he should go? Leave her abominable, interminable dinner party and go over to that quiet kitchen to eat pancakes! Violet would think he was crazy—would perhaps take steps to put him in the insane asylum, would at least consult a physician. What a fraud life was! A man was never his own master in this world!

A servant tapped at the door.

"Mrs. Van Rensselaer says will you please come down at once. The guests have arrived."

There was a smack of insolence in the maid's voice. She knew who was mistress in that house.

As he turned away from the simple vision, a figure stole down the alley, furtively looking this way and that, and slipped like a shadow close to the bright kitchen window, peering in, a white anxious face, with a cap drawn low over the eyes, and a reckless set to the expensive coat worn desperately hunched above crouching shoulders.

If Charles Van Rensselaer had lingered just a second longer at the window, he might have seen that creeping figure, might have—!

But he turned sharply at the servant's call and went down to play the polished host, to entertain his unwelcome guests with witty sarcasm and sharp repartee, to give the lie to his heart sorrow, and one more proof to the world that he belonged to a great and old family and bore a name that meant riches and fame and honor wherever he went.

Chapter 3

When Murray Van Rensselaer slid out from the hospital door into the night, he had no fixed idea of where he was going or what he was going to do. His main thought was to get away.

It had been years since he had had to walk anywhere, much less run. There had always been the car. But the car was in pieces, and he dared not take a taxi. His feet, so long unused for real work, were nimble enough in dancing and in all sorts of sports, but now when necessity was upon him, somehow they seemed to fail him. They lagged when he would hasten forward. It seemed to him he crawled.

The blocks ahead of him looked miles away. When he came to another corner and rounded it into the next street he felt a great achievement, yet shrank from the new street, lest he meet some acquaintance. It was impressed on him with letters of fire, written with a pen of iron in his soul that he was a murderer, and he must escape from justice. Therefore his unwilling feet were carrying him through the night to a place he knew not, to a place he would not. It came to him suddenly that he despised himself for fleeing this way, but that he knew his own soul, and that it was not in him to stand and face a murder trial. He could not bear the scorn in his beautiful mother's face, the bitterness in his father's eyes. He shrank from the jeers or pity of his companions, from the gentle, sad eyes of Bessie's mother, from the memory of Bessie's white face. He could not face a court and a jury, nor fight to save his life. He could not bear the horror of the punishment that would be measured out to him. Even though money might make the penalty light, never again could he face the world and be proud of his old family name and carry out life with others with a high hand because he was Murray Van Rensselaer; because he had a right to be deferred to, and to rule others, because he had been born into a good and honorable and revered family. He had severed connection with that family! He had smirched the name he bore! He had ruined himself for life! He was a murderer!

These thoughts pursued him through the night as he hurried onward, not knowing where he went.

Cars shot by him in the street. Twice he ducked away because a familiar face looked out at him from some passing vehicle. Like a dart the thought went through him that he could go their way no longer, be in their world no more. He must always shy away from the face of man. He would never be free again! He had lost everything! The brand of Cain was upon him! Who was Cain?

Where had he heard that phrase, "the brand of Cain"?

And then he came within the shadow of his own home.

He had been busy with his terrible thoughts. He had not been thinking where he was going, not realizing where his frantic feet were carrying him. Now as he turned the corner sharply, almost knocking over another pedestrian in his flight, he saw the great marble structure ahead of him; its shaded lights, its dim familiar beauty, its aloofness, its pride, impressed him for the first time. What had he done? Brought down the pride of this great house! Blighted his own life! He did not want to come here! He must not come here! The marble of the walls was as unfriendly and aloof as the marble halls from which he had fled. The cold clarity of the ether still clung to his garments like the aroma of the grave. Why had his feet carried him here, where there was no hiding for him, no city of refuge in that costly marble edifice? His father and his mother were bitter against him anyway for past offenses. Little follies they seemed to him now beside the thing that he had so unwittingly done. Had some devil led him here to show him first what he had lost before it flung him far away from all he had held dear in life?

Yet he could not turn another way. It seemed he must go on. And now as he passed the house, across the way a shining car drew up, and people in evening coats got out and went in, and he remembered. There was to have been a dinner—his mother had begged him to come—Gwendolen Arlington—she was the girl in coral with the silver shoes—a pretty girl—how she would shrink from him now! She must not see him—! He shied around the corner as if some evil power propelled him in a vain attempt to get away into some dark cranny of the earth—Gwendolen—she would be sitting at his mother's table, in his place perhaps, and his chair vacant beside her—oh no, his mother would supply someone else, and he perhaps—where would he be? While the news boys on the street cried out his name in shame—and his mother smiled her painted smile, and his father said the glittering sarcasms he was famous for, and he—was out in the cold and dark—*forever*!

Not that he had ever cared particularly for home, until now, when it was taken from him! There had always been a hunger in his heart for something different. But now that he was suddenly alienated from all he knew, it became strangely precious.

Ah! Now he knew where the devil was carrying him. The old alley! Bessie's house! He knew deep in his heart he could not have gotten away without coming here. He would have to see it all to carry it with him forever, and always be seeing what he had destroyed. Yes, there was the kitchen window, the shutters open. Mrs. Chapparelle never closed those shutters while Bessie was out. It was a sort of signal that all was well in the house, and every child safely in when those shutters were closed. He could remember as a little boy when he watched from his fourth-story back nursery window, always with a feeling of disappointment when those shutters that shut out the cheeriness of the Chapparelle home were closed for the night.

Yes, and there was the flat stone where he and Bessie used to play jacks under the gutter pipe, just as of old. He hadn't been out in the alley since he came back from college, and that was before he went to Europe. It must be six or seven years now! How had he let these dear friends get away from him this way? His mother of course had managed at first. She never liked him to go to the side street for company—but later, he had chosen his own companions, and he might have gone back. Why hadn't he?

Somehow, as he made his stealthy way down the paved walled alley, thoughts came flocking, and questions demanded an answer as if they had a personality, and he was led where he would not.

Surely he did not want to come here now of all times. Come and see this home from which he had taken the sunshine, the home that he had wrecked and brought to sorrow! Yet he must.

Like a thief he stole close and laid his white face against the window pane, his eyes straining to see every detail, as if precious things had been lost from his sight and must be caught at, and all fragments possible rescued, as if he would in this swift vision make amends for all his years of neglect.

Yes, there she was, going about getting supper just as he remembered, stirring at a great bowl of batter. There would be pancakes. He could smell the appetizing crispness of the one she was baking to test, to see if the batter was just right. How he and Bessie used to hover and beg for these test cakes, and roll them around a bit of butter and eat them from their hands, delicious bits of brown hot crispness, like no other food he had ever tasted since. Buckwheats. That was the name they called them. They never had buckwheats at his home. Sometimes he had tried to get them at restaurants and hotels, but they brought him sections of pasty hot blankets instead that had no more resemblance to the real things than a paper rose to a real one. Yes, there was the pitcher of milk, foaming and rich, the glass syrup jug with the little silver squirrel on the lid to hold it up—how familiar and homely and dear it all was! And Bessie—Bessie—lying still and white in the hospital, and the police hunting the city over for her murderer!

Somebody must tell her mother!

He looked at the mother's face, a little thinner, a trifle grayer than when he knew her so well and she had tied up his cut finger. The crinkles in her hair where it waved over her small fine ears were sprinkled with many silver threads. He remembered thinking she had prettier ears than his mother, and wondering about it because he knew that his mother was considered very beautiful. She wore an apron with a bib. The kitten used to run after her and play with the apron strings sometimes, and pull them till they were untied and hung behind. There was an old cat curled sedately on a chair by the sink. Could that be the same kitten? How long did cats live? Life! Death! Bessie was dead, and there was her mother going about making hotcakes for supper, expecting Bessie to come in pretty soon and sit at that white table and eat them! But Bessie would never come in and eat at that table again. Bessie was dead, and he had killed her! He, her murderer, was daring to stand there and look in at that little piece of heaven on earth that he had ruined.

He groaned aloud and rested his forehead on the windowsill.

"Oh God! I never meant to do it!" The words were forced from his lips, perhaps the first prayer those lips had ever made. He did not know it was a prayer.

The cat stirred and pricked up its ears, opening its eyes toward the window, and Mrs. Chapparelle paused and glanced that way, but the white face visible but a moment before was resting on the windowsill out of sight.

The busy hum of the city murmured on outside the alley where he stood, but he heeded it not. He stood overwhelmed with a sense of shame. It was something he had never experienced before. Always anything he had done before, any scrape he found himself in, it had been sufficient to him to fall back on his family. The old, honored name that he bore had seen him through every difficulty so far, and might even this time if it were exerted to its utmost. Had Bessie been a stranger, it would probably have been his refuge still. But Bessie was not a stranger, and there was grace enough in his heart to know that never to his own self could he excuse, or pass over, what he had done to her and to her kind, sweet mother, who had so often mothered him in the years that were past.

A little tinkling bell broke the spell that was upon him—the old-fashioned doorbell in the Chapparelle kitchen just above the door that led to the front of the house. He started and lifted his head. He could see the vibration of the old bell on its rusty spring just as he had watched it in wonder the first time he had seen it as a child. Mrs. Chapparelle was hastening with her quick step to open the door. He caught the flutter of her apron as she passed into the hall. And what would she meet at the door? Were they bringing Bessie's body home, so soon—! Or was it merely someone sent to break the news? Oh, he ought to have prepared her for it. He ought to be in there now lying at her feet and begging her forgiveness, helping her to bear the awful sorrow that he had brought upon her. She had been kind to him, and he ought to be brave enough to face things and do anything there was to do—but instead he was flying down the alley on feet that trembled so much they could scarcely bear his weight, feet that were leaden and would not respond to the desperate need that was upon him, feet that seemed to clatter on the smooth cement as if they were made of steel. Someone would hear him. They would be after him. No one else would dash that way from a house of sorrow save a murderer! Coward! He was a *coward*! A sneak and a coward!

And he loved Bessie! Yes, he knew now that was why he was so glad when he saw her standing on the corner after all those years—glad she finally yielded to his request and rode with him, because she had suddenly seemed to him the desire of his heart, the conclusion of all the scattered loves and longings of his young life. How pretty she had been! And now she was dead!

His heart cried out to be with her, to cry into her little dead ear that he was sorry, to make her know before she was utterly gone, before her visible form was gone out of this earth, how he wished he was back in the childhood days with her to play with always. He drew a breath like a sob as he hurried along, and a passerby turned and looked after him. With a kind of sixth sense he understood that he had laid himself open to suspicion, and cut sharply down another turn into a labyrinth of streets, making hairbreadth escapes, dashing between taxis, scuttling down dark alleys, and across vacant lots, once diving through a garage in mad haste with the hope of finding a car he could hire, and then afraid to ask anyone about it. And all the time something in his soul was lashing him with scorn. Coward! Coward! it called him. Bearing a lofty name, wearing the insignia of wealth and culture, yet too low to go back and face his mistakes and follies, too low to face the woman he had robbed of her child and tell her how troubled his own heart was and confess his sin.

Murray Van Rensselaer had been used to boasting that he was not afraid of anything. But he was afraid now! He was fleeing from the retribution that he was sure was close upon his footsteps. Something in his heart wanted to go back and do the manly thing but could not! His very feet were afraid and would not obey. He had no power in him to do anything but flee!

Chapter 4

$\mathcal{S}$ometime in the night he found himself walking along a country road. How he got there or what hour it was he did not know. He was wearier than he had ever been in his life before. The expensive shoes he was wearing were not built for the kind of jaunt he had been taking. He had been dressed for an afternoon of frivolity when he started out from home. There had been the possibility of stopping almost anywhere before dinnertime, and he had not intended a hike when he dressed. His shoes pierced him with stabs of pain every step he took. They were soaked with water from a stream he had forded somewhere. It was very hazy in his mind whether the stream had been in the gutter of the city where the outflow from a fire engine had been flooding down the street or whether he had sometime crossed a brook since he left the outskirts of town. Either of these things seemed possible. The part of him that did the thinking seemed to have been asleep and was just coming awake painfully.

He was wet to the skin with perspiration and was exhausted in every nerve and sinew. He wanted nothing in life so much as a hot shower and a bed for twenty-four hours. He was hungry and thirsty. Oh! *Thirsty!* He would give his life for a drink! Yet he dared not try to find one. And now he knew it had been a brook he had waded, for he remembered stooping down and lapping water from his hand. But it had not satisfied. He wanted something stronger. His nerves under the terrible strain of the last few hours were crying out for stimulant. He had not even a cigarette left—and he dared not go near enough to human habitation to purchase any. Oh yes, he had money, a whole roll of it. He felt in his pocket to make sure. He had taken it out of his bank that morning, cashed the whole of his allowance check, to pay several bills that had been hounding him, things he did not want Dad to know about. Of course there were those things he had bought for Bessie and had sent to her. He was glad he had done that much for her before he killed her. Yet what good would it ever do her now? She was dead. And her mother would never know where they came from. Indeed Bessie would not know either. He had told her they were for a friend and he wanted her help in selecting them. Perhaps Bessie would not have liked his gift after all. He had not thought of that before. Girls of her class—but she was not any class—no type that he knew—just one of her kind, so how could he judge? But somehow it dawned upon him that Bessie would not have taken expensive gifts even from him, an old friend. That entered his consciousness with a dull thud of disappointment. But then, Bessie would never know now that he had sent them. Or did they know after death? Was there a hereafter? He knew Mrs. Chapparelle believed in one. She used to talk about heaven as if it were another room, a best room, where she would one day go and dress up all the time in white. At least that was what his childish imagination had gleaned from the stories she used to read to him and Bessie. But then, if Bessie knew about the gifts, she would also know his heart—Wait! Would he want her to know his heart—all his life?

He groaned aloud and then held his breath lest the night had heard him. Oh, he was crazy! He must find a spot to lie down, or else he might as well go and give himself up to justice. He was not fit to protect himself. He was foolish with sleep.

He crept into a wood at last, on a hillside above the road, and threw himself down exhausted among some bushes quite hidden from the road in the darkness.

He was not conscious of anything as he drifted away into exhausted sleep. It was as if he with all his overwhelming burden of disgrace and horror and fear was being dragged down through the ooze of the earth out of sight forever, being obliterated, and glad that it was so.

He woke in the late morning with a sense of bewilderment and sickness upon him. The light was shining broad across his face and seemed focused upon his heavy, smarting eyes. He lay for an instant trying to think what it was all about, chilled to the bone and sore in every fiber. A ringing sound was in his ears, and when he tried to rise, the earth swam about him. His whole pampered being was crying out for food. Never in his life before had he missed a meal and gone so far and felt so much. What was it all about?

And then his memory reminded him sharply of the facts. He was a murderer, an outcast from his father's house upon the face of the earth, and it was necessary that he should go without food and go far, but where, and to what end? There would be no place that he could go but that he would have to move farther. Why not end it all here and be done with it? Perhaps that would be a good way to make amends to Bessie. He had killed her; he would kill himself, and if there was a place hereafter he would find her and tell her it was the only decent thing he could do, having sent her, to come himself and see that she was cared for. Yet when he toyed with the thought somewhat sentimentally in his misery, he knew he had not the courage to do it even for gallantry. And it seemed a useless kind of thing to do. Nothing was of any use anyway! Why had he ever gotten into such a mess? Only yesterday morning at this time he was starting off for the country club and an afternoon's golf. He took out his watch and looked at it. It had stopped! The hands were pointing to ten minutes after one. Probably he had forgotten to wind it. It must be later than that.

A sudden roar came down the road below him, growing in volume as it approached. He struggled to a sitting posture and looked out from his hiding place. It was a truck going down the road, and behind it came two other cars at a little distance apart. One carried a man in uniform. He could see the glitter of brass buttons and a touch of brightness on his cap. He drew back suddenly and crouched, his fear upon him once more. Perhaps that was an officer out to hunt for him. If it was late in the day, by this time the newspapers had gotten word of it! He could see the headlines: SON OF CHARLES VAN RENSSELAER A MURDERER! DRIVES GIRL TO HER DEATH. TAKES BODY TO HOSPITAL AND ESCAPES.

He shuddered, and a ghastly pallor settled upon him. Incredible that such a fate could have overtaken him in a few short hours, and he should have been reduced to hiding in the bushes for safety! He must get out of here, and at once! Now while there were no more cars in sight. The road appeared to be comparatively free from travelers. Perhaps he could keep under cover and get to some small town where he might venture to purchase some food. He certainly could not keep on walking without eating. He struggled to his feet in a panic and found every joint and muscle stiff and sore and his feet stinging with pain as soon as he stood upon them. He glanced down and saw that his handsome overcoat was torn in a jagged line from shoulder to hem, and a bit of fur was sticking out through the opening. That must have been done when he climbed that barbed-wire fence in the dark!

He passed his hand over his usually clean-shaven face and found it rough and bristly. He tried to smooth his hair and pull his hat down over his eyes, but even this movement was an effort.

How was he to go on? Yet he must. He was haunted by a prison cell and the electric chair, preceded by a long, drawn-out trial, in which his entire life would be spread to public gaze. His beautiful mother and haughty, sarcastic father would be dragged in the dust with their proud name and fame, and Mother Chapparelle in her black garments would sit and watch him with sad, forgiving eyes. Strange that he knew even now in his shame that her eyes would be forgiving through their sorrow.

Yet paramount to all this was the piercing, insistent fact that he was hungry. He had never quite known hunger before. He felt in his pockets in vain hope of finding a stray cigarette, but only old letters and programs, souvenirs of his carefree life, came to his hand. Then it came to him that he must destroy these, here where he was in shelter and the ground was wet. He could make a hasty fire and destroy everything that would identify him if he should be caught.

He felt for his little gold matchbox and, stooping painfully, lighted a small pile of letters and papers and bits of trinkets. He burned his tie and a couple of handkerchiefs with his initials. There were his watch and cufflinks, and the gold cigarette case, all bearing initials. He could throw those in the bushes if there was danger. Perhaps he had better get rid of them at once, however, while there was a chance. What if he should bury them? He looked about for something with which to dig. Digging had never been a pastime with him. He awkwardly turned up a few chunks of mud with his hands then took out his knife, a gold one attached to his watch chain, and burrowed a little farther, not getting much below the surface. He put the trinkets into his glove and laid them into the earth with a strange feeling that he was attending the burial of something precious. Then after he had walked a few steps he deliberately returned and unearthed the things, restoring them to his pocket. He had had a sudden realization that he was parting with what he might need badly. There was not enough money in his pocket to carry him far, nor keep him long, and these trinkets would help out. They were no more an identification than all the rest of him. Why throw them away? He looked regretfully at the ashes of his two fine handkerchiefs, the last he would ever have with that initial. And he would need them. He turned and looked back over the road he had traveled in the night and seemed to see all the things he was leaving, his home, his friends, his club, his comfortable living! What a fool he had been. If he had not angered his father and annoyed his mother, and "got in bad" with all his relations everywhere, they would have stood by him now and helped him out of this scrape somehow, just as they had always done before.

Then in the middle of the distance where the panorama of his life had been passing, there arose a face, smiling and sweet, with a rose flush on the cheeks, a light in the eyes, sunshine in the hair, and he remembered! As he looked the face grew white, and the lids fell over the blue eyes, and she was gone!

Sick with the memory, he turned and fled; on feet that were sore, with limbs that were aching, with eyes that were blinded with unaccustomed tears, he stumbled on across rough fields, through woods and meadows and more woods, always woods when he could strike them.

And coming out toward evening with a gnawing faintness at the pit of his stomach, where he could see across a valley, he noted a little trolley car like a toy in the distance sliding along the road, and a small village of neat little houses about a mile away. Eagerly he watched the car as it slid on across the land, almost as small as a fly it seemed, and soon it was a mere speck on the way to the village. Where there was one trolley there were more. Could he dare try for the next one and go to that village for something to eat? He could not go on much longer without food. Or else he would fall by the wayside, and the publicity which his mother so hated—that kind of publicity which was not pretty—would be sure to find him out. He must not drag down his mother's and his father's name. He must hold out to save them so much at least.

His mind had grown clearer through the day, as he had tramped painfully hour after hour and thought it out. He knew that the only thing to do was to get far away, to someplace where law could not find him out and fetch him back for punishment. To do that successfully he must disguise himself somehow. He must get rid of his clothes little by little and get other clothes. He must grow a beard and change his haircut and act a part. He had been good at acting a part for fun in the old days. He was always in demand for theatricals. Could he do it now when Fear was his master?

He stumbled across the meadows one by one, painfully over

the fences, and at last stood in the ditch by the side of the shining rails with the long, low sunset rays gilding them into bright gold. He waited with trembling knees and watched eagerly for the coming of the car, and when at last a faint hum and a distant whistle announced that it was not far off, he began to fairly shake in his anxiety. Would there be many people on board? Would he dare take the risk? Still, he must take it sometime, for he could not hold out much longer.

There were only three women on board, and they did not notice the haggard young fellow who stumbled into the backseat and pulled his hat down over his eyes. They were talking in clear intimate voices that carried a sense of their feeling at home in the car. They told about Mary's engagement, and how her future mother-in-law was giving a dinner for her, and how proud John was of her and was getting her a little Ford coupe to run around in. They talked of the weather and little pleasant everyday things that belonged to a world in which the man in the backseat had no part of. They whispered in lower tones of how it was rumored that Bob Sleighton was making money in bootlegging, and he got a glimpse for the first time in his life of how the quiet, respectable, nondrinking world think of people who break the law in that way. And then they told in detail how they scalloped oysters and made angel cake, and just the degree of brownness that a chicken should be when it was roasted right, until Murray Van Rensselaer, sitting so hungry in his backseat, could fairly smell them all as they came out of the oven, and felt as if he must cry like a child.

Chapter 5

It was dusk when he slid stealthily out of the car, having waited with his head turned toward the darkening window till each of the three women had gotten off at her particular corner. He had spotted a bakery window, and there he made his way, ordering everything they had on their meager menu. But then when he had gotten it, he could only eat a few bites, for somehow Bessie's white face as he carried her into the hospital kept coming between him and the food and sickened him. Somehow he could not get interested in eating any more, and he paid his bill and left a tip that the girl behind the counter did not in the least understand. She ran out to find him and give it back, but he had gone into a little haberdashery shop, and so she missed him.

He bought a cheap cap of plain tweed and a black necktie. Somehow it did not seem decent going around without any necktie. He walked three blocks and threw his old hat far into a vacant lot, then boarded the next trolley, and so went on, where he did not know. He had not known the name of the little town where he had eaten. He began to wonder where he was. He seemed a long way from home, but when a few minutes later the motorman called a name, he recognized a town only about thirty miles from his home city. Was it possible he had walked all that time and only gotten thirty miles away? He must have been going in a circle! And the newspapers would have full descriptions of him by this time posted everywhere! He was not safe anywhere! What should he do? Where go? Why go anywhere?

He lifted his eyes in despair to the advertisements overhead, for it seemed to him that every man in the car was looking at him suspiciously. He tried to appear unconcerned. He felt his chin to see if his beard had grown any, but his face was unsuitably smooth. He tried to make himself read the advertisements, Chiclets and chewing gum, and baked beans. Toothpaste, and wallpaper, and cigarettes.

Then suddenly his attention was riveted on the sign just across from where he sat. The letters stood out so clearly in red and black on the white background as if they were fairly beckoning to get his attention, as if somebody had just written them to attract his eye; as if it were a burning message for his need: YE MUST BE BORN AGAIN!

A strange thing to be in a trolley car. He never stopped to wonder how it came there, or what it meant to the general public. He took it just for himself. It suggested a solution to his problem.

He must be born again. Sure! That was it, exactly what he needed! He could not live in the circle where he had been first born. He had ostracized himself. He had been disloyal to the code and cast a slur on the honorable name with which he had been born, and it was no more use for him to try to live as Murray Van Rensselaer any longer. He would just have to be born all over again into someone else. Born again! How did one do it? Well, he would have to be somebody else, make himself over, get new clothes first, of course, so he would look like a new man, and the clothes that he could find for what money he had would largely determine the kind of man he was to be made into. This cap was the start. It was a plain, cheap working man's cap. It was not the kind of cap that played much golf or polo, or was entitled to enter the best clubs, or drove an expensive car. It was a working man's cap, and a working man he must evidently be in the new life. It was a part of being born that you didn't choose where you should see the light of day, or who should be your parents. A strange pang shot through him at the thought of the parents whom he might not call his own anymore. The name he had borne he would no longer dare to mention. It was the name of a murderer now. He had dishonored it. He would have to have a new name before it would be safe for him to go among men.

A policeman boarded the car in a few minutes and eyed him sharply as he passed to the other end of the car. Murray found his whole body in a tremble. He slid to the back platform and dropped off the next time the car slowed down, and walked a painful distance till a kindly voice from a dilapidated old Ford offered him a ride. Because he felt ready to drop and saw no shelter nearby where he might sleep awhile, he accepted. It was too dark for the man to see his face clearly anyway. He seemed to be an old man and not particularly canny. A worldly wise man would scarcely have asked a stranger to ride at that time of night. So Murray climbed in beside him and sank into the seat, too weary almost to sigh.

But the old farmer was of a social nature and began to quiz him. How did he come to be walking? Was he going far? The young man easily settled that.

"Car broke down!" That was true enough. His car would never run again.

But the old man wanted to know where.

Not being acquainted with the roads around there, Murray could not lie intelligently, and he answered vaguely that he had been taking a cross-cut through a terrible road that did not seem to be much traveled.

"'Bout a mile back?" asked the stranger.

"About."

"Hmm! Copple's Lane, I reckon. In bad shape. Well, say, we might go back and hitch her on and tow her in. I ain't in any special hurry." And the man began to apply the thought to his brakes for a turn around.

The young man roused in alarm.

"Oh, no," he said energetically. "I've got an appointment. I'll have to hurry on. How far is it to a trolley or train? I'll be glad if you'll let me out at your home and direct me to the nearest trolley to the city. I'll send my man back for the car. It'll be all right," he added, reverting in his anxiety to the vernacular of his former life.

His worldly tone made its immediate impression. The stranger looked him over with increasing respect. This was a person from another world. He talked of his man as of a slave. The fur collar on the fine overcoat came under inspection. He didn't often have fur-lined passengers in his tin Lizzie.

"That's a fine warm coat you've got on," he admired frankly. "Guess you paid a pretty penny for that?"

The young man became instantly alarmed. Now, when this man got home and read his evening paper with a description of that very overcoat, he would go to his telephone and call up the police station. He must get rid of that coat at all costs. If the man had it in his possession perhaps he would not be so ready to make known the location of the owner.

"Don't remember what I paid," he answered nonchalantly. "But it doesn't matter. I have to get a new one. This one got all cut up in the wreck," and he brought to view the long rip where the coat had caught on some barbed wire when he tried to climb a fence.

The stranger looked at the jagged tear sharply.

"My wife could mend that," he said speculatively. "Ef you wantta stop at the house and leave it, she'll darn it up so you won't scarcely know it's been tore. Then when you get your car fixed up, you can come along back and get your coat. I'll loan you mine while you're gone. That's a mighty fine coat. I'd like to own one like it myself. Sorry you can't remember the price. Now I paid twenty-seven fifty at a bargain sale fer this here one, and it's a real good piece of cloth."

Young Van Rensselaer stared in the dark. He did not know there were coats for twenty-seven fifty.

"Nice coat," he said nonchalantly. "How'd you like to exchange? I'm going away tonight on a little trip, and I'm afraid I couldn't take the time to come back, and I wouldn't have time to wait to have it mended. I do hate to go with a torn coat, too."

"H'm!" said the man with a catch in his breath as if he could not believe his ears, but he did not mean to let anybody know it. "But that wouldn't be altogether fair. Your coat is lined with fur. It must have cost 'most fifty dollars."

"Oh, well, I've had it some time, you know, and your coat is new; that squares it all up. I'm satisfied if you are."

"It's a bargain!" said the man, stopping his car with alacrity, beginning to unbutton his overcoat. A bargain like that had better be taken up before the young gentleman retracted his offer.

Murray Van Rensselaer divested himself of his expensive coat and crawled into the harsh gray coat of the stranger, and said to himself eagerly, "Now I'm becoming a new man," but he shivered as the car shot forward and the chill air struck through him. Fur lining did make a difference. It never occurred to him before that there were men who could not have fur coats when they needed them for comfort. And now he was one of those men! How astonishing!

The new owner of the fur coat decided that it would be wise not to take the strange young man to his house. He would drop him at the first garage, which was a mile and a half nearer than his home. Then if he thought better of his exchange, he could not possibly hunt him up and demand his coat back again. So the young man was let out in the night before a little garage on the outskirts of town, and the Ford disappeared into the darkness, its taillight winking cunningly and whisking out of sight at the first corner. No chance for that fur coat to ever meet up with its former owner again. And Murray Van Rensselaer stood shivering in the road, waiting till his companion was out of sight that he, too, might vanish in another direction. He had no use for a garage, and he groaned in his spirit over the thought of walking farther with those infernally tight shoes. He almost had a wild notion of taking them off and going barefoot for a while.

Then suddenly a brilliant headlight mounted the hill at the top of the road, and a motorcycle roared into view, heading straight toward him. He could see the brass buttons on the man's uniform, and he dodged blindly out of the path of the light and ducked behind the garage in frantic haste, forgetful of his aching feet, and made great strides through the stubble of an old cornfield that seemed acres across, his heart beating wildly at the thought that perhaps the man with his overcoat had already stopped somewhere to telephone information about him. He was enveloped in panic once more and stumbled and fell and rose again regardless of the bruises and scratches, as if he were struggling for the victory in a football game. Only in this game his life was the stake.

A phrase that he had heard somewhere in his past came to his mind and haunted him. Like a chant it beat a rhythm in his brain as he dragged his weary body over miles of darkness.

"The mark of Cain!" it said. Over and over again: "The mark of Cain!"

Chapter 6

Grevet's was a fine old marble mansion just off the avenue with its name in gold script and heavy silken draperies at the plate-glass windows. It had the air of having caught and imprisoned the atmosphere of the old aristocracy that used to inhabit that section of the city. The quiet distinction of the house seemed to give added dignity to the fine old street, where memories of other days still lingered to remind old residents of a time when only the four hundred trod the sacred precincts of those noble mansions.

Inside the wrought-iron grill-work of its outer entrance, the quiet distinction became more intense. No footstep sounded from the deep pile of imported carpets that covered the floors. Gray floors, lofty walls done in pearl and gray and cream. Upholstery of velvet toning with the walls and floor. And light—wonderful perfect light—softly diffused from the walls themselves, seemingly, making it clear as the morning, yet soft with the radiance of moonlight. A pot of daffodils in one window, just where the silken curtain was slightly drawn to the street. A crystal bowl of parma violets on a tiny table of teakwood. An exquisite cushion of needlepoint blindingly intricate in its delicate design and minute stitches. One rare painting of an old Greek temple against a southern sky and sea. That was Grevet's.

And when you entered there was no one present at first. It was very still, like entering some secret hall of silence. You almost felt like an intruder unless you were of the favored ones who came often to have their wants supplied.

A period of overwhelming waiting, of hesitation lest you might have made a mistake after all, and then Madame, in a costume of stunning simplicity, would glance out from some inner sanctum, murmur a command, and out would come a slim attendant in black satin frock and hair, cut seemingly off the same piece of cloth, and demand your need, and later would come forth the mannequins and models wearing creations of distinction that would put the lily's garb to shame.

It was in the mysterious sidelines somewhere, from which they issued forth unexpectedly upon the purchaser of garments, that a group of these attendants stood conversing, just behind Madame's inner sanctum, in low tones because Madame might return at any moment, and Madame did not permit comments on the customers.

"She was a beautiful girl," said one whose high color under tired eyes, and boyish haircut on a mature head, were somehow oddly at variance. "She was *different!*"

"Yes, different!" spoke another crisply with an accent. "Quite different, and attractive, yes. But she had no style. She wore her hair like one who didn't care for style. Pretty, yes, but not at all the thing. *Quite out.* She didn't seem to belong to him at all. She was not like any of the girls he has brought here before."

"And yet she had distinction."

"Yes," hesitating, "distinction of a kind. But more the distinction of another universe."

"Oh, come down to earth, Miss Lancey," cried a round little model with face a shade too plump. "You're always up in the clouds. She had no style, and you know it. That coat she wore was one of those nineteen-ninety-eight coats in Simon's window. I see them every night when I go home. I knew it by those tricky little pockets. Quite cute they are, with good lines, but cheap and common, of course. She was nothing but a poor girl. Why try to make out she was something else? She has a good figure, of course, and pretty features, if one likes that angelic type, but no style in the world."

"She was stunning in the black velvet," broke in the first speaker stubbornly. "I can't help it—I think she had style. There was something—well, kind of gracious about her, as if she were a lady in disguise."

"Oh, Florence, you're so hopelessly romantic! That's way behind the times. You don't find Cinderellas nowadays. Things are more practical. If a lady *has* a disguise, she takes it off. That's more up to date."

"Well, you know yourself she was different. You can't say she wasn't perfectly at home with those clothes. She wore them like a princess."

"She had a beautiful form," put in an older salesperson. "That's a whole lot."

"It takes something more than form," said the girl persistently. "You know that Charlotte Bakerman had a form. They said she was perfect in every measurement, but she walked like a cow, and she carried herself like a gorilla in a tree when she sat down."

"Oh, this girl was graceful, if that's what you mean," conceded the fat one ungraciously.

"It wasn't just grace, either," persisted the champion of the unknown customer. "She didn't seem to be conscious she had on anything unusual at all. She walked the same way when she came in. She walked the same way when she went out in her nineteen ninety-eight. She sort of glorified it. And when she had on the Lanvin green ensemble, it was just as if she had always worn such things. It sort of seemed to belong to her, as if she was born with it, like a bird's feathers."

"I know what you mean," said the woman with tired eyes and artificial blush. "She wasn't thinking about her clothes. They weren't important to her. She would only care if they were suitable. And she would know at a glance without discussing it whether they were suitable. You saw how she looked at that flashy little sports frock, the one with the three shades of red stripes and a low red leather belt. She just turned away and said in a low tone: 'Oh, not that one, Murray!' as if it hurt her."

"Did she call him Murray?" asked the fat one greedily.

"Yes. They seemed to know each other real well. She was almost as if she might have been a sister, only we know he hasn't got any sisters. She might have been a country cousin."

"Perhaps he's going to marry her!" suggested the fat one.

"Nonsense!" said the first girl sharply. "She's not his kind. Imagine the magnificent Mrs. Van Rensselaer mothering anything that wore a nineteen-ninety-eight coat from Simon's! Can you? Besides, they say he's going to marry the Countess Lenowski when she gets her second divorce."

"I don't think *that* girl would marry a man like Murray Van Rensselaer," spoke the thoughtful one. "She has too much character. She had a remarkable face."

"Oh, you can't tell by a face," shrugged a slim one with sinuous body and a sharp black lock of hair pasted out on her cheek. "She can't be much, or she wouldn't let him buy her clothes."

"She didn't!" said the first speaker sharply. "I heard her say, 'I wouldn't think she would like that, Murray. It's too noticeable. I'm sure a nice girl wouldn't like that as well as the blue chiffon.'"

"Hmm!" said the slim one. "Looks as if she must be a relative or something. Did anybody get her name?"

"The address on the box was Elizabeth Chapparelle," contributed a pale little errand girl who had stood by listening.

"Elizabeth!" said the thoughtful one. "She looked like an Elizabeth."

"But if they weren't for her, that wouldn't have been her name," persisted the fat one.

"I thought I heard him call her Bessie once," said the little errand girl.

"Then he was buying for one of his old girls who is going to be married," suggested the slim one contemptuously. "Probably this girl is a friend of them both."

"Hush! Madame is coming! Which one did he take? The Lanvin green?"

"Both. He told Madame to send them both! Yes, Madame, I'm coming!"

A boy in a mulberry uniform with silver buttons entered.

"Say, Lena, take that to Madame, and tell her there's a mistake. The folks say they don't know anything about it."

Lena, the pale little errand girl, took the heavy box and walked slowly off to find Madame, studying the address on the box as she went.

"Why!" She paused by the thoughtful-eyed woman. "It's her. It's that girl!" Madame appeared suddenly with a frown.

"What's this, Lena? How many times have I told you not to stop to talk? Where are you carrying that box?"

"Thomas says there's a mistake in the address. The folks don't know anything about it."

"Where is Thomas? Send him to me. Here, Thomas. What's the matter? Couldn't you find the house? The address is perfectly plain."

"Sure, I found the house, Madame, but they wouldn't take it in. They said they didn't know anything about it. It wasn't theirs."

"Did they say Miss Chapparelle didn't live there? Who came to the door?"

"An old woman with white hair. Yes, she said Miss Chapparelle lived there. She said she was her daughter, but that package didn't belong to her. She said she never bought anything at this place."

"Well, you can take it right back," said Madame sharply. "Tell the woman the young lady knows all about it. Tell her it will explain itself when the young lady opens it. There's a card inside. And Thomas," she added, hurrying after him as he slid away to the door and speaking in a lower voice, "Thomas, you leave it there no matter what she says. It's all paid for, and I'm not going to be bothered this way. You're to leave it no matter what she says, you understand?"

"Sure, Madame, I understand. I'll leave it."

The neat little delivery car, with its one word, Grevet's, in silver script on a mulberry background, slid away on its well-oiled wheels, and the service persons in their black satin straight frocks turned their black satin bobbed heads and looked meaningfully at one another with glances that said eagerly: "I told you so. That girl was different!" and Madame looked thoughtfully out of her side window into the blank brick wall of the next building and wondered how this was going to turn out. She did not want to have those expensive outfits returned, and she could not afford to anger young Van Rensselaer; he was too good a customer. He had expected her to carry out his instructions. It might be that she would have to go herself to explain the matter. Anyone could see that girl was too unsophisticated to understand. Her mother would probably be worse. She would have notions. Madame had had a mother once herself, so long ago she had forgotten many of her precepts, but she could understand. Madame was clever. This was going to be a case requiring clever action. But Madame was counting much upon Thomas. Thomas, too, could be clever on occasion. That was why he wore the silver buttons on the mulberry uniform and earned a good salary. Thomas knew that his silver buttons depended on his getting things across when Madame spoke to him as she had just done, and Madame believed Thomas would get this across.

In the early dusk of the evening when it came closing time at Grevet's, the service women in chic wraps and small cloche hats flocked stylishly out into the city and made their various ways home. The thoughtful one and the outspoken one wound their way together out toward the avenue and up toward obscure streets tucked in between finer ones, walking to save carfare; for even those who worked at Grevet's, there were circumstances in which it was wise in good weather to save carfare.

Their way led past the houses of wealth, a trifle longer perhaps, but pleasanter, with a touch of something in the air which their narrow lives had missed but which they liked to be near and enjoy if only in the passing. Their days at Grevet's had fostered this love of the beautiful and real, perhaps, that made a glimpse into the windows of the great a pleasant thing: the drifting of a rare lace curtain, the sight of masses of flowers within, the glow of a handsome lamp, and the mellow shadows of a costly room, the sound of fine machinery as the limousines passed almost noiselessly, the quiet perfect service of the butler at the door, the well-groomed women who got out of the cars and went in, delicately shod, to eat dinners that others had prepared, with no thought or worry about expense. These were more congenial surroundings to walk amid, even if it took one a block or two farther out of the way, than a crowded street full of common rushing people, jostling and worried like themselves, and the air full of the sordid things of life.

They were talking about the events of the day, as people will, the happenings of their little world, the only points of contact they had in common out of their separate lives.

"How much have you sold today, Mrs. Hanley?" questioned the girl eagerly. "I had the biggest sale this month yet."

The sad-eyed one smiled pleasantly.

"Oh, I had a pretty good day, Florence. This is always a good time of year, you know."

"Yes, I know. Everybody getting new things." She sighed with a fierce longing that she, too, might have plenty of money to get new things. A sigh like that was easily translatable by her companion. But for some reason Mrs. Hanley shrank tonight from the usual wail that the girl would soon bring up about the unfairness of the division of wealth in the world, perhaps because she, too, was wondering how to make both ends meet and get the new things that were necessary. She roused herself to change the subject. They were passing the Van Rensselaer mansion now, well known to both of them. She snatched at the first subject that presented itself.

"Why do you suppose Madame is so anxious to please that young man when everybody says he doesn't pay his bills?"

"Oh," said Florence almost bitterly, "she knows his dad'll pay 'em. It's everything to have a name like that. He could get away with almost anything if he just told people who he was."

"I suppose so," said Mrs. Hanley almost sadly. "But I hope that girl doesn't keep those clothes. She's too fine for such as he is."

"Yes, isn't she?" said Florence eagerly. "I suppose most folks would think we were crazy talking like that. He's considered a great catch. But somehow I couldn't see a girl like that getting soiled with being tied up to a man that's got talked about as much as he has. She's different. There aren't many like that living. That is the way she looks to me. Why, she's like some angel just walking the earth because she has to; at least that's the impression her face gave to me. Just as if she didn't mind things us other folks think so much about; she had higher, wonderful things to think about. I don't often see anyone that stirs me up this way and makes me think about my mother. I guess I ain't much myself, never expected to be, but when you see someone that is, you can't help but think!"

After that incoherent sentence, Florence, with a cheerful good night, turned off at her corner, and Mrs. Hanley went home to a little pent-up room high up in a fourth-rate boardinghouse, to wash off her makeup and prepare a tiny supper on a small gas stove, and be a mother for a few brief hours to her little crippled son, who lay on a tiny couch by the one window all day long and waited for her to come.

Chapter 7

More than four hundred miles away, a freight train bumped and jerked itself into the town of Marlborough and lumberingly came to a halt. With its final lurch of stopping, a hasty figure rolled from under one of the empty cars and hurried stiffly away into the shadows as if pursued by a fear that the train upon which he had been riding without a right might come after him and compel him to ride farther.

The train was over an hour late. It was due at five. It had been held up by a wreck ahead.

It was the first time that Murray Van Rensselaer had ever taken a journey under a freight car, and he felt sure it would be the last. Even though he might be hard pressed, he would never resort to that mode of travel again. That the breath of life was still in him was a miracle, and he crawled into the shadow of a hedge to take his bearings.

There were others who had stolen rides in that manner, for thousands of miles, and seemed to live through it. He had read about it in his childhood and always wanted to try it, and when the opportunity presented itself just in the time of his greatest need, with a cordon of policemen in the next block and his last dollar from the ample roll he started with spent, he had lost no time in availing himself of it. But he felt sure now that if he had been obliged to stay under that fearful rumbling car and bump over that uneven roadbed for another ten minutes, he would have died of horror, or else rolled off beneath those grinding, crunching wheels. His head was aching, as if those wheels were going around inside his brain. His back ached with an ache unspeakable, and his cramped legs ached as if they were being torn from his aching body. He had never known before how many places there were in a human body to ache.

He had eaten no breakfast nor dinner. There was no buffet in the private berth he had chosen, and he had no money in his pocket to purchase with if there had been. It was his first realization of what money meant, of what it was to be utterly without it. For the moment, the fear that was driving him in his flight was obliterated by the simple pangs of hunger and weariness. He had started for the far West, where he hoped to strike some remote cattle ranch where men herded whose pasts were shady, and where no questions were asked. He felt that his experience in polo would stand him in good stead among horses, and there he could live and be a new man. He had been planning all the way, taking his furtive path across the country, half on foot and half by suburban trolleys, until his money gave out and he was forced to try the present mode of transportation. He had entertained great hopes of a speedy arrival among other criminals, where he would be safe, when he crawled under that dirty freight car and settled himself for his journey. But now, with his head whirling and that desperate faintness at the pit of his stomach, he loathed the thought of going farther. If there had been a police station close at hand, he would have walked in gratefully and handed himself over to justice. This business of fleeing from justice was no good, no good in the world.

He stood in the shelter of a great privet hedge that towered darkly above him, and shivered in the raw November air, until the train had jolted itself back and forth several times and finally grumbled on its clattery way again. He had a strange fancy that the train was human and had discovered his absence, was trying to find him perhaps, and might still compel him to go on. He almost held his breath as car after car passed his hiding place. Each jolt and rumble of the train sent shivers down his spine and a wave of sickness over him, almost as if he had been back underneath that dreadful car above those grinding wheels. It was with relief unspeakable that he watched the ruby gleam of the taillight disappear at last down the track around a curve. He drew a long breath and tried to steady himself.

Down the road, across the tracks, some men were coming. He drew within his shelter until they were passed and then slid round the corner into a street that apparently led up over the brow of a hill.

He had no aim, and he wondered why he went anywhere. There was nowhere to go. No object in going. No money to buy bed or bread with, nothing on him worth pawning. He had long ago pawned the little trinkets left in his pockets when he started. Eventually this going must cease. One had to eat to live. One couldn't walk forever on sore feet and next to no shoes. Flesh and bones would not keep going indefinitely at command of the brain. Why should the brain bother them longer? Why not go up there on the hill somewhere and crawl out of sight and sleep? That would be an easy way to die, die while one slept. He must sleep. He was overpowered with it like a drug. If he only had a cigarette, it would hearten him up. It was three days since he had smoked— he who used to be always smoking, who smoked more cigarettes than any other fellow in his set. It was deadly doing without! And to think that the son of his father was reduced to this! Why, even the servants at home had plenty to eat and drink and *smoke*!

He plodded on up the street, not knowing where he was going, nor caring, scarcely knew that he was going. Just going because he had to. Some power beyond himself seemed to be driving him.

Suddenly a bright light shone out across the walk from a big stone building set back from the street. It was a church, he saw as he drew nearer, yet it had a curious attachment of other buildings huddled around it, a part of the church, yet not so churchly. He wondered vaguely if it might not be a parochial school of some sort.

There were lights in low windows near the ground and tall shrubs making shelter about, and from the open doorway there issued a most delectable odor, the smell of roasting meat.

Straight to the brightness and appetizing odor his lagging feet led him without his own conscious volition. It was something that he had to do, to go to that smell and that comfort, even though it led him into terrible danger. A moment more and he stood within the shelter of a great syringa bush looking down into the open window of a long, lit basement room, steadying himself with his trembling hand against the rough stone wall of the building, and just below his eager hand was a table with plates and plates full of the most delectable-looking rolls and rows of wonderful chocolate cakes and gleaming frosted nut cake.

He could hear voices in the distance, but no one was in sight, and he reached down suddenly and swiftly and with both hands gathered two little round white frosted cakes and a great big buttered roll and, sliding behind the syringa bush, began to eat them voraciously, snatching a bit from one hand and then the other.

He had never stolen anything before, and he was not conscious of stealing now. He ate because he was famished and must eat to live.

Down in the basement a church supper was in preparation.

Great roasts were in the parish oven; potatoes were boiling for the masher. The water was on for lima beans, and a table stood filled with rows of salad plates, on which one of the church mothers was carefully placing crisp lettuce and red-ripe tomatoes stuffed with celery and bits of nuts. Another church mother was ladling out mayonnaise from a great yellow bowl in which she had just made it. A kettle of delicious soup was keeping hot over the stove.

They never did things by halves in the Marlborough Presbyterian Church, and this was a very special occasion. It was the annual dinner of the Christian Endeavor Society, and they had always made a great deal of it. In addition to this, a new man was coming to town, a young man, well heralded, notable among young church workers in the city where he had spent his life, already known for his activity in Christian Endeavor work and all forms of social and uplift labor. They felt honored that he was coming to their midst. As a teller in the bank, he would have a good financial and social standing as well, and moreover his name was well remembered, as his father and mother used to live in Marlborough years before. There had been a letter commendatory and introductory from the city pastor to Rev. Dr. Harrison, the pastor of the Marlborough church, and the annual church affair had been postponed a week that it might be had on the night of his arrival, that he might be the guest of honor and be welcomed into their midst properly. Not a few of the girls in the Christian Endeavor had new dresses for the occasion, and the contributions for the dinner had been many and unusually generous. It seemed that all the girls were willing to make cakes galore, and each vied with the other to have the best confection of the culinary art that could be produced. Some of the mothers had offered their best linen and silver to make the tables gorgeous, and there had been much preparation for the program, music, speeches, and even a dramatic monologue. The vice president, who was poetically inclined, had written a poem that was intended as a sort of address of welcome to the stranger, and an introduction to their members, and many a clever hit and pun upon names embellished its verses. No one who had come to town in years had had the welcome that was being prepared for Allan Murray, the new teller in the Marlborough National Bank, and State Secretary of the Christian Endeavor Society in his home state.

The big basement dining room of the church was all in array with tables set in a hollow square. Two girls were putting on the finishing touches.

"Anita, oh, Anita! Has Hester May's sponge cake come yet?" called the taller of the two, a girl rather apt to wear many beads.

"Yes, it's here, Jane, real gummy chocolate frosting on top. Mmmm! Mmmm! I could hardly keep from cutting it. It looks luscious. Is your mother going to get here in time to make the coffee?"

"Oh yes, she'll be here in half an hour. You ought to put an apron on, Anita. You'll get something on that lovely blue crêpe dress. My, but you look scrumptious with that great white collar over the blue. Did you make that collar yourself? It's wonderful! Say, how did you embroider that? Right through the lace border and all? Oh, I see! My, I wish I was clever like you, Anita!"

"Oh, cut it, Jane! We haven't time for flattery! I've got to finish setting this table. Are the forks over there? Where's Joseph? Go ask him if we haven't any more forks. He washed them after the Ladies' Aid luncheon. Perhaps he put them away."

"They're in the lower drawer. I saw them when I got out the napkins to fold. Here they are. Wouldn't it be dreadful if the guest of honor didn't get here after all, when everything is coming out so fine? Did you know Mrs. Price was sending roses out of her conservatory? A great armful. I brought down mother's cut-glass bowl to put them in, and we'll put them at the speaker's table, right in front of Mr. Harrison and the guest. Oh dear, I hope he gets here all right!"

"Why, why shouldn't he, Jane? What an idea! Didn't he write and say he expected to arrive this afternoon? Mrs. Summers said she had his room all ready, and his trunk came last night, so of course he'll be here."

"But there's been an awful wreck on the road. Didn't you hear about it, Anita? Yes, it's terrible, they say. Doctor Jarvis telephoned he couldn't come to lunch. He went on a special relief train. It's somewhere down around Smith's Crossing. The rails spread, or something, and the express telescoped the way train, or else it was the other way round, and a lot of people got hurt, and some killed, or at least there was a rumor they did."

"Mercy!" said Anita, stopping in her work. "Why, that's awful! Allan Murray might have been on the train, you know."

"No, I guess not," said Jane. "He telegraphed last night he was arriving here late in the afternoon. That would mean he would take the train at Alton at noon. This wreck was the morning train. But then, he might have been delayed by it. You know it takes a long time to clear the tracks. Oh well, he's likely at Mrs. Summers' now unpacking, or we would have heard. We ought to stop talking and get to work. The celery has to be put in the glasses and the nuts in the dishes. One of those nut dishes is broken, too. Isn't there another dish up on that high shelf that will do?"

"I brought over some silver nut dishes. They will do for the middle table. Did they say any Marlborough people were on that train?"

"Yes, Dick Foster and some college friend coming home for the weekend, but they phoned they were all right. They were in the last car and only a little shaken up. Mr. Foster took the car and ran down to Smith's Crossing after them. Then there was that lame shoemaker from under the drugstore, that little shop, you know, and Mrs. Bly, the seamstress. Nobody knows anything about them. At least I didn't hear."

"Oh, Mrs. Bly," said Anita sympathetically. "I hope no harm came to her, poor thing. She's sewed for us ever since I was a child. Say, Jane, does your brother know this Mr. Murray? He went to the same college, didn't he?"

"Yes, but it was after Allan Murray left. He saw him once though. He was just adored in college. He was a great athlete, though very slender and wiry, Bob says, and he was awfully clever.

Made Phi Beta Kappa and all that, and was president of the YMCA, and head of the student gov, and stunningly handsome. Bob didn't say that though. It was Marietta's cousin said that. Her brother was in Allan Murray's class and brought him home once, and she thought him just a perfect Greek god, to hear her talk, but when I asked Bob about it, he said, oh yes, he was a looker he guessed. He never took particular notice. And I simply couldn't get a description, though I tried hard enough. He couldn't even remember the color of his eyes, said they were just eyes, and what difference did it make. But Marietta said he was dark and had very large dark eyes, slender—no, *lean*, that was the world she used— and awfully tanned and fit. She said he had a smile, too, that you never could forget, and fine white teeth, and was careful about his appearance, but not much of a dresser. She said he had worked his way through college. His father had lost money, and he was going in for thrift and didn't give much time to social things but was awfully good company."

"Hmm! That's just about what the minister said when he told us he wanted us to make him feel at home. I don't really approve of it myself, this taking a stranger and carrying him around on a little throne before you've tried him out, but when Mr. Harrison asked us to arrange this Christian Endeavor banquet on the night of his arrival to give him a kind of welcome to our town, why of course it had to be done. And of course Mr. Harrison knows what he's talking about, or he wouldn't suggest it. But it makes it just a little embarrassing for us girls to seem to be so very eager to welcome another young man into our midst that we fall all over ourselves to let him know it right off the first night."

"Now, Anita! You're always so fussy and prudish! As if he would think anything about it at all. Besides, his having been an active Christian Endeavorer in his home church and his father having been a member of our church years ago when he was a boy makes it kind of different—don't you think?"

"Oh, I suppose so," said Anita thoughtfully. "Only I do hope he won't be stuck on himself. The young men are all so sure of their welcome anyhow these days, it doesn't seem as if it was hardly necessary. And it's enough to turn a young man's head anyway to have the whole town bowing down to him this way. Teller in the town bank, taken in to board at one of the best houses in town just because Mrs. Summers knew his mother when she was a girl, and given a church supper on the night of his arrival. I'm sure I hope he will be worth it all, and that we won't spoil him right at the start."

"Oh, Anita! You're so funny! What do you care if he is spoiled, anyway, if we have a good time out of it? I'm sure I don't. And it'll be nice to have another fellow around; so many of our boys have gone off to college or to work in the city. And those that are left don't care a cent for the church affairs. I have to fairly hire Bob and Ben to come to anything we have here, and this Murray man, they say, is crazy about church work. If it proves true, I think the society will grow by leaps and bounds."

"Well, what kind of a growth is that? Just following after a new man! That's not healthy growth. When he goes, they'll go with him if that's what they come for. Who is that outside? Perhaps it's the man with the ice cream. It ought to be here by this time. Go out and look. It may be some of those tormenting boys that live across the street. And the cakes and rolls are all under that window. I declare, I should think church members would teach their children better than to *steal*! Go quick, Jane. I don't want to leave this butter now till I get it all cut in squares. But for pity's sake, forget that new man, or you'll be bowing down to him just like everybody else!"

"Oh, Anita! You're perfectly hopeless," giggled Jane as she fled up the basement stairs to the outside door to reconnoiter.

A moment more and Anita heard her friend's voice ring out clearly in an eagerly hospitable voice among the syringa bushes outside the chapel window:

"Isn't this Mr. Murray? Mr. Allan Murray? Won't you come right in? We're all expecting you."

Anita, cutting butter into squares in the pantry window in the basement, turned away with a curl of her pretty lip and slammed down the window. If Jane wanted to make a fool of herself with this stranger, she, Anita, was not going to be a party to it. And she carried the cakes to be cut to the far table in the kitchen quite away from the dining room and went to work with set lips and a haughty chin. The new man should not think *she* was after him, anyway.

Chapter 8

Outside the church Murray Van Rensselaer, somewhat fortified within by the stolen bun and the two frosted cakes, whose crumbs were yet upon his lips, started in astonishment.

Of the unexpectedly warm greeting he caught only one word, "Murray," his own name, and as he took it in, thinking at first that he had been recognized, it came to him what it would mean. The whole careful fabric of his intricate escape was undone. Unless he disappeared at once into the darkness, he would be brought speedily out into the light and have to explain. Some dratted girl he had probably met at a dance somewhere and didn't remember. But everybody knew him. That was the trouble with belonging to a family like his and being prominent in society and clubs and sports. His picture had been in the paper a thousand times—when he took the blue ribbon at the horse show, when he played golf with a visiting prince at Palm Beach, on his favorite pony playing polo, smashing the ball across the net to a world champion tennis player; the notable times were too numerous to mention. She didn't know. She hadn't seen the city papers yet or hadn't noticed. Probably didn't think it was the same name. It wouldn't take long for the news to travel, even four hundred miles. That was nothing. He must get out of here!

He made a wild dash in the other direction but came sharply in contact with a stiff branch of syringa, which jabbed him in the eye smartly, and for an instant the pain was so great that he could do nothing but stand still.

The girl in the doorway was tall and slim, and she stood where the light from the chapel shone full behind her and silhouetted a very pleasant outline. Also she knew that the light caught and scintillated from her crystal necklace, which hung to her very long indefinable waist, and that she presented thus a trim appearance. But she might as well have been short and fat for all he saw of her as he stood and held his eye and groped about with his other hand on what seemed an interminable stone wall behind him. Was there no way to get out of this?

Jane was not a girl to give up the vantage she had gained of being the first to welcome this new hero to town. He had backed off into the shrubbery, shy perhaps, and had not answered, but she was reasonably sure of her man. Of course it must be he. He was likely reconnoitering to be sure he was in the right place, and it wouldn't do to let him slip away. He might be one of those who were shy of an open welcome and needed to be caught or he would escape. So Jane proceeded to catch him.

With nimble feet she descended the three stone steps and was upon him before he knew it, with a slim white hand outheld.

"Your name is Murray, isn't it? I was sure it must be"—as he did not dissent. "Mine is Jane Freeman, and we're awfully glad you've come to town. We're expecting you to supper, you know, and you might as well come right in. Everybody else will be here pretty soon, and we'll just have that much more time to get acquainted. Won't the girls be humming though when they find out I met you first! But I had a sort of right, because my mother and your mother were schoolmates together, you know! Were you trying to find the right door? It is confusing here. Doctor Harrison's study is that door, and that one goes into the choir room, and this enters the kitchen and dining rooms. We go over to this other door and enter through the chapel. Everyone gets lost here at first."

"Yes, I guess I did lose my way," murmured Murray Van Rensselaer, feeling it imperative to say something, under the circumstances, and casting furtive glances behind him to see how he could get away.

"Come right around this way," went on Jane volubly. "Here's the path. Have you been over to Mrs. Summers' yet? Isn't she coming over? I thought she would have shown you the way."

"No, I haven't been to Mrs. Summers' yet," he said, catching eagerly at the idea. "But I really can't go in this way. I've—you see, there was a wreck on the road—"

"Oh, were you *really* in the wreck after all? How wonderful!

And you got through? How ever did you do it? Why, the relief train hasn't come back yet—at least it hadn't when I came over."

"Oh, I walked part of the way and got on the freight—"

"Oh really! How thrilling! Then you can tell us all about the wreck. We haven't heard much. Come right in and meet Anita. I want you to tell her about the wreck." But the young man halted firmly on the walk.

"Indeed," said he decidedly, "it's quite impossible. I'm a wreck myself. I've got to dress before I could possibly meet anybody, except in the dark, and I think you'll have to excuse me tonight. My trunk hasn't come yet, you know, and I'm really not fit to be seen. You don't know what a wreck is, I guess."

"Oh, were you really in it like that!" exclaimed Jane adoringly. "How wonderful that you escaped! But you're mistaken about your trunk. It came yesterday. Mrs. Summers told me this morning it had arrived, and it's over in your room. If you really must dress first, I'll show you the way to Mrs. Summers', but it wouldn't be necessary, you know. You would be all the more a hero. You could come right in the church dressing room and wash and comb your hair. It would be terribly interesting and dramatic for you to appear just as you came from the wreck, you know."

"Thank you," said the young man dryly. "Much too interesting for me. I'll just get over to my trunk, if you don't mind," he suggested soothingly. "Which way is the house? I won't have any trouble finding it. It's not far away, you say?"

"Oh no, it's right here," she said excitedly with a vague wave of her hand. "Come right across the lawn. It's shorter. I don't mind running over in the least. In fact, I've got to go and see if I can't borrow another vase for some roses that just arrived. You must be very tired after such an exciting afternoon. Was it very terrible at first? The shock, I mean?"

"Oh! Terrible? Yes, the wreck. Why, rather unpleasant at first, you know. The confusion and—and—"

"I suppose the women all screamed. They usually do when they are frightened. I never can see why. Now, I never scream. When I'm frightened I'm just as cool. My father says he can always trust me in a crisis because I keep still and do something. You look as if you were that way, too. But then men are, of course."

She was steering him swiftly toward a neat Queen Anne house of somewhat ancient date, perhaps, but very pretty and attractive, in spite of the fact that the maples with which it was surrounded were bare of leaves. There were little ruffled curtains at the window, and plants, and old-fashioned lamps with bright shades, and a gray-haired woman moving about in a bay window watering a fern. It was a picture of a sweet, quiet home, and something of its peace stole out into the November night with its soft lights like a welcome. Murray looked with hungry eyes. There would be beds in that house, and warmth, and a table with good things to eat. The bite he had stolen had only whetted his appetite. How good if he had a right to enter this home as the boy who was expected would do soon, welcomed, a festive supper prepared, perhaps a place where he might earn enough to live, and friends to make life worth the living. It was the first time in his life he had ever felt an urge to work. His father's business had seemed a bore to him. He had pitied him now and then when he happened to think of it at all, that he was old and had to go downtown every day to "work"—not that he had to. Murray knew his father could retire a good many times over and not feel it. But he had pitied him that he was old and therefore had nothing to interest him in life but dull business. Now business suddenly seemed a haven to be desired.

But all this was merely an undercurrent of thought while he was really casting about in his mind how he might rid himself of his pest of a girl, and was furtively observing the street and the lay of the bushes that he might suddenly dodge away and leave her in the darkness. He hesitated to do it lest she might even pursue him, and he felt that in case of fleeing his strength would probably leave him altogether, and he would drop beside some dreary bush and be overtaken.

He could not quite understand his attitude toward this girl. He had been somewhat of a lady-killer, and no girl had held terrors for him in the old life. He knew they always fell for him, and he could go any way he liked and they would follow. Now here was a girl, just a common little country girl, filling him with terror. She seemed to possess almost supernatural power over him, as if she had eyes that could see through to his soul and would expose him to the scorn of the world if he for one moment angered her and let her get a chance to look into his poor shaken mind. *Murray*

Van Rensselaer! Why, Murray, what's the matter with you? he said to himself. And then, *But I'm not Murray Van Rensselaer anymore. I'm a murderer fleeing from justice! I must get away!*

Then right before him, what he thought was a long french window turned into a glass door and opened in front of his unwilling feet, and there stood in the broad burst of light the woman with the gray hair whom he had seen through the window going about the room.

She stood there with a questioning look upon her face, and she had kind eyes—eyes like Mrs. Chapparelle's—*mother* eyes. They looked into the darkness of the yard as if they were waiting for him, searching, expecting him, and he found his feet would go no further. They would not take the dash into the darkness of the shrubbery that his situation required. They just stopped and waited. It had been growing in his consciousness for some time that this thing would happen pretty soon, that he would stop and get caught, and he wondered almost apathetically what he would do then. Just wait, and let them do with him what they pleased?

But Jane's voice rang out triumphantly: "He's come, Mrs. Summers. He didn't get hurt after all. He came through all right. Isn't that great? But he's all messed up, and he wants to clean up. I told him I was sure his trunk had come. It has, hasn't it?"

"Oh, is that you, Jane? Yes, his trunk has come," said the lady with a smile. Then she turned toward the shivering youth and put out both hands eagerly, taking his cold ones in hers that felt to him like warm little veined rose leaves. She drew him without his own volition across the brick terrace into the light.

"So this is Allan Murray!" she said, and her voice was like a mother's caress. "My dear boy! I'm so glad to have you with me! You don't know how precious your dear mother was to me! And I shall be so glad if you will let me take her place while you are here, as much as anyone could take the place of a woman like your mother!"

Now was the time for him to bolt, of course, if he was ever going to get away, just jerk his hands from her frail touch and bolt! But his feet didn't seem to understand. They just stood! And his eyes lingered hungrily on her loving ones. He longed, oh, how he wished that this woman really was a friend of his mother— that he had had a mother who could have been a friend of a woman like this one, that he might now be befriended by her. And his hands warmed to the soft vital touch of those little frail rose-leaf hands. They seemed to be warming his very soul, clear to the frightened center where he knew he was a murderer and an outlaw. But he hadn't vitality enough left to vanish. He would have been glad if some magic could have made him invisible, or if he could have suddenly died. But nothing like that happened to men who were in trouble.

Then, his hands and his feet having failed him in this predicament, he tried his lips, and to his surprise words came, fluently from long habit, with quite a nice sound to his voice, modest and grateful and polite and apologetic.

"So kind of you!" he murmured safely, the old vernacular

returning from habit to his lips. "But I'm not fit to be touched. It's been awful, you know—smoke and soot and cinders and broken things. I'm torn and dirty—I'm not fit to be seen!"

"Why, of course!" said the dear lady with understanding. "You don't want me to look you over and see how much you resemble your mother till you've had a bath and a shave. I know. I've had a boy of my own, you know. He died in the war"—with the breath of a sigh—"but come right up to your room. Everything is all ready, and there's plenty of hot water. The bathroom is right next to your room, and your room is at the top of the stairs on the right. There are towels and soap and everything you need. If I'd only had your trunk key, I would have presumed to take out your clothes and hang them in the closet for you. It would have been such a pleasure to get ready for a boy again. And it would have taken out the wrinkles. But I've my electric iron all ready, and I can press anything that needs it while you are taking your bath. Suppose I go up with you and you unlock the trunk and hand me out your suit, and I'll just give it a mite of a pressing while you're in the bathroom. It won't take a minute, and I'd love to."

She led him as she spoke to the foot of the stairs, where a soft light above invited to the quiet restfulness of upstairs, and a gleam of a white bathroom lured unspeakably his tired body. But his brain was functioning again. He saw a way of escape from this delightful but fearful situation.

"That's the trouble," he said. "I have lost my keys! They were in my bag, and the bag rolled down the embankment into the burning cars."

"Oh!"

"Ah!" from the two women as he hurried on.

"I am sorry to disappoint you, but I guess I'll have to forgo the supper. It will take too long to get that trunk open and get ready. You two just better go over to the church, and I'll stick around here and get shaped up for tomorrow. You know I've been through a pretty rough time and—"

"I know you have," broke in the gentle voice firmly, "but I'm afraid you'll really have to go to that supper. It's all been prepared as a welcome for you on account of your father and mother, you know, and it's pretty much for a church and a town to remember and love people like that through thirty years of absence. Besides, Mr. Harper, the president of the bank, will be there, and I don't suppose it would be a very good thing for your future as the new teller if you were to stay away. You see, really, they are honoring you and will be terribly disappointed—"

Murray Van Rensselaer began to feel as if he really were the person who was being waited for over at that church supper, and his natural savoir-faire came to his assistance.

"Oh, in that case of course," he said gallantly, "it wouldn't do to disappoint them, but how can I possibly manage it? You don't happen to have a suit of your son's that you'd be willing to loan me?"

He said it with just the right shade of depreciation and humility. It was a great favor, of course, to ask for the suit of her dead son. But she flashed a pleasant, tender look at him.

"No, dear, I haven't. I gave them all away where they would be useful. But I am sure we can get that trunk of yours open."

"Couldn't we pick the lock?" said Jane, wishing she still wore hair pins. It would be so romantic to lend the hair pin that opened the new hero's trunk.

But Mrs. Summers opened a little cabinet by the foot of the stairs and took out a hammer and screwdriver.

"I think we'll manage with these," she said pleasantly. "Jane, if you'll just take those two vases and that maple cake and run over to the church and tell them we'll be a few minutes late, but we're coming, then I needn't stop to go over just yet. Now, Allan Murray, come on!" she said, and started up the stairs.

Murray Van Rensselaer hesitated and looked toward the door, but the reluctant Jane, with arms full of cake and vases, was still filling it, eyeing him blissfully, and there was no escape that way. Perhaps if he once got in the room above with the door locked, he could climb from the window and get away in the dark. So he dragged himself up the stairs after his hospitable hostess and was ushered into a bedroom, the like of which for sweetness and restfulness had never met his eye before.

There were thin white smooth curtains at three low windows, a white bed with plump pillows that looked the best thing in the world for his weary body, a little stand beside it with a shaded lamp, and a Bible. Odd! A Bible! Across the room was a fireplace under a white mantel, and drawn up beside it under a tall shaded lamp was a big luxurious chair with a bookcase full of books beside it.

Then he turned to the inner side of the room, and there a bureau with a great mirror suddenly flung his own image back to him and startled him.

The last time he had seen himself in a mirror was at his tailor's trying on a new suit that had just been finished for his order. He could see the trim lines of his figure now, the sharp creases of well-pressed garments, the smart cut, the fine texture of the material, his own well-groomed appearance, his handsome careless face, shaven and sure of himself and his world, the grace of his every movement. He had not known he was particularly vain of himself, but now as he gazed on this forlorn, unshaven object, with bloodshot eyes, with coarse, ill-cut garments, and a shapeless cap crushed in his dirty, trembling hand, he was suddenly filled with a great shame.

Mrs. Summers was down on her knees beside a neat trunk, making strong, efficient strokes with a hammer on the lock.

I don't belong here! The words were as audible to his ears as if he had spoken them aloud, and he turned with a swift motion to glide out the door and away, but too late. The lock of the trunk had given way with a rasping sound, and Mrs. Summers rose with a little smile of triumph on her lips and looked toward him. He could not flee with those kind mother eyes upon him.

"Now, if you'll help me pull it out from the wall, we can open it," she said pleasantly, and there was nothing for him to do but acquiesce, although he really was very little help with that trunk, for his arms were weak, and when he stooped, a great dizziness came over him, so that he almost thought he was going to fall.

Mrs. Summers swung the top of the trunk open deftly.

"We can have Mr. Klingen, the locksmith, up in the morning to fix that lock before we put the trunk away in the attic for the winter," she said, smiling. "Now, which is the suit you want to wear tonight? This blue one right on top? We've got to hurry a little because it's getting late. And I'll tell you a secret. I've got three big pans of scalloped oysters downstairs piping hot and just ready to be eaten, and I want you to help me carry them over to the church. They're a surprise. They don't know they're going to have scalloped oysters. They think they're only having roast lamb and mashed potatoes, but I just thought I'd have a little celebration on myself, so I made these without telling. Do you like scalloped oysters?"

"Do I like scalloped oysters?" beamed Murray, forgetting his role of outlaw and realizing his empty stomach. "Lead me to 'em."

His hostess smiled appreciatively.

"All right, you hurry then, and I'll have your clothes up in a jiffy! Here's the bathroom, and this is the hot water." She turned the faucet on swiftly. "And this knob controls the shower. Bob always liked a shower. Do you?"

"I certainly do!" said Murray fervently.

"Well, now, hurry up! I'll have your suit up in no time. Let's run a race!"

She ran smiling down the stairs as if she were an old comrade, and he stood still in the cozy little bathroom with the steam of the nice, hot water rising in the white tub, and what seemed like a perfect army of clean, luxurious towels with big embroidered S's on them, and Turkish washrags with blue crocheted edges, and cakes of sweet-smelling soap all calling him to the bath that his aching body so much desired, and yet now was the time when he ought to be going! He *must* be going!

He glanced back from the door and down the stairs. He could just see an ironing board beyond the dining room door, right in the doorway, and the blue suit lying across it, the trousers folded in a most acceptable manner, and there was her step. She was standing right in the doorway with the iron in her hand and facing toward the stairs! He could not get away without passing her, at least not by going down the stairs. And, well—why not take a bath? He certainly needed it. There would be a way to get away later. And oh, scalloped oysters, and those good things he had seen through the windows! But of course he couldn't go to that supper! Still, there was the bath all ready, and no telling when he would ever get a chance again.

So he locked the door and began swiftly to take off the alien garments that in the three weeks of his wanderings he had managed to acquire. At least, here was a bath, and why not take the goods the gods provided?

Chapter 9

Murray Van Rensselaer was roused from the relaxation which the luxury of soap and water had brought to him by the sound of Mrs. Summers' voice and a tap at the bathroom door.

"Your suit is ready on the bed, and I took the liberty of laying out some underclothes and things that I found in the trunk. Will it take you long to dress? I don't want my oysters to get tough."

"I'll be with you in no time now," he called lightly as he scrubbed away feebly with one of the big Turkish towels. He was beginning to realize all he was in for. Where would he get shaving things? He was not used to shaving himself often, either. He had depended on his man so long. But perhaps that trunk would have some things in it. Darn it all! Suppose that suit didn't fit after she had taken so much trouble pressing it. He would simply have to make a dive out of the window if it didn't. Or wait. He could say they had sent the wrong trunk! Only how would she account for the fact that he hadn't noticed it when she took out the suit? Well, he needn't cross the bridge till he came to it.

He gathered up his coarse garments, enveloped himself in a towel, and with a hasty survey of the hall, made a dive into "his room," feeling as if he had already weathered several storms.

There on the bed lay garments, and fearfully he put forth his hand and examined them. They were pleasant garments, smooth and fine, not perhaps so fine as the heir of the house of Van Rensselaer had been used to wearing, and still, good enough to feel luxurious after the ones he had picked up by the way on his journeys and used as a disguise. He climbed tentatively into them and found that they fit very well—a little loose on his lean body, grown leaner now with enforced privation, but still a very respectable fit.

Everything was there, even to necktie and collar, even to buttons put onto the shirt. What a mother that woman was! Fancy his mother doing a thing like that, putting buttons on a shirt! And hunting out all those garments just as if she had been a man! Well, this woman was great! He had a passing regret that he could not remain and enjoy her longer, but at least he was thankful for this brief touch with a life like that. Well, he would remember it, and sometime, when—no! There would never be any time when he could, of course. He was a murderer and an outlaw. But if there had been, she would have been a sweet memory to put by to think of, a kind of ideal in a world that knew no ideals. There had been fellows in college, a few that looked as if they had homes and mothers like this. He hadn't realized then what made them different, but this must have been it. They had homes and mothers. He began to envy the chap whose name was Allan Murray. What a winter he would have in this room, sitting by that fire reading those books. He had never been much of a reader himself, but now as he slid his feet into the shoes that were a whole size too large for him and glanced up at the comfortable chair and the light and the gleaming blue and red and gold of the backs of those books, he thought it might be a pleasant occupation. In fact, almost anything that kept one at home and gave one rest and peace seemed heaven to him now. The bath had refreshed him and given him a brief spurt of strength, and now that he was again attired in clean garments, and looked fairly like a respectable young man once more, his courage rose. He had managed the old-fashioned razor very well indeed for one as unskilled in caring for himself as he was, and his clean-shaven face looked back at him now from the big old mahogany-framed mirror with a fairly steady glance. He wasn't so bad-looking after all. There were heavy shadows under his eyes, and he looked thin and tired, and there was an almost irritating resemblance to his mother in his face that he had never noticed before, but still, nobody would ever look upon him just casually and take him for a murderer. And here, for the time being, he was protected by another man's identity and name. If that chap Allan Murray only didn't turn up in the midst of proceedings, why, perhaps he could even venture to get a little dinner, if things didn't get too thick. Of course he could always bolt if there were any signs of the other fellow coming to life. It was to be hoped that he at least had sustained a sprained ankle in the wreck that would keep him till morning, or till a late train that night. He hated the idea of having to go off with the other fellow's clothes. They might be some he was fond of, and maybe he couldn't afford to buy many. But he had a good job ahead of him, and he'd probably pull through—teller of a bank! That must bring a fairly large salary. And anyhow, if a fellow was a murderer, why not be a thief also? One was an outlaw anyway. Might as well be hung for a sheep as a lamb. Besides, would that other fellow stop at a suit of clothes if his life was at stake? And the reputation of his fine old family? I ask you.

His meditations were broken by a pleasant voice chanting: "Are you ready, Allan Murray? My oysters will be tough if they have to wait another minute!" and there was that something in her voice that made him respond cheerily much in the same spirit:

"Yes, I'm coming, Mrs. Summers. Be with you immediately." And that was the first that his real inner consciousness knew or had admitted that he really meant to dare to go to that supper.

He snatched a nice white hairbrush and brushed his hair vigorously, parting it in a way he had never done before, and bungled a knot in the blue tie she had laid out; then, grasping a gray felt hat that seemed to wink at him from the tray of the trunk, he hurried downstairs, as pleasant-appearing a young man as ever one would need to see. He caught a glimpse of himself in a long old mirror between two windows in the living room as he came downstairs, and he said to himself: *Why, I don't look in the least like myself. I look a new man. Nobody would ever dream that I'm a murderer!*

He carried two pans of scalloped oysters across the lawn to the church, while Mrs. Summers walked beside him and carried the third and guided him to the church kitchen door. Now, here would be a good chance to escape when she went inside the kitchen, only he would simply have to take one of those pans of oysters with him, for they were making him giddy now with their delicious odor. He wished he had remembered to bring his old overcoat with him, for it was cold out here in the chill November air.

But Mrs. Summers gave him no chance to escape. She swung the door open and ushered him inside, where he was surrounded by a bevy of young people, who fairly took him into their arms with welcome and almost carried him on their shoulders into a great banquet hall, where tables were set with flowers and overflowing plates of good things, and the odors of wonderful food were more than a starving man could resist. He let them shut the door and draw him inside. Only when he lifted his eyes and met the eyes of one girl in blue whom they introduced as Anita, and who looked at him as if she knew he was a sham, and despised him, did he come to himself and wish he could run away.

But Anita dealt her glancing blows and passed indifferently, and he was hurried eagerly into the banquet room and placed in the seat of honor beside the minister, who had also just arrived.

There was a great excitement, for someone had just come in

with grave face and open evening paper, stating that the name of Allan Murray was among those who were seriously injured in the wreck.

Murray couldn't help feeling a twinge of relief and security as he heard that. At least he could eat his dinner in peace, without any more likelihood than there had been for the last three weeks that he would be apprehended and lodged in jail before the meal was over.

But his relief was but short-lived, for another difficulty approached. The minister leaned over, smiling, and said in a low tone: "Murray, they're going to call on you to ask a blessing."

Murray's heart stood still, and he felt a trembling sensation creeping over him, as if the enemy after a brief respite had him in sight again. Whatever a blessing was, he didn't know. If the man had asked him to "say grace," he might have understood. But a "blessing"! Well, whatever it was, he had best keep out of it, so, gripping his self-control together again, he endeavored to look as if nothing extraordinary had been asked of him and leaned engagingly toward the minister.

"Doctor, I hope you'll excuse me from doing anything tonight. I'm simply all in. That wreck—!"

"Oh, certainly," the minister hastened to assure him. "I shouldn't have asked, and of course everybody will understand. But you are so well known as an active Christian worker, you know, that it was only natural to feel it appropriate. Still, of course I understand. I'll just tell the young president of this affair how it is, and she'll excuse you. I guess you must have a good appetite by this time if you've just arrived from the wreck?" he finished kindly.

"I'll say!" said Murray, glad that there was one question he could answer truthfully.

Then, suddenly, a silence spread over the entire chattering company, and Murray looked up to see the girl in blue, the one who had looked through him with scorn, whom they called Anita, standing at the middle table on the opposite side of the room, about to speak.

"Mr. Harrison, will you ask God's blessing?"

Her voice rang clear, and her eyes seemed to sweep the speaker's table where he sat and touch him with a slight look of disapproval. Somehow he felt that that girl was suspecting him. It was almost like having a police officer standing over there looking at him. It gave him a feeling that if he should dare get up and try to slide away unnoticed, she would immediately call the whole company to order and have him arrested.

These things had for the moment engrossed his mind so that he had not taken in what the girl had been saying. But all at once he noticed that everybody in the room but himself was sitting with bent head in an attitude of prayer. At least, everybody except one girl. It was perhaps the ardent furtive glance of Jane's eyes raised from a bent head to watch him that finally called him to himself and made him involuntarily close his eyes and bend his head. He felt as if he had been caught thinking by Jane, and that there was no knowing but she would interpret his thoughts. She seemed so almost uncanny in her ability to creep into intimacy without encouragement.

But once his eyes closed, the words of Anita came back to him like an echo, especially that word "blessing." It was the same unusual word the minister had used, and he had used it in much the same phrase, "Ask a blessing." So this was what they meant— make a prayer! Gosh! Was that what they had wanted him to do? What he was supposed to be able to do? He had indeed assumed a difficult character, and one he would never have voluntarily chosen. What should he do about it? Would it happen again? And could he invent another excuse, or would that lay him open too much to suspicion? What did they say when they made a prayer over a table like that? Could he fake a prayer? He had tried faking almost everything. He was known at home as a great mimic. But to mimic something about which he knew nothing would be a more difficult task than any he had ever undertaken before. He set his mind to listen to the words that were being spoken.

The first thing he noticed about this "blessing" business was that the minister was talking in a conversational tone of voice, as if addressing some other mortal, though with a deferential tone as to One in authority, yet on a familiar, friendly basis. The tone was so intimate, so assured, as if addressed to One the speaker knew would delight to honor his request, that Murray actually opened the fringes of one eye a trifle to make sure the man by his side was not addressing a visible presence.

There was something beautiful and strong and tender about

the face of the minister with his eyes closed, standing there in the hush of the candlelit tables, the tips of his long, strong fingers touching the tablecloth, the candlelight flickering on his rugged face, peace upon his brow, that impressed Murray tremendously in the brief glance he dared take. And the words from those firm lips were no less awe-inspiring. A thrill of something he had never quite experienced before ran down his spine, a thrill not altogether unpleasant.

Those words! They sank into his soul like an altogether new lesson that was being learned. Could he ever repeat it and dare to try to get away with a prayer like that?

"We thank Thee for the new friend that has come among us to live, who is not a stranger, because he is the son of those whom we have long loved and known. We thank Thee for the beautiful lives of his honored father and mother, who at one time walked among us, and the fragrance of whose living still lingers in the memory of some of us who loved them. We thank Thee also that he is not only born of the flesh into the kingdom, but that he has been born again, of the Spirit, and therefore is our brother in Christ Jesus—"

There was more to that "blessing," although the stranger guest did not hear it. He felt somehow strangely ashamed as these statements of thanksgiving fell from the pastor's lips, as though he were being held to honor before One who knew better, who was looking him through and through with eyes that could not be deceived. So now there were two in that room whose eyes were hostile, who knew that he was false, that he did not belong there, the girl they called Anita and the Invisible One whose blessing was being invoked. And while he felt a reasonable assurance that he could escape and flee from the presence of that scornful girl, he knew in his heart that he could never get away from the other, who was the One they called God. God had never been anything in his life but a name to trifle with. Never once before had he felt any personality or reality to that name God. It filled him with amazement that was appalling in its strangeness. He felt that life until then had not prepared him for anything like a fact of this sort. Of course he knew there were discussions of this sort, but they had never come near enough to him for him even to have recognized an opinion about them before. Why they did now he did not understand. But he felt suddenly that he must get out of that room; even if he starved to death or was shot on the way, he must get away from there.

He opened his eyes cautiously, glanced about furtively for the nearest unguarded exit, and saw the eyes of Jane watching him greedily. She even met his glance with a feather of a smile flitting across her mobile young lips, a nice enough comradely smile, if he only had been in the mood to notice, and if she hadn't been so persistent and forward, but it annoyed him. He closed his eyes quickly as if they had not been opened, and when he tried to glance about again, he looked the other direction, where he thought he remembered seeing a door into a passageway.

But a dash of blue blocked the passageway. Somehow Anita, in the blue gown, had gotten there from her position at the other end of the room. She was standing, leaning against the door frame almost as if she were tired. Her shapely little head rested against the wall, and her eyes were closed. There was almost a weary look in the droop of her lips and the way she held the silver tray down by her side. Somehow she seemed different now when she was not looking at him. There was something attractive about her, a sweet, good look that made him think of something pleasant. What was it? Oh! *Bessie!*

Like a sharp knife the thought went through his heart. Yes, Bessie had a good, sweet look like this girl, and Bessie would have had eyes of scorn for anyone who was not true to the core. Up in heaven somewhere, if there was such a place as heaven—and now that he was sure he had lost it, he began to believe that there was—Bessie was looking down on him with scorn. A murderer, he was, and a coward! Here he was, sitting at a meal that was not his, wearing a suit and a name that were not his, hearing God's blessing invoked upon him and his, and too much of a coward to confess it and take his medicine. Obviously he could not steal out now with that blue dress blocking the way. He must stay here and face worse perhaps than if he had never run away. What had he let himself in for in assuming even for a brief hour another man's name and position in life? It was clear that this Allan Murray, whom he was supposed to be, was a religious man, had come from religious parents; so much of his newfound character he had learned from the minister's prayer. Now how was he to carry out a character like that and play the part? He with the burden of a murderer's conscience upon him!

The "blessing" was over, to his infinite relief, and a bevy of girls in white aprons, with fluttering ribbon badges and pretty trays, were set immediately astir. The minister turned to him with a question about the wreck, and he recalled vaguely that there had also been a word of thanksgiving in that prayer about the great escape he was supposed to have made. He grasped at the idea eagerly and tried to steer the conversation away from himself and into general lines of railroad accidents, switching almost immediately and unconsciously to the relative subject of automobile accidents, and then stopping short in the middle of a sentence, dumb, with the thought that he had killed Bessie in an automobile accident, and here he was talking about it—telling with vivid words how a man would drive and take risks and get used to it. Where was it he had heard that a guilty man could not help talking about his guilt and letting slip out to a trained detective the truth about himself?

His face grew white and strained, and the minister eyed him kindly.

"You're just about all in, aren't you?" he said sympathetically. "I know just how it is. One can't go through scenes like that without suffering, even though one escapes unscathed himself. I was on a train not long ago that struck a man and killed him. It was days before I could get rested. There is something terrible about the nerve strain of seeing others suffer."

And Murray thankfully assented and enjoyed a moment's quiet while he took a mouthful of the delicious fruit that stood in a long-stemmed glass on his plate.

But the minister's next sentence appalled him:

"Well, we won't expect a speech from you tonight, though I'll confess we had been hoping in that direction. You see, your fame has spread before you, and everybody is anxious to hear you. But I'll just introduce you to them sometime before the end of the program, and you can merely get up and let them see you officially. I know Mr. Harper will be expecting something of that sort, and I suppose you'll want to please him. You see, he makes a great deal of having found a Christian young man for a teller in his bank."

The minister looked at him kindly, evidently expecting a reply, and Murray managed to murmur, "I see," behind his napkin, but he felt that he would rather be hung at sunrise than attempt to make a speech under these circumstances. So that was his new character, was it? A Christian young man! A young Christian banker! How did young Christian bankers act? He was glad for the tip that showed him what was expected of him, but how in thunder was he to get away with this situation? A speech was an easy enough matter in his own set. It had never bothered him at all. In fact, he was much sought after for that sort of thing. Repartee and jest had been his strong points. He had stories bubbling full of snappy humor on his tongue's tip. But when he came to review them in his panic-stricken mind, he was appalled to discover that not one was suitable for a church supper on the lips of a young Christian banker! Oh gosh! If he only had a drink! Or a cigarette! Didn't any of these folks smoke? Weren't they going to pass the cigarettes pretty soon?

Chapter 10

Sometime about half past ten that supper was over. It seemed more like a week to the weary wanderer, though they professed to by hurrying through their program because he must be tired.

He really had had a very good time, in spite of the strangeness of the situation and his anxiety lest his double might appear on the scene at any moment to undo him. He had tried to think what he would say or do in case that should happen, but he could only plan to bolt through the nearest entrance, regardless of any parishioner who might be carrying potato salad or ice cream, and take advantage of the natural confusion that would arise in the event of the return of another hero.

Having settled that matter satisfactorily, his easy, fun-loving nature actually arose to a moderate degree of enjoyment of the occasion. He had always taken a chance, a big chance, and in this kindly, admiring atmosphere, his terror, which had driven him from one point to another during the last few weeks, had somewhat subsided. It was more than halfway likely that the man he was supposed to be was either hurt seriously or dead, seeing that they had had no direct word from him, and it was hardly probable he would appear at the supper at this late hour, even if he did get a later train to Marlborough. So, gradually, the tense muscles of his face relaxed, the alert look in his eyes changed to a normal twinkle, for he was a personable young man when he was in his own sphere, and his tongue loosened. As his inner man began to be satisfied with the excellent food, and he drank deeply of the black coffee with which they plied him, he found a feeble pleasure in his native wit. His conversation was not exactly what might have been termed "religious," but he managed to keep out of it many allusions that would not have fitted the gathering. He was by no means stupid, and some inner sense must have guided him, for he certainly was among a class of people to whom his previous experience gave him no clue. They were just as eager and just as vivacious over the life they were living and the work they were doing as ever the people with whom he was likely to associate were over their play. In fact, they seemed somehow to be happier, more satisfied, and he marveled as he grew more at his ease among them. He felt as if he had suddenly dropped out of his own universe and into a different world, run on entirely different principles. For instance, they talked intermittently, and with deep concern, about a man whom they called John, who was suffering with rheumatic fever. It appeared that they went every day to see him, that he was of great importance to their whole group; some of them spoke of having spent the night with him and of feeling intensely his suffering, as if it were their own, and of collecting a fund to surprise him with on his birthday. They spoke of him with honor and respect, as if he were one with many talents whom they deeply loved. They even spoke of his smile when they came into his sick room and of the hothouse roses that someone had sent him, how he enjoyed them. And then quite casually it came out that the man was an Italian day laborer, a member of a mission Sunday school which this church was supporting! Incredible story! Quite irrational people! Love a day laborer! A foreigner! Why, they had spoken of him as if he were one of their friends!

He looked into their faces and saw something beautiful; perhaps he would have named it "love" if he had known more about that virtue, or maybe he might have called it "spiritual" if he had been brought up to know anything but the material in life. As it was, he named it "strange" and let it go at that. But he liked it. They fascinated him. A wild fancy passed through his mind that if he ever had to be tried for murder, he would like it to be here, among a people who thought and talked as these people did. They thought him like themselves, and he was not. He did not even know what they meant by some of the things they said.

Between such weird thought as this, he certainly enjoyed his dinner, wineless and smokeless even though it was. There was a taste about everything that reminded him of the days when he used to go up to Maine as a little boy and spend the summers with his father's maiden sister, Aunt Rebecca, long since dead. Things had tasted that way there, wonderful, delectable, as if you wanted to eat on forever, as if they were all real and made with love. Odd how that word *love* kept coming to him. Ah! Yes, and there was Mrs. Chapparelle. She used to cook that way, too. It must be when people cooked with their own hands instead of hiring it out that it tasted that way. Mrs. Chapparelle and the pancakes, and the strawberry shortcake with cream, made of light puffy biscuit with luscious berries between and lots of sugar. Mrs. Chapparelle! Her face had begun to fade from his haunted brain since the night he had looked into her kitchen window and had seen her go briskly to the door in answer to the ring. What had she met when she opened that door? A white-robed nurse, and behind her men bearing a corpse? Or had they had the grace to send someone to break the news first?

The thought struck him suddenly from out of the cheerfulness of the evening, and he lifted a blanched face to Anita as she put before him his second helping of ice cream and another cup of coffee.

And he was a murderer! He had killed poor Bessie Chapparelle, a girl a good deal like this Anita girl, clean and fine, with high ideals. What would these people, these kind, good people, think of him if they knew? What would they do? Would they put handcuffs on him and send for the police? Or would they sit down and try to help him out of his trouble? He half wished that he dared put himself upon their mercy. That minister now. He looked like a real father! But of course he would have to uphold the law. And of course there wasn't anything to do but hang him when he had killed a girl like Bessie! Not that he cared about the hanging. His life was done. But for the sake of his mother, who had never taken much time out of her social duties to notice him, and the father who paid his bills and bailed him out, he was running away, he told himself, so that they would not have to suffer. Just how that was saving them from suffering he didn't quite ever try to explain to himself. He was running away so there would not be any trial to drag his father and mother through. That was it.

He ate his ice cream slowly, trying to get ahold of himself once more, and across the room Anita and Jane happened to be standing together for an instant in a doorway.

"Isn't he stunningly handsome, Anita? Aren't you just crazy about him?" whispered Jane effusively.

"He's good-looking enough," admitted Anita, "but I'm afraid he knows it too well."

"Well, how could he help it, looking like that?" responded the ardent Jane, and she flitted away to take him another plate of cake.

But the crowning act of his popularity came when Mr. Harper, president of the bank, senior elder in the church, and honored citizen, came around to speak with the young man and welcome him to the town. He had been detained and came in late, being rushed to his belated supper by the good women of the committee. He had only now found opportunity to find the new teller and speak to him.

Murray rose with a charming air of deference and respect and stood before the elder man with all the ease that his social breeding had given him. He listened with flattering attention while the bank president told him how glad he was to have a Christian young man in his employ, and how he hoped they would grow to be more than employer and employed.

Murray had dreaded this encounter if it should prove necessary, as he feared the president would have met his young teller before this occasion and would discover that he was not the right man. But Elliot Harper stood smiling and pleased, looking the young man over with apparently entire confidence, and Murray perceived that so far he was not discovered.

It was easy enough to assent and be deferential. The trouble would come when they began to ask him questions. He had settled it in his mind quite early in the evening that his strong point was to be as impersonal as possible, not to make any statements whatsoever about himself that could possibly not be in harmony with the character of the man he represented, as he thought they knew him, and to make a point of listening to others so well that they should think he had been talking. That was a little trick he learned long ago in college when he wanted to get on the right side of a professor. It came back quite naturally to him now.

So he stood with his handsome head slightly bowed in deference and his eyes fixed in eager attention, and the entire assembly fastened their eyes upon him and admired.

That might possibly be called the real moment when the town, at least those representatives of the town that were present, might be said to have opened their arms and taken him into their number. How he would meet Mr. Harper was the supreme test. With one accord they believed in Mr. Harper. He stood to them for integrity and success. They adored Mr. Harrison, their minister, and confided to him all their troubles; they had firm belief in his creed and his undoubted faith and spirituality; they knew him as a man of God and respected his wonderful mind and his consistent living. But they tremendously admired the keen mind, clear business ability, coupled with the staunch integrity, of their wealthy bank president, Elliot Harper. Therefore they awaited his leading before they entirely surrendered to the new young man who had come to live in their midst.

Murray Van Rensselaer felt it in the atmosphere as he sat down. He had not lived in an air of admiration all his life for nothing. This was his native breath, and it soothed his racked nerves and gave him that quiet satisfaction with himself that he had been accustomed to feeling ever since he was old enough to know that his father was Charles Van Rensselaer, the successful financier and heir of an ancient family.

He had stood the test, and the time was up. Now, anytime, in a moment or two, he could get away, melt into the darkness, and forget Marlborough. They would wonder and be indignant for a day or a week, but they would never find him nor know who he was. He would simply be gone. And then very likely in a day or two the other man whom he had been representing for the evening would either turn up or have a funeral or something, and they would discover his fraud. But there would in all probability be an interval in which he could get safely away and be no more. He had gained a dinner and a pleasant evening, a little respite in the nightmare that had pursued him since the accident, and he had a kindly feeling toward these people. They had been nice to him. They had showed him a genuineness that he could not help but admire. He liked every one of them, even the offish Anita, who had a delicate profile like Bessie's, and the ridiculous Jane, who could not take her eyes from him. Now that he was an outcast, he must treasure even such friendliness, for there would be little of that sort of thing left for him in the world going forward. He could not hope to hoodwink people this way the rest of his life.

He felt a sudden pang at the thought of throwing this all away. It had been wonderfully pleasant, so different from anything he had ever experienced among his own crowd—an atmosphere of loving kindness like what he used to find at the Chapparelles', which made the thought of stolen evenings spent in the company of Bessie seem wonderfully fresh and sweet and free from taint of any selfishness or sordidness. How different, for instance, these girls were from the girls at home. Even that Jane had an innocence about her that was refreshing. How he would enjoy lingering to play with these new people who treated him so charmingly, just as he had lingered sometimes in new summer resorts for a little while to study new types of girls and frolic awhile. It would be pleasant, *how* pleasant, to eat three good meals a day and have people speak kind words and try to forget that he was a murderer and an outlaw. If he were in a foreign land now, he might even dare it. But four hundred miles was a short distance where newspapers and telegraph and radio put everything within the same room, so to speak. No, he must get out, and get out quickly. There would likely be a late train, and perhaps his other self would arrive on it. If possible he would have to get away without going back to Mrs. Summers', but at least if he went back he must not linger there. He could make some excuse, run out for medicine to the drugstore, perhaps, or if worse came to worst, pretend to go up to bed and then steal away after she was asleep. There would be a way!

His resilient nature allowed him to feel wonderfully cheerful as he arose from the table at last and prepared to make his adieus.

But it was not easy, after all, to get away. Mrs. Summers came to him and asked him if he would mind carrying a basket home for her—she wouldn't be a minute—and then pressed him into service to gather up silver candlesticks and a few rare china dishes.

"You see, they're borrowed," she explained, "and I don't like to risk leaving them here lest someone will be careless with them in the morning before I could get over, or mix them up and take them to the wrong person. I wouldn't like them to get broken or lost under my care."

They walked together across the lawn under a belated moon that had struggled through the clouds and was casting silver slants over the jeweled brown of the withered grass.

"It's been so lovely having you here," said Mrs. Summers gently, "almost like having my boy back again. I kept looking at you and thinking, 'He's my boy. He's coming home every night, and I can take care of him just as I did with my own.'"

Murray's heart gave a strange lurch. Nobody had ever spoken to him like that. Love, except in a tawdry form, had never come his way, unless his father's gruffness and continual fault-finding might be called love. It certainly had been well disguised so that he had never thought of it in that light. It had rather seemed to him, when he thought about it at all, that he stood to his father more in the light of an obligation than anything else. His mother's love had been too self-centered and too irritable to interest him. There had been teachers occasionally who had been fond of him, but their interest had passed when he used them to slide out of schoolwork. There had been a nurse in his babyhood that he barely remembered, who used to comfort him when he was hurt or sleepy, and sometimes when he was sick cuddle him in her arms as if she cared for him, but that was so very far away. He had sometimes watched the look between Bessie Chapparelle and her mother when he would be there playing games in the evenings with Bessie, a look that had made him think of the word *love*, but that also was far away and very painful now to think about. Strange how one's thoughts will snatch a bit from every part of one's life and blend them together in an idea that takes but an instant to grasp, just as a painter will take a snatch of this and a dab of that color and blend them all into a tint, with no hint of the pink or the blue, or the black, or the yellow, or the white, that may have gone to form it, making just a plain gray cloud. Murray was doing more thinking these last few days than he had ever done in the whole of his life before. Life, as it were, was painting pictures on his mind; wonderful living truths that he had never seen before were flashing on the canvas of his brain, made up of the facts of his past life which at the time had passed over him unnoticed. He had gone from his cradle like one sliding downhill and taking no note of the landscape. But he found now that he had suddenly reached the bottom of the hill and had to climb up (if indeed he might ever attain to any heights again), that he knew every turn of the way he had come and wondered how he could have been oblivious before. It occurred to him that his experience might be called "growing up." Trouble had come, and he had grown up. Life had turned back on him and slapped him in the face, and he began to see things in life, now that he had lost them, that he had not even recognized before.

As he slipped his arm through the big basket and stood waiting for Mrs. Summers to decide whose cake pan the big square aluminum one was, he looked wistfully about him on the disarray of tables, kind of hungering in his heart to come here again and feast and bask in the cheery comforting atmosphere. Good and sweet and wholesome it all was, a sort of haven for his weary soul that was condemned to plod on throughout his days without a place for his foot to remain, forevermore. He had a strange, tired feeling in his throat as if he would like to cry, like a child who has come to the end of the good time, and whose bubbles are broken and vanished. There would be no more bubbles for him anymore. The bowl of soapsuds was broken.

And so as they walked toward the little cottage with its gleaming light awaiting them from the dining room window, he felt strangely sad and lonely, and he wished with all his heart that he might walk in and be this woman's boy. If only he could be born again into her home and claim her as his mother and take the place as her son and be a new man, with all his past forgotten! He thought—poor soul, he had not yet learned the subtlety of sin and the frailty of human nature—he thought if he could be in this environment, with such people about him, such a home to come to, and such a mother to love him, he could learn to fit it. If it hadn't been for the possibility of the other man coming, he would have dared to try it and keep up his masquerade.

Chapter 11

He helped her unpack the basket and put her things away, and he gave a wistful look about the pretty, cozy room. He had never supposed there were homes like this anywhere. There was nothing formal about the place, and yet there were bits of fine old furniture, pictures, and bric-a-brac that spoke of travel and taste. It just seemed a place where one would like to linger and where *home* had been impressed upon everything around like a lovely monogram worked into the very fabric of it.

"Now," said Mrs. Summers as she whirled about from the cake box, where she had been bestowing a dozen lovely frosted sponge cakes that had been left over and she had brought home, "you must get to bed! I know you are all worn out, and you've got to be on hand early tomorrow morning. What time did Mr. Harper say he wanted you at the bank? Was it nine o'clock? I thought so. So I won't keep you up but a minute more. I thought it would be nice if we just had a bit of a prayer together the first night, and a verse. I always like a verse for a pillow to sleep on, don't you? Even if it is late. Will you read, or shall I?" and she held out a little limp-covered book that looked, like everything else in the house, as if it had been used lovingly and often.

"Oh, *you!*" gasped Murray embarrassedly, looking at the book as if it had been a toad suddenly lifting its head in the way, and wondering what strange new ceremony now was being thrust at him. There seemed no end to the strange things they did in this pleasant, unusual place. Take that thing they called "blessing" and was a prayer! It was like that book his nurse used to read him in his childhood, called *Alice in Wonderland*. You never knew what you would be called upon to do next before you could eat or sleep. Did they do these things all the time, every day, or just once in a while, when they were initiating some new member? It must be a great deal of trouble to them to keep it up every day, and must take up a good deal of time.

"Very well," said Mrs. Summers. "You sit in that big chair, and I'll just read a little bit where I left off last night."

They did it every night, then! Like massaging one's face and putting on night garments, as his mother always did, lovely gauzy things with floating scarfs like wings. This must be a sort of massaging for the soul.

He settled down in the comfortable chair and watched the white fingers of the lady flutter open the leaves of the book, familiarly and lovingly.

He liked the shape of her lips as she spoke, the sound of her voice. There was fascination in watching her, so sweet and strong and pleasant.

"There was a man of the Pharisees, named Nicodemus, a ruler of the Jews: The same came to Jesus by night, and said unto him, Rabbi, we know that thou art a teacher come from God: for no man can do these miracles that thou doest, except God be with him."

Murray heard the words, but they meant nothing to him. He was not listening. He was thinking what it would have been like if he had been born into this home. Then suddenly into his thoughts came those words, so startling. Where had he heard them before? "Jesus answered and said unto him, Verily, verily, I say unto thee, Except a man be born again, he cannot see the kingdom of God."

Why! How very strange! Those were the words he had seen in the streetcar. Almost the identical words, "Ye must be born again!" He would never forget them, because that had seemed the only way out of his difficulty. And now she was reading again, this time identical: "Marvel not that I said unto thee, Ye must be born again."

Why! It was like someone answering his thoughts. What did it all mean? He listened and tried to get the sense. It appeared to be an argument between one named Nicodemus and one Jesus. There was talk of wind blowing and water and a Spirit. It was all Greek to him. A serpent lifted in the wilderness, of believing and perishing, and eternal life. He almost shuddered at that. Eternal life! Who would want to live forever when he was a murderer and an outcast? "For God sent not his Son into the world to *condemn* the world," went on the steady voice, "but that the world through him might be *saved.*"

Astonishing words! They got him! Condemnation was what he was under. Saved! He almost groaned. Oh, if there were but a way for him to be saved from this that had come upon him!

"He that believeth on him is not condemned."

Strange words again, and of course it all meant nothing—nothing that could apply to his case. Depression came upon his soul again. The condemnation of the law overshadowed him. He looked restlessly toward the door. Oh, if he could get away now and go—go swiftly before condemnation overtook him and got him in its iron grip forever!

The little book was closed, and the astonishing little lady suddenly rose from her chair and knelt down beside it. He was embarrassed beyond measure. He wanted to do the proper thing and excite no suspicions, but how was one to know what to do in a situation like this? Kneeling down in a parlor beside a Morris chair! How could anyone possibly know that that was the thing expected? Or was it expected?

Then he began slowly, noiselessly, to move his weary, stiffened muscles, endeavoring to transfer his body into a kneeling posture without the slightest sound, the least possible hint that he had not of course been kneeling from the start.

Strange happening for this onetime social star to be kneeling now in this humble cottage, hearing himself (or what was supposed to be himself) prayed for earnestly, tenderly, with loving chains of prayer "binding his soul about the feet of God." He grew red and embarrassed. He felt tears stinging his eyes. How was it that a possibility of anything like this being done anywhere in the universe for him never entered his mind before? It was indeed as if he was born into a new universe, and yet he still had the consciousness of his old self, his old guilt, upon him. It was intolerable. He never had felt so mean in his life as while he knelt there, hearing himself brought to the presence of God and knowing that he had cheated this wonderful woman who was praying for him, and that he was soon going to steal from her house in the night and never be seen by her anymore. What would she think? And how would she meet her God the next time she prayed? Would she curse him, perhaps, and would worse punishment come upon him than had come already? And how would a God feel about it? He had never been much concerned about God, whether He was or was not, but now he suddenly knew as this woman talked with Him with that assurance, that face-to-face acquaintance, that intimacy of voice, that there *was* a God. Whatever anybody might say, he knew now that there *was*! It was as if he had seen Him, he had felt Him, anyway, in a strange convincing power like the look from a great man's eyes, whom one had never met before, nor heard much of, yet recognizes at the first glimpse as being mighty! Well! There was a Power he hadn't counted on! The Power of God! He knew the details of the power of the law. But what if he also was in danger from the Power of God? What if this deception, just for the sake of a bath and a supper, should anger God and turn the vengeance of heaven and hell upon his soul? He vaguely knew that there were yet unfathomable depths of misery that he had not even tapped the surface of, and his burden seemed greater than he could bear. If he only might become someone else, be born again, as the book had said, so that no one would ever recognize him, not even God! But would that be possible? Could one be born at all without God about?

Floundering amid these perplexities, he suddenly became aware that the lady had risen, and, red with embarrassment, aware of tears upon his face which he could not somehow wipe away quickly enough, he struggled to his own feet.

She was not looking at him. She had moved across the room to a pitcher of ice water she had prepared before she began to read, and now she poured a glass and handed it to him. He was struck with the look of peace upon her lips. It seemed a look that no one he had ever known before had worn. Wait, yes, Mrs. Chapparelle sometimes had looked that way, even when they had very little for supper. Once he had stayed with them when there were only potatoes and corn bread. No butter, only salt for the potatoes, and a little milk, two glasses, one for him and one for Bessie. She must have gone without herself, and yet she had that look of peace upon her lips! Had even smiled! What was it? Talking with God that made it?

He got himself up the little white staircase with the mahogany-painted rail and the softly carpeted treads of gray carpet, and locked himself inside his room. He knew he had said good night and agreed upon something about when he would come to breakfast in the morning. As he did not intend to be present at breakfast the next morning, he had paid little heed to what she had said. His soul was in turmoil, and he was weary to the bone. He dropped into the big chair and gazed sadly about him on the pretty room.

He had it in mind to make a little stir of preparation for bed and then wait quietly until the house was still and he could steal down the stairs or out the window, whichever seemed the easiest way, and be seen no more. But he felt a heaviness upon him that was overpowering. He looked at the white bed with the plump pillows and the smooth sheets that had been turned back for his use. His eyes dwelt upon the softness of blankets and the immaculate cleanness of everything, and he longed with inexpressible longing to get into it and go to sleep, but he knew he must not yield. He knew that it would not be safe for him to linger till the morning. The news of him would have spread even by this time, and someone somewhere would say that he knew that the man he was supposed to be was dead or hurt, or else was coming in the morning. No, he must get up and get into his coarse clothes at once and be ready to depart. It would not do to be quiet now and noisy later. She would think it strange of him to be long in getting to bed. He must hurry! He took off the shoes that were a bit too large for him and crinkled his tired toes luxuriously. He took off the suit that was not his and folded it for the trunk tray. He took off the collar and necktie and put them back in the trunk. Then he looked at the pile of soiled underwear that he had brought back from the bathroom after his bath, and his soul rebelled. If the fellow he was supposed to be ever came back from the wreck and got his good job and his good home, he might thank his lucky stars and not bother if he was minus a pair of undergarments. He couldn't go in those soiled, tattered things any longer. And besides, if he was a murderer, why not be a thief, too, to that extent, anyway? He was sure if he was in the other fellow's place he wouldn't begrudge a poor lost soul a few of his clothes.

So he gathered the soiled clothes into a bundle, laid them on the coals that were still red in his fireplace, and watched them blaze up into flames with weary satisfaction. Then he turned out the light and tiptoed over to the window. He raised the shade and looked out to reconnoiter.

The window overlooked the street, and there was a great arc light hung in the trees, so that it shone full upon his windows. Moreover, there were people passing, and cars flying by, not a few. Marlborough had by no means gone to bed, even though the Presbyterian church social was over and the last member of the committee gone to her home. It was no use to try to escape yet. He must wait till after midnight.

So he tiptoed back, intending to turn on the light and begin to get together the rest of his things. But the flickering firelight from a charred stick that had broken in two and fallen apart to blaze up again feebly fell invitingly over the white bed and played with the shadows over the pillow. An inexpressible longing came over him to just see how it felt to lie down in that soft clean whiteness and rest for five minutes. He would not stay for more than five minutes or he might fall asleep, and that would be disastrous, but he must rest a moment or two while he was waiting, or he would not be able to travel—he was so tired. He would open the window so that when he was ready to go, he would not be making a noise again, and then he would rest.

So, just as he was, he lay cautiously down and drew the soft blankets around him, with the fragrant sheet against his face, and closed his weary eyes.

The night wind stole softly in and breathed restfully upon him, filling his lungs with clean, pure air and fanning his hot forehead, and the little charred stick collapsed with a soft shudder and went out, leaving the room in darkness, and Murray Van Rensselaer slept.

Chapter 12

When he awoke eons might have passed. He didn't know where he was, and a broad band of sun was streaming across his bed. The wind was blowing the muslin curtain out like a streamer across the room, and Mrs. Summers was tapping at the door with crisp, decided knocks, and calling to him: "Mr. Murray! Mr. Murray! I'm sorry to have to disturb you, but it's getting very late. You ought to be eating your breakfast this minute. You don't want to be late the first morning, you know!"

He opened blinded eyes and tried to locate himself. Who in thunder was Mr. Murray, and why didn't he want to be late the first morning? Was that his man calling him? No, it was a woman's voice. He blinked toward the window and saw the outlines of a church against the brightness of the sunny sky and saw people going down a strange street. He turned his head on his pillow and closed his eyes. What the dickens did it matter, anyhow? He was tired and was going to sleep this heaviness off. He must have been out late the night before. Hitting the pace pretty hard again! Must be at some club, or one of the fellows took him home. What was the little old idea, anyhow, trying to wake him up? Couldn't they let a fellow sleep till he was ready to wake up?

But the knocking continued, and he was about to tell the person at the door what he thought of him in most forcible language, when he opened his eyes again with his face the other way and saw the old rough coat he had been wearing for the past three weeks lying across the nice comfortable chair by the side of the fireplace awaiting him. Then it all came back to him like a slap in the face.

He sprang to a sitting posture and gazed hurriedly about him, a growing alarm in his eyes.

"Mr. Murray! Mr. Murray! Are you awake? Breakfast is ready. It's very late!" reiterated the pleasant but firm voice. "I'm afraid Mr. Harper will think—are you almost ready?"

"Oh—I—why, yes, Mrs. Summers," he answered then, half abashed, with a growing comprehension in his tone. "Why, yes," crisply, "I'll be with you in just a moment. I'm nearly dressed. I must have overslept."

Mrs. Summers, relieved, retired from the door, and Murray slid cautiously from the bed and grasped what garments came to hand, which proved to be the suit he had worn the night before. He couldn't go down in those old rags in broad daylight, of course. He had to make a getaway the best way possible, now that he had messed all his plans by falling asleep. Poor old guy, he would miss a suit also, but what's a suit of clothes in an emergency!

Murray dressed at lightning speed, giving little time to the brushing of hair or arrangement of tie, and was soon hurrying downstairs.

She had his coffee all poured, and there was oatmeal with cream and granulated sugar. There was half a grapefruit, too, all cut and ready for eating, and he was hungry as a bear. Yet in spite of all her talk about hurrying, she stopped to say that prayer before eating. Odd. It seemed to be a matter of course, like breathing—a habit that one couldn't stop. He almost bungled things by beginning a bite of his fruit in the middle of it. But she didn't seem to notice. She was bringing hot buttered toast and scrambled eggs and wonderful-looking fried potatoes. He could have hugged her, they all looked so good, and he had been hungry, hungry, hungry so many days before that!

Then right into the middle of that wonderful breakfast there came a sharp ring at the door. He became conscious that he had heard a high-power car drive by and stop, and panic seized him. He was caught at last, caught in his own trap, baited by sleep. What a fool he had been! He set down his cup of coffee and sprang to his feet, looking wildly about him.

"I must go!" he murmured vaguely, feeling he must say something to his hostess.

But she was already on her feet, going swiftly to the door.

"Get your coat and hat," she said in a low tone as she went.

"Too bad, right in the middle of your breakfast. But he won't want to wait—"

He dashed toward the stairs, thinking to make his escape out of a window from above somewhere while the officers entered below, but almost ran into the arms of Mr. Elliot Harper, smiling and affable, with extended hand.

"Sorry to have to hurry you the first day," he said pleasantly, "but I didn't think to mention it last night. There's a conference this morning, and I thought I'd like to have you attend. I drove around in the car to pick you up. Don't let me take you away till you've finished breakfast, however—!"

"Oh, I've finished," said the young man, uneasily glancing up the stairs and wondering if his best chance lay up there or through the kitchen door. He seemed to be always just about to make a dash and escape. It was amusing when one stopped to think of it, how he got more and more tangled in a web. Hang it all! If he only hadn't fallen asleep last night! If he only could think of a reasonable excuse to get away! It wouldn't do to just bolt with this keen-eyed businessman watching him. He was the kind to set the machinery of the law moving swiftly. He must use guile.

"I meant to go back and polish my shoes," he said deprecatingly. "If you can wait just a moment—"

"Oh, let that go till we get to the bank!" said the president genially. "There's a boy down there just dotes on polishing shoes. Save your strength, and let him do it. This your hat? I'm sorry to hurry you, but I promised to see a man before the conference, and the time's getting short. If you can just as well come now, I'll take it as a favor. . . ."

He went. How could he do otherwise with Mrs. Summers smilingly blocking the way of escape upstairs, and the determined bank president urging him toward the door? He would just ride down to the bank. There could be no danger in that, and then while Harper was seeing his man he would melt away quietly into the landscape and be seen no more.

He climbed into the luxurious car with a sense of pleasure as of coming to his own surroundings once more and rode down the pretty village street, his companion meanwhile drawing his attention to the buildings they were passing.

"This is the minister's house. You'll like Mr. Harrison, I'm sure. He's a marvelous, humble, great man. If it weren't for his humility, he'd be nabbed up by some of the great city churches. Here the senior elder lives. He has two daughters you'll meet. Nice girls. One's engaged to my nephew. The big stone house on your right belongs to Earl Atherton, one of our directors. Made his money in oil. Keen man. Next is the Stapletons'. Have a son in Harvard. You must have heard of him in athletics, Norton Stapleton. Fine lad! Good sense of balance. Comes home every year still unspoiled. Says he's coming back to go in business with his dad. Not many like him. Over there's the Farrington-Smiths'. You won't care for them. The girls all smoke cigarettes and drink, and the boys are a speedy lot. The town as a whole disapproves of them. They moved here from the city, but I hear they don't care for it, call it dull.

They'll probably invite you. They are trying hard to get in with our best people, and the girls are really quite attractive in a dashing, bold sort of way, but you won't want to accept. Thought it was just as well to let you know how the land lies. There! That's the bank in the distance, that gray-stone front. We've made it on time after all. Now we'll go right in, and I'll introduce you to the vice president. He'll take you to our conference room. Mr. Van Lennup, I wrote you about him, you know. He's immensely pleased at your coming. He was another one who knew your father, you know. This way. Walk right in this side door!"

There was no escape, though he glanced furtively either way. The street was full of passersby, and the sunlight was broad and clear. A man suddenly dashing away from his companions would excite much attention in the quiet town. He could not hope to make any possible getaway that way. He must bide his time and watch for a side door, a byway somewhere.

They led him across a marble floor down aisles of mahogany partitions, through silently swinging doors to an office beyond, where he was introduced to the vice president. They went down a marble hall to an elevator and shot up several stories to a dim and silent room with thick velvet underfoot and a polished table of noble proportions set about with lordly chairs. He perceived that he was in the inner sanctum of the directors of the bank, and when the heavy door swung back with something like a soft sigh, he felt as if prison walls had closed behind him.

A young man who had been writing at the table rose, went to

the wide plate-glass window, and drew up the shade a little higher. Murray perceived that the window overlooked the street and was too many stories above it to allow climbing out and escaping that way. He was evidently in for a directors' conference unless there might be a chance when the others were all coming in for him to slip out as they entered and make his way by the stairs to the regions below. Strange, he hadn't expected this town was large enough to boast of high office buildings for its banks. But then, he had seen it only in the dark. It must be larger than he had supposed.

Then the vice president shoved forward a chair for him to be seated and paralyzed him by remarking: "They tell me you were in college with Emory Hale, and that you two went to France together. That'll be pleasant for both of you, won't it? Emory has, I think, decided to remain in Marlborough all winter. He is doing some intensive study along scientific lines, you know, and thinks Marlborough's quiet will be a favorable atmosphere for his work. He's going to write a book, you know. Great head he has. By the way, you knew his father was one of our directors? He'll be here this morning. I met him as I came down. He says Emory wrote home that it had a great deal to do with his decision for the winter, your being here!"

Murray's brow grew moist with a cold perspiration, and he sidled over to the window as his companion turned to greet a newcomer. Perhaps, after all, the window was his best chance. Perhaps it was the best thing to risk it. They couldn't arrest a dead man, could they, even if they did recognize him? But yet, if he should break both legs, say, and have to lie in the hospital and have officers visiting him. . . Hang it all! However did he get into a scrape like this? All for a row of buns and cakes! And a foolish girl who thought she recognized him! If he ever got out of this, he would run so far and so fast that nobody would ever catch up with him again. He would change clothes with the first beggar whom he met and chop wood for a living. He would do something so that he would never again run the risk of being recognized and hauled back to his home for disgrace.

And then the door opened, and half a dozen clean-shaven, successful-looking men entered, followed almost immediately by several more, and the conference convened.

He was given a chair at the far side of the table away from both window and door, and surrounded by strong, able-bodied men, who acknowledged the introductions to him with pleasant courtesy and the right hand of welcome. Before he knew it, he found himself glowing with the warmth of their friendliness and his heart aching almost to bursting that he could not stay and take refuge behind all this genial welcome. If only he were sure that that bird Allan Murray was dead, really dead, so he could never come to life and turn up inconveniently any old time, he believed he would chance it. He would take his name and his place and make a new spot for himself in the world and try to make something of himself worthwhile. A tingle of ambition burned in his veins. It intrigued him to watch all these businessmen who seemed so keen about their part in the work of the world. He had never touched the world of business much. He had not supposed it would interest him. He found himself wondering what his superior, sarcastic father would think of him if he should succeed in business someday and, having made a fortune, should return home and let him know what he had done. And then it came to him that even if he did make a new name and fortune, he would never dare return. He would only bring shame and disgrace upon his father and mother, because he was a murderer, and even if they tried to protect him, they would have to do it by hustling him off out of the world again where he would be safe.

A wave of shame brought the color into his pale face, and he looked quickly around the group of earnest men to see if any of them had noticed him, but they were intent upon some knotty discussion that seemed to have to be decided at once before they could proceed with the day's program, and he retired into his own thoughts once more and tried to plan an escape to be put into effect as soon as he should be freed from the zealous watchfulness of these men who thought he was their new teller. There was that Emory Hale, too, they had talked about, who was supposed to have been with him in France. He must get away before he turned up.

Two hours later he thought his moment had come.

They had all just come down in the elevator, and he was about to be shown to the location of his new duties. He came out of the elevator last and noticed an open door at the end of the hall only a few feet away and an alcove with a chair obviously for the comfort of the elevator boy during slow times. Deftly he swung himself back into this alcove till the other men had passed and the boy had clashed the steel door of the elevator shut and whirled away into the upper regions for another load. For a brief instant the coast was clear, and he glided to the doorway and was about to pass out into the sunshine, regardless of the fact that he was hatless. A second more and he could have drawn a full breath of relief, dashed around the corner, and sped up till he was somewhere out of town in the wide-open country.

But in that instant's passing he came face-to-face with Jane, smartly coated and hatted in green, with brown fur around her neck, the color of her eyes and hair, and unmistakable joy in her eyes.

"Why, Allan Murray!" she cried. "Good morning! Where are you going without your hat? You look as if you were running away from school."

He came to himself with a click in his heart that reminded him of prison bars and bolts, and turned to greet her.

Somehow he summoned a smile to his ashy lips.

"Not at all," he answered cheerfully, glancing behind him at the still-empty hallway. "I was—ah—just looking for the postman." A door opened somewhere up the hall, and footsteps came out briskly.

"Excuse me," he said to the lingering girl, "I must go back. We're very busy this morning. I can't stop!"

He turned and dashed back again, coming suddenly face-to-face with Elliot Harper, who surveyed him in mild surprise.

"Oh, is that you, Murray? I was just going back for you! I must have missed you somehow."

"Yes," said nimble Murray, "I just stepped to the door to get my bearings! I always like to know how the land lies, that is, the building I'm in, you know."

"Well, we'll go right in now. McCutcheon is ready to show you your duties. We go through this side door."

Murray followed him because there was nothing else he dared do, and the steel gateway swung to with a click behind him as he entered the inner precincts of the bank itself. And once more he heard dimly the echo of bolts and bars and approaching prison walls about him. He walked to the little grated window that was to be his, so cell-like with its heavy grill, and saw an open drawer with piles of clean money lying ready for his unskilled hand. He felt almost frightened as he stood and listened, but he kept his calm exterior. It was part of his noble heritage that he could be calm under trying circumstances. He was even jaunty with a feeble joke upon his mobile lips and a pleasant grin toward the man who was endeavoring to teach him what he had to do. The trouble was the man seemed to take it for granted that he already knew a great deal about the matter, and he had to assent and act as if he did. Here he was, a new man, new name, new station, new portion in life. Yet the odds were so against him, the chances so great that he would soon be caught and put under lock and key

for an impostor, that he would have given anything just then even
to be back riding under the freight train and dodging policemen
at every turn of his way.

Chapter 13

The day that Bessie Chapparelle had met her old playmate, Murray Van Rensselaer, for the first time in seven years had been her birthday. She was twenty-one years old and feeling very staid indeed. It is odd how very old twenty-one can make itself seem when one reaches that milestone in the walk of life. A girl never feels half so grown-up at twenty-five as when she reaches twenty-one. And Bessie was counting back over the years in the way a girl will, thinking of the bright and sad epochs, and looking ahead eagerly to what she still hoped to attain. She was wondering how long it would be before she could give her beloved mother some of the luxuries she longed for her to have, and as she stood on the street corner waiting for a trolley, she watched the shining wheels of a new car come flashing down the street and wished she were well enough off to begin to buy a car. Just a little Ford roadster, of course, or maybe a coupe. A second hand one, too, but there were plenty of nice, cheap, second hand ones. It would be so nice to take Mother for a ride in the park in the evenings when she got home from her work. They could prepare a lunch and eat it on the way in the long summer twilights. What wonderful times they could have together! Mother needed to get out more. She was just stuck in the house sewing, sewing, sewing all the time. Pretty soon she would be able to earn enough so that Mother would not have to sew so much, perhaps not at all. Mother was getting to the age when she ought to rest more and have leisure for reading. The housework was really all she ought to be doing. If only she could get a raise within a year and manage to buy some kind of a car so they could take rides!

Bessie Chapparelle had been tremendously busy during those seven years since she and Murray Van Rensselaer used to play games together in the evenings and listen to the books her mother read aloud to them when they grew tired of chess and cards and crokinole. Murray had gone off to prep school, and Bessie had studied hard in high school. She had not even seen him at vacations. He had been away at a camp somewhere in the West or visiting with some schoolmate. He had remembered her graduation day, for they had talked about it before he left, and he had sent back a great sheaf of roses, which were brought up to her on the platform after she read her essay. Everybody wondered and exclaimed over the beauty and quantity of those roses, sent across the continent with a characteristic greeting tied on the card: *Hello, Pal, I knew you'd win out! Murray.*

The roses had brought other roses to her cheeks and a starry look to her eyes as she came forward with wonder in her face and received the two tributes of flowers, one of tiny sweetheart rosebuds and forget-me-nots, small and exquisite, and this other great armful of seashell-pink roses with hearts of gold. She was almost smothered behind their lavish glory, and her little white dress, simple and lovely, made by her mother, looked like a princess's robe as she stood with simple grace and bowed with a gravely pleased smile toward the audience. She took the roses over her arm and looked out from above them, a fitting setting for her happy face, but the little nosegay of sweethearts and forget-me-nots she held close to her lips with a motion of caressing, for she knew they came from her mother. They were like the flowers her mother had received from her father long ago when he was courting her, and they meant much to the girl, who had listened, fascinated by the tales of her mother's girlhood, and treasured every story and incident as if it had been a part of her very own life story. Oh, she knew who sent the forget-me-nots and sweetheart rosebuds! No one but her dear, toiling mother could have done that, and it filled her heart with tender joy to get them, for she knew they meant much sacrifice, and many hours' overwork, far into the night, perhaps, to earn the money for those costly little blossoms. She knew how much they cost, too, for she had often wanted to buy some for her mother and had not dared. But she did not know nor guess who had sent the larger mass of roses, not till she got by herself in the dressing room for a second and read the brief inscription on the card and Murray's name. Then something glowed in her face that had not been there before, a dreamy, lovely wonder, the foreshadowing of something she could not name and did not understand—a great gladness that Murray, her playmate, had not forgotten her after all this time, a revelling in the lavishness of his gift, and the wonder of the rare flowers, which she knew were more costly than anything else she had ever had in her life before. Not that she measured gifts by costliness or prized them more for that, but her life had been full of anxious planning to make a penny go as far as possible for the dear mother who toiled so hard to give her an education and all that she needed, and money to her meant toil and self-sacrifice and love. She would not have been a girl if it had not given her a thrill to know that her flowers were more wonderful than any flowers that had been sent up to that platform that day. Not that she was proud or jealous, but it was so nice to have them all see that somebody cared.

It was only a moment she had for such reflection, and then the girls came trooping in, and she had barely time to hide the little white card in the folds of her dress before they all demanded to know who sent them. They had not expected her to have such flowers. They were almost jealous of her. She was a brilliant scholar—was not that enough?

She had been popular enough, though too busy to form the friendships that make for many flowers at such a time. They had conceded her right to the place of honor because of her scholarship, but they felt it their right to shine before the public in other ways.

But Bessie was radiantly happy and gave them each a rose, such wonderful roses! They all openly declared there had never been such roses at a high school commencement before in all their knowledge. And she went her way without ever having told them the name of the sender, just vaguely saying, "Oh, from a friend away out West!" and they looked at one another wonderingly as she passed out of the dressing room and into the cool dusk of the night, where her mother waited in the shadow of the hedge for her. Then she had friends out West! Strange she never mentioned anyone before! Yet when they stopped to think, they realized Bessie never talked about herself. She was always quietly interested in the others, when she was not too busy studying to give attention to their chatter. And perhaps they had not given her much opportunity to talk, either. They never realized it before.

Then she passed from their knowledge, except for an occasional greeting on the street. They were fluttering off to the seashore and the mountains, and later on to college. But Bessie went to work.

Her first job was as a substitute in an office where a valued secretary had to be away for several months with an invalid mother.

She did not know shorthand and had only as much skill on the typewriter as one can acquire in high school, and with no machine of one's own, but she worked so diligently at night school and applied herself so carefully to the typewriter in the office that long before the absent secretary returned, she had become a valued asset to that office.

As fast as a helper in an office can climb, she had climbed, working evenings on a business course, and getting in a little culture also along the way. But she had not had time nor money for parties and the good times other young people had. One cannot study hard in the evening and take courses at a night school, then get up early and work conscientiously all day, and yet go out to dances and theaters.

Moreover, her life interest was not in such things. She had been brought up in an old-fashioned way, in the way that is condescendingly referred to as "Victorian." She still believed in the Bible and honored her mother. She still believed in keeping the laws of the land and the law of purity and self-respect. She had not bobbed her hair nor put makeup on her face, nor gone to any extreme in dress.

And yet when Murray Van Rensselaer saw her standing on that corner that morning of her twenty-first birthday, waiting for her trolley, she was sufficiently attractive to make him look twice and slow down his speed, even before he recognized her for the playmate of his childhood's days.

There had been no more roses, no letters even passing between them, and Bessie had come to look back upon her memory of him as a thing of the past, over forever. She still kept the crumpled rose leaves folded away in tissue paper in her handkerchief box and smiled at them now and then as she took her best handkerchiefs out for some formal occasion, drawing a breath of their old fragrance, like dried spices, whose strength was so nearly gone that it was scarcely recognizable. Just sweet and old and dear, like all the pleasant things of her little girlhood. Life had been too real and serious for her to regret the absence of her former friend or even to feel hurt at his forgetfulness. He had passed into college life and travels abroad. Now and then his name was in the paper in connection with college sports, and later as a guest of some young prince or lord abroad. She and her mother read these articles with interest and a pleasant smile, but there was no bitterness nor jealousy in their thought of the boy who used to find a refuge in their kitchen on many a stormy evening when his family had left him alone with servants, and he had stolen away for a little real pleasure in their cozy home. It was what was to have been expected when he grew up. Was he not Murray Van Rensselaer? He would have no time now, of course, for cozy pancake suppers and simple stories read aloud. His world expected other things of him. He was theirs no longer. But they had loved the little boy who had loved them, and for his sake they were interested in the young man he had become, and now and then talked of him as they turned out their own lights and looked across the intervening alley to the blazing lights in the big house where his mother entertained the great ones of the city.

His coming back to his own city had been heralded in the papers, of course, and often his name was mentioned in the society columns, yet never had it happened that they had met until this morning. And Bessie was heart-whole and happy, not expecting young millionaire princes to drop down on her doorstep and continue a friendship begun in lonely babyhood. She was much too sane and sensible a girl to expect or even wish for such a thing. Her mind now was set upon success in her business world and her ambition to put her mother into more comfortable circumstances.

She met him with a smile of real pleasure, because he had cared to stop and recognize her for old times' sake, yet there was just the least tinge of reserve about her that set a wall between them from the start. He had recognized her with a blaze of unmistakable joy and surprise on his face and brought his car to such an abrupt stop that a taxi behind him very nearly ran up on the top of his car and climbed over him, its driver reproaching him loudly in no uncertain terms. But Murray had sprung from his car and taken her by the hand, his eyes devouring her lovely face, taking in every detail of her expression. Clear, unspoiled eyes, with the old glad light in them; fresh, healthy skin, like velvet, flushed softly at the unexpected meeting; lips that were red enough without the help of lipstick; and hair coiled low and arranged modishly, yet without the mannish ugliness put on by so many girls of the day; trim lines of a plain tailored suit; unconscious grace, truth, and goodness in her looks. To look at her was like going into the glory of a summer day after the garishness of a night in a cabaret.

He would have stood a long time holding her hand and finding out all that had been happening to her during the interval while they had been separated, but the traffic officer appeared on the scene and demanded that he move his car at once. He was not allowed to park in that particular spot where he had chosen to stop and spring to the pavement.

"Where are you going? Can't I take you there?" he pleaded, with one foot on the running board and his eyes still upon her face.

She tried to say she would wait for the trolley—it was not far away now—but he waved her excuses aside, said he had nothing in the world to do that morning, and before she realized it she was seated in the beautiful car whose approach she had watched so short a time before. As she sank down upon the cushions, she thought how wonderful it would be if sometime she could buy a car like this. Not with such a wonderful finish, perhaps, but just as good springs and just as fine machinery. How her mother would enjoy it!

The car moved swiftly out of the traffic into a side street, where they had comparatively a free course, and then the young man had turned to look at her again with that deep approval that had marked his first recognition.

"Where did you say you wanted to go?" he asked, watching the play of expression on her face and wondering about it. She did not seem like the girls he knew. She was so utterly like herself as he used to know her when they were children, that it seemed impossible.

"You don't have to get somewhere immediately, do you?" he asked eagerly. "Couldn't we have a little spin first?"

She hesitated, her better judgment warning her against it. Already she was reproaching herself for having gotten into the car. She knew her mother would have felt it was not wise. They were not of the same walk of life. It would be better to let him go his way. Yet he had been so insistent, and the traffic officer so urgent to clear the way. There seemed nothing else to do.

"Why, I was going to the library for a book I need this evening in my study," she said pleasantly. "My employer is out of town and gave me a vacation. I'm making use of it doing some little things I never have time for."

"I see," said Murray with his pleasant, easy smile that took everything for granted. "Then I'm sure I'm one of the things you haven't taken time for in a good many years. You'll just give a little of your time, won't you? Suppose we go toward the park, where we'll have more room."

While she hesitated, he shot his car up a cross street and was soon whirling on the boulevard toward the entrance of the park, enjoying the light in her eyes as the car rolled smoothly over the asphalt. It was so apparent that she loved the ride! She looked as she used to look when he brought her over the canary in the gold cage that he had bought with some of his spending money one Christmas. He began to wonder why he had let this delightful friend of his drop out of his acquaintance. Why, come to think of it, he had not seen her since the night his mother made him so mad telling him he was disgracing the family by running to play with little "alley" girls, that he was too big to play with low-born people anymore. He remembered how he tried to explain that Bessie did not live in the alley, as his mother's maid had informed her, but just *across* the alley, and how he tried to force her to go to the window and look out across the back area, where she could see quite plainly the neat two-story brick house, with the white sheer curtains at the windows, and a geranium between the curtains. It had all looked so pleasant to him he felt sure his mother would understand for once if she would only look. He could not bear that she should think such thoughts about these cozy friends of his who had given so many happy hours to him that his mother would have left desolate. But she shook him off angrily and sent him from the room.

That had been the last time he had seen Bessie. They told him the next day that he was to go to a summer camp, and from there he was sent to boarding school in the far West. It had all been very exciting at first, and he had never connected his mother's talk with his sudden migration. Perhaps the thought only vaguely presented itself in his mind now as a link in the chain of his life. He was not inclined to analyzing things, just drifting with the tide and getting as much fun out of it all as possible. But now, with Bessie before him, he wondered why it was that he had allowed seven whole years to drift by apart from her. Here she had been ripening into this perfect peach of a girl, and he might have been enjoying her company all this time. Instead he had solaced his idle hours with anyone who happened to drift his way. Bah! What a group they had been, some of them! Something in him knew that this girl was never like those. Something she had had as a little girl that he admired and enjoyed had stayed with her yet. He was not like that. He was sure he was not. He was quite certain he had been rather a fine chap in those early days before the evil of life had been revealed to him. A faint little wish that he might have stayed as he was then faltered through his carefree mind, only he flippantly felt that of course that would have been impossible.

Bessie was enjoying her ride. She exclaimed over the beauty of the foliage, where some of the autumn's tints were still left clinging to the branches. She drank in the beauty of cloud and distant river, and her cheeks took on that delicate flush of delight that he had noticed in her long ago. He marveled that a human cheek could vary in its coloring so exquisitely. He had unconsciously come to feel that such alive-looking flesh could only be on the face of a child. Every woman he knew wore her expressions like a mask that never varied, no matter what emotion might cross her countenance. The mask was always there, smooth and creamy and delicate and unmoved. He had come to feel it was a state that came with maturity. But this girl's face was like a rose whose color came and went in delicate shadings and seemed to be a part of the vivid expression as she talked, as the petals of a rose showed deeper coloring at their base when the wind played with them and threw the lights and shadows in different curves and tintings.

Murray as a rule did little thinking, and he would have been surprised and thought it clever if someone had put this idea into words for him. But the impression was there in his mind as they talked. And then he fell to wondering how she would look in beautiful garments, rich silks and velvets and furs. She was simply and suitably dressed, and might be said to adorn her garments, but she would be superb in cloth of silver and jewels. How he would enjoy putting her in her right setting! Here was a girl who would adorn any garment, and whose face and figure warranted the very greatest designers in fashion's world.

An idea came to Murray.

They often came that way by impulse, and sometimes they had their origin in the very best impulses. He leaned toward her with a quick, confidential air. They were on their way back now, for the girl had suggested that she had taken enough of his time.

"I wonder if you won't do something for me?" he said in his boyish, pleasant tone that reminded her of other days together.

"Why, surely, if I can," she complied pleasantly.

"You certainly can," he answered cheerfully. "No one could do it better. I want you to come with me to a shop I know and help me to select something for a gift for a friend of mine. You are her figure to an inch, and you have her coloring, too. I want to see how it will look on you before I buy it."

There was perhaps just the least shade of reserve in her voice as she graciously assented. Naturally she could not help wondering who the gift was for. Not his mother, or he would have said so. He had no sister, she knew. A cousin, perhaps? No, he would have called her cousin. Well, it was of no consequence, of course. It gave her just the least little bit of an embarrassed feeling. How could she select something for one in his station of life? But she could at least tell what she thought was pretty. It was on the whole quite exciting, come to think of it, to help in the selection of something where money did not have to be considered—just for once to let her taste rule. It would be wonderful!

Then they turned from the avenue onto the quieter street and drew up suddenly before Grevet's. She drew her breath with pleasure. Ah! Grevet's! She had often wondered what a shop like this was like inside, and now she was to know! It was like playing a game, to have a legitimate reason for inspecting some of the costly wares that were here exclusively displayed. She stepped from the car with quiet composure, however, and no one would have dreamed that this was her first entrance into these distinguished precincts.

Chapter 14

In a little cottage on the outskirts of a straggling town about half a mile from the scene of the railroad wreck, a sick man lay tossing on a hard little bed in a small room that could not easily be spared from the needs of a large family. A white-capped nurse, brought in by the railroad, stooped over him to straighten the coarse sheet and quilt spread over him, and tried to quiet his restless murmurings.

"Teller!" he murmured deliriously. "Teller!"

"Tell who?" asked the cool, clear voice of the nurse.

"M'ry!" he mumbled thickly. "Teller!"

"You want me to tell Mary?" asked the nurse crisply.

The heavy eyes of the man on the bed opened uncomprehendingly and tried to focus on her face.

"Yeh! Teller! M'ry. Bank!"

"Mary Banks?" asked the nurse capably. "You want me to send word to Mary Banks?"

The patient breathed what seemed like assent.

"Where?" asked the nurse clearly, taking up the pencil that lay by her report and writing in clear little script, "Miss Mary Banks."

"Bank!" said the patient drowsily. "Bank! Teller!"

"Yes, I will tell her," responded the nurse. "Where—does—she—live?" enunciating slowly and distinctly.

The man's head paused in its restless turning, and the eyes tried to focus on her face again, as if he were called back by her words from some far wandering.

"Marlborough!" He spoke the word clearly and drowsed off again as if he were relieved.

That night by the light of a sickly gas lamp whose forked flame she had shaded with a newspaper from the patient's eyes, she wrote a note to Mary Banks in Marlborough, telling her that a young man with curly red hair and a tweed suit was calling for her and asking that she be told that he had been injured in a wreck. She stated that the patient's condition was serious and that if he had any friends, they had better come at once. It was impossible to find any clue to his name, as he wore no coat when he was picked up, having evidently pulled it off to assist others worse injured than himself and having fainted before he got back to it. The pockets of his trousers had nothing in them but a little money, a railroad ticket, a knife, a few keys, and a watch marked with the initials A.M.

The letter was given to the doctor to mail the next morning when he came on his rounds, and in due time it reached the

Marlborough post office. After reposing some days in the general delivery box, it was finally put up in a glass frame in the outer post office among uncalled-for letters. But the patient lay in a deep deathlike stupor, and knew nothing of all this. After his efforts to speak that one word, Marlborough, he had seemed satisfied, and the doctor and nurse tried in vain to rouse him again to consciousness of the world about him. It was thought that he had been injured around his head and that an operation might be necessary, but the doctor hesitated to take that step without first consulting with some of the sick man's friends or relatives. The doctor even went so far as to write a note to a fellow physician in the town of Marlborough, asking him to look up this "Mary Banks" and endeavor to get a line on the man and his friends, if possible.

But no Mary Banks could be found in all the town of Marlborough. Strange as it may seem, however, a young woman of romantic tendencies, by the name of Banks, who admitted that her middle name was Marie—Rose Marie Banks—was at last discovered, and induced to take the journey of some thirty miles to the bedside of the unconscious man, that she might identify him. It was a handsome young doctor who entreated her, anxiously, to please a former head and great colleague in the profession. He had just bought a new shiny blue car, and the day was fine. Rose Marie consented to go "just for the ride" and alighted happily before the cottage, stood an awed moment beside the sickbed, and gazed half frightened on the solemnity of the living death before her. Then she shrank back with a "No, I ain't never seen him before," and hurried out to the waiting car, glad to be back in the sunshine of life once more. The sick man lay burning with fever and moaning incoherent words to the distracted nurse, who had done her best, and the days went on and on monotonously.

Chapter 15

It was strange how many circumstances could combine to hedge in Murray Van Rensselaer's pathway so that there was no way of escape.

They led him into the mahogany-lined cage with its bronze bars at the little window and inducted him into the mysteries of the duty of a bank teller, and he was fascinated. It was like a new game. He always was dead to the world for a time when he met with a new form of amusement. They never could get him to pay attention to anything else until he had followed out its intricacies and become master of its technique. And this playing with crisp new bills of fascinating denominations and coins in a tray of little compartments was the best he had ever tried. Poker chips and mah-jongg tiles weren't nearly as interesting. These were real. They suddenly seemed the implements with which the world's big battles were fought. He had a vague perception of why his father stayed in the game of business when he had enough money to buy himself out many times. It was for the fascination of it.

Also, as he cashed checks and counted money, he had a realization that he was doing something for the first time in his life that was really worthwhile to the world. Just why it was valuable to the world for him to stand there and hand out money in return for checks he did not figure out. He only knew he liked it immensely. He felt as if he were doing these people a personal favor to give them money when they asked for it. He was so smiling and affable, and took so much trouble to give the fussy old lady exactly the right number of five- and ten-cent pieces that she asked for in change, and was so pleasant to the children who came with their Christmas savings accounts and had to have different things explained to them, that the other officials, watching him furtively as they went about their own business, raised approving eyebrows at one another. They nodded as they passed with a tilt of the head toward the new member of their corps, as much as to say: "He'll do all right; he's going to be a success."

It is true he often did not know how to explain the things they asked of him and had to make them up or manage to get out of answering entirely. He asked very few questions, however, of his fellow workers, for he did not wish them to suspect he did not know it all. Only now and then he would say: "Oh, I say, Warren," to the man who had been assigned to coach him, "just what is your custom here about this?" making it quite plain that where he came from they had a method of their own, and he did not wish to vary from the usual habit here.

It was remarkable how often he could skate like that on thin ice and not fall through. Of course his college practice had made his mind nimble in subterfuges, but on the other hand, the situation was quite different from any he had ever met with before. He found it the more interesting because of these various hazards, and he came to feel a new elation over each person whom he succeeded in serving satisfactorily without help. It was quite a miracle that he made no more mistakes than he did.

The morning passed swiftly, and when he was told that it was the noon hour, he came to himself with a sudden realization that now was his chance to escape. He had almost forgotten that he had wanted to escape—*needed* to. He was enjoying himself hugely and liked the idea of going on and becoming a banker. He saw himself winning out and becoming a champion in the game of banking—just as he had won out and become a champion in tennis and golf and polo.

But with the relief from his little cage window and the piles of fascinating coins came the remembrance of his terrible situation, came as if it were new all over again, and settled down upon his soul in crushing contrast to the happiness of the morning. Why, men had liked him, been pleased with what he did, showed him that he was going to be a success. The long lines of men and women, even boys and girls, outside his window, looking at him as if he were someone who held their fate in his hand, had eyed him with pleasant cordiality. Everywhere men had acknowledged his smile, as if it were worth something to know him. He had been used to all that, of course, at home, only there had been a new tang to this friendliness—a kind of respect that had never been granted to him before. Was it because he was doing real work? Or was it partly because of what they thought he was—that religious business that almost everyone managed to get in a hint about? He did not quite understand it, but it somehow gave him a new angle on life, a new respect for righteousness and right living. How odd that he had never thought before that there were compensations in being what men called "good."

But to have experienced this new deference and then to be let down to reality again was a tremendous blow. Of course he had known it was not his; he was only sort of playing at being a man and a bank employee, but it had been great! And now he had to go out and sneak away like a thief and disappear! He looked down at the piles of money he was leaving with a wistful regret. Suppose he was a thief! Suppose he should sweep all that with one good motion into his pocket and disappear. He could do it. It would be a good game, interesting to see if he could get away with it, but how loathsome to think about afterward! He almost shivered at the thought of himself doing a thing like that. That money had come to have a sort of personality and value of its own apart from what it might be worth to him personally. He had never looked at money before in any but the light of his own needs. There had always been plenty of it so far as he was concerned, and he had always seemed to feel he had a right to as much as he pleased. But now he suddenly saw that money was a necessity to the daily life of the community. He had seen it pay a gas bill and a telephone bill today, and he had seen small checks brought forth from worn wallets in trembling hands, and the cash carried away with a look that showed it was to be used for stern necessity. One could tell by the shabbiness of some of the owners that with them a little money had to go a long way.

Now all this swept through his mind in a kind of hurried surge as he turned to follow the man Warren out to lunch. He knew none of the words to express these thoughts to himself, but the thoughts themselves left their impression on his soul as they surged through him.

And now, the murderer, who had played at being a bank teller for a brief time, must go out supposedly to lunch, must shake this man Warren somehow and get away, never to return, and he did not want to go. He did not want to go back to being a runaway murderer. He felt like a small boy who wanted somebody to show him the way home and comfort him. He decided the quickest way to shake Warren was to say that he must run back to Mrs. Summers' for lunch, as she would be expecting him, and he needed to get something he had left in his other coat, some papers he must show to Mr. Harper at once.

But he found no opportunity for such stratagem. The man Warren was in complete command of the situation. He was sent by Mr. Harper to bring Murray to the top floor, where lunch was to be served to the directors today, and where the president was awaiting him and wanted him to sit beside him. They were joined almost at once by one or two others who had been more or less in his vicinity all the morning, so there was no chance whatever of escape unless he wished to try the astonishing method of making a dash. This matter of making a bold dash had become almost an obsession in his mind. He saw it was a thing that was impossible. They would think he was crazy. They would immediately cry out. He would be caught at once and have to explain. It might work in the darkness, perhaps, but not in broad daylight in a bank. So he followed meekly and was shot up in the elevator to the top floor and given a fine lunch and more of the pleasant deference that had soothed his overwrought nerves all the morning, until he was even able to rally and make several bright sallies in response to the conversation of the men about him. He could see again that they liked him and were pleased with his ready speech.

Back to the window again and the pleasant game that was so fascinating. There was only one unpleasant occurrence, just before closing time, when the girl Anita came in to make a deposit and looked at him with her clear eyes. A distant, formal recognition she gave him, but no more, and again he felt her likeness to Bessie, poor Bessie Chapparelle, with her white face against his shoulder as he carried her into the hospital.

It swept over him with a sickening thud: Bessie was dead. Why hadn't he gone back to Bessie Chapparelle long ago? This girl Anita had that same sweet reserve about her that Bessie had put between himself and her while they were driving. He had wanted to break down that reserve, but he liked her for it. He could see that Anita would be a good girl to know. She would be somewhat like Bessie, perhaps. But because of Bessie he shrank from even looking at her. And somehow that odd fancy that she could look through him, that she might even read that he had killed a girl, took more and more possession of his mind. He must get away from this town!

But Mr. Harper came to him just at closing time, and said he wanted to take him home to dinner that night, that there were one or two matters he wanted to talk over with him, and besides his wife and daughters were most anxious to meet him. They would leave the bank around five o'clock. His duties would be about over for the day then, and they would take a little drive around the town and vicinity of Marlborough, if that was agreeable to the young man. Then they would drive to the Harper home and dine and spend the evening.

There was nothing to do but assent, of course, but his mind was so troubled trying to think how to get away that he scarcely paid heed to the routine of his work, which they were trying to teach him, and once or twice made bad calculations which he knew must have made them wonder that he did not know better. He saw they were being very nice to him, but he fancied a look of surprise passed over their faces that he had not understood more quickly.

The day's agenda was carried out without a break. He actually went through that entire day, ride and dinner and evening and all, and was returned to Mrs. Summers' house late that night and ushered to the very door, which she herself opened for him, so that there was no instant in which he could have gotten away unnoticed.

As he stood by the bedroom window in the soft light of the little bed lamp and looked out into the pleasant street once more, as he had done twenty-four long hours before, he was amazed at the supervision that had followed him from early morning to late at night. It seemed almost uncanny. He was beginning to wonder if perhaps there was some secret reason for it, that he should be caught in this maze of deceit, and then to add this also to his already-heavy offense. Could it be possible that a kind Providence, or some other great unseen Power, if there was such a thing in the universe, had provided this way of escape from his terrible situation and prepared a new place and a new name for his wayward self to begin again?

He looked around the pleasant, friendly little room that seemed already to have somehow become his, to the deep easy chair with the soft light falling on a magazine laid close at hand, to the comfortable white bed, with its sheets turned down again, ready for his entrance, and suddenly his heart failed him. How could he go out into the world again and hide away from men when here was this home and this place in the world awaiting him? He would never find another place where everything would be so easy to fit into. He might stay at least until something was heard of the other fellow. He would take pains to inquire about that wreck. He would profess to be anxious about some of his fellow passengers, and they would talk, and he would find out a lot of things—where the other fellow really lived—and perhaps there would be a way of tracing him. If he had really died, the way would be clear for him. The man seemed to have come from a distance, from the way they spoke of his trains, and his trunk coming on ahead. It was likely there would be a good chance of his never being found out. Why not take the chance?

Now, Murray Van Rensselaer had been taking chances all his life. He loved chances. He was a born gambler in life, and if it had not been for the white face of Bessie Chapparelle that haunted him everywhere he turned and suddenly appeared to him out of the most unexpected thoughts and occurrences, he would have just delighted in entering into this situation and seeing if he could get away with it. The little white haunting face spoiled everything for him everywhere. There had never been anything in his life before that really took the fun and the excitement out of living.

There was one other occurrence of the day that set its searing touch upon his troubled mind, and that was when he had been returning from lunch. He had lifted his eyes to the wall beyond the table where patrons were standing writing checks and had seen a large sign hanging on that wall beyond the table in full sight of all who entered the bank, bearing the picture of a young man, and underneath the picture the words, in large letters, $5,000 REWARD—

He read no more. To his distorted vision the picture seemed to be one of himself. Yet he was not near enough to see it, and he dared not go nearer. It had been like a nemesis staring him in the face all the afternoon as he worked away at the game of money, every time he looked up, and tried not to see the sign upon the wall with the face and the words upon it, yet always saw them.

He thought of the sign now as he stood by the window and looked out, thinking how he could get across that tin roof silently, and down to the ground by way of the rose trellis.

Then the thought presented itself that perhaps, after all, he was safer there, in the bank, even if it proved to be his own picture staring across at him, than he would be out in the world trying to run away from people who were hunting for him and wanting to get that reward. No one would think of looking for that face behind the teller's window. He was bearing an honored name, and behind that name he was safe. He must stay. That is, unless the other man turned up, and then—? Well, then it would be time enough to decide what to do. At least his situation could be no worse than it was now. He would go to bed and to sleep like other people, and tomorrow he would get up and go to the bank and play that enticing game of money again and see if he could get away with it all. At least it would keep his mind occupied, so that he would not always have to see Bessie Chapparelle lying huddled beneath that overturned car.

He turned from the window and looked toward the tempting bed again. He was not used to resisting temptations. It had been his habit always to do exactly as he pleased, no matter what the consequences. Let the consequences take care of themselves when they had arrived. Ten to one they would never arrive. It had been his experience that if you kept enough things going, there was no room for consequences. Habit is a tremendous power. Even in the face of a possible arrest for murder, it swayed him now. And he was tired—deadly tired. The excitement of the day, added to the excitement of the days that had gone before, had exhausted him. Add to that the fact that he had been without stimulants of any kind, unless you could call coffee a stimulant. It was a strange thing, all these people who did not drink and did not approve of smoking. How did they get that way?

He had thought that as soon as he got out in the world again somehow he would manage to get a pack of cigarettes. But at the breakfast table Mrs. Summers had told him how the one thing that had held her back at first from being ready to take him in was that she hated smoking in her house, but when Mr. Harper had boasted that he was a young man who never smoked, that decided her.

"And he was so pleased about it," she added. "You know, though he smokes himself, he said it was a sign of great strength of character in you that you had gone all through the war even without smoking, and you were said not to be a sissy, either."

He had paid little heed to her words while he was eating breakfast, because his mind was engrossed with how he could get away, but down at the bank Mr. Harper, at noon, lighting his cigar, looked at him apologetically and said: "I know you don't smoke, Murray, but I hope you'll pardon us older fellows who began too young in life to cut it out now. I admire your strength tremendously."

He had opened his mouth to disclaim any such strength, to say that they had been misinformed, for his whole system was crying out for the comfort of a smoke, but a distraction suddenly occurred, and caution held him back from contradicting it later. Besides, the entire company seemed to have heard it about him that he did not smoke, and he dared not attempt to invent a story that would show they were mistaken. If he was supposed to be that kind of young man, better let it stand. He could all the more easily slip away unobserved without their immediate alarm.

So now in the quiet of his own room, he longed fiercely for a smoke. But he had not a cent in his pocket. There had not been a chance for an instant all day when he could have purchased cigarettes unobserved, and if he had them in his hand he would not dare to smoke there in Mrs. Summers' house. She hated it. She would smell it. She would think him a hypocrite. Somehow he did not want Mrs. Summers to think ill of him. Of course he was a hypocrite, but somehow he didn't want her to know it. She had been kind to him, and he liked her. She was what seemed to him like a real mother, and he reverenced her. If he stayed and enjoyed her home and the position which he was supposed to fill, he would also have to live up to the character he was supposed to be, and that would include not smoking, even when he got a chance and the money to purchase the smokes. Could he stand it? Was it worth the trouble?

And yet when he came to think about it, was not that perhaps the very best disguise he could have, not to smoke? He had been an inveterate smoker. Everybody who knew him knew that. If he was made over into a new man, the old man in him unrecognizable, he must seek to obliterate all signs of the old man. Well, could he do it?

He had settled down into the big chair to think, to decide what to do, and suddenly a great drowsiness overtook him. With a quick impulse of old habit he got up and began to undress without more protest. He would have another good night's rest before he did anything about it anyway. He could not run far with sleep like this in possession of his faculties. And in three minutes he snapped out the light and was in bed. At least he was probably safe till morning. The man Murray could not very well turn up at that time of night.

Chapter 16

Murray wondered again the next morning when Warren stepped in with a note from Mr. Harper while he was eating his breakfast, and insisted on waiting and walking down to the bank with him. It did seem uncanny. Were all these people in collusion somehow to prevent his being left alone an instant?

It would have been a startling thought to him had someone suggested that each one was working out the divine will for his good, and that though he might flee to the uttermost part of the earth, even there an all-seeing care would be about him, reaching to draw him to a God he had never known.

Murray liked Warren. He seemed quite companionable. He wondered if he played golf or had a car. But it annoyed him to be under such continual supervision. Although he had about decided to remain in Marlborough for the present, at least until he got his first week's pay, if that were possible, still he did not like the feeling that he was being forced to do this. He cast about in his mind for an excuse that would leave him free, but Warren was so altogether genial that there seemed nothing else to do but make the best of it. Surely they would not have lunch parties on the roof of the bank building every day of the week. There would certainly come a letup sometime.

So they walked downtown together, and Murray discovered that Warren was married and lived in a little cottage two blocks above Mrs. Summers. Warren said they wanted him to come to dinner some night just as soon as Elizabeth got back. Elizabeth was away in Vermont, visiting her mother.

Elizabeth! Would he never get away from thoughts of Bessie Chapparelle?

Warren confided in Murray that he was saving for a car, just a little coupe—he couldn't afford anything else yet—but it would be nice for Elizabeth to take the baby out in. There was a nice, eager, domestic air about him that was different from anything Murray had experienced among his young men friends, even the married ones. He did not remember that any of them had babies, or if they had they did not speak about them. They were tucked away somewhere with their nurses out of sight till they should be old enough to burst upon the world full-fledged in athletics or society. There was something pleasant about the thought of a girl taking her baby out for a ride in a little coupe, even if it was a cheap one. And a cottage! He had never been to dinner at a cottage. It occurred to him that Bessie would have been the kind of mother who would have taken her baby out for a ride. Bessie! Oh Bessie! Why had he not thought of Bessie before and kept in touch with her? But when he did find her, he had killed her! He had thought this terrible depression at remembrance of her would pass away in a few days, but it did not. It only grew worse! Someday it might drive him mad! This was no way to begin a day!

But he entered the bank committed to take a hike with Warren that afternoon after closing time, and Warren was to come home to dinner that night with him. Mrs. Summers had asked him at the breakfast table. So the pleasant ties that were binding him to Marlborough multiplied and weakened his purpose of leaving, and from day to day he held on, each day thinking to go the next. If he had had money, even a little, or any sense of where he might go, it would have been different, perhaps, for ever over him hung the fear of the return of the real Murray, though each day, no, each hour that passed in security weakened his realization of it and at times almost obliterated the thought of it as a possibility.

Then there began to happen the strangest things that he had to do, things utterly alien to all of his former life.

There was the first Sunday. It came like a shock to him.

Saturday afternoon he and Warren took a hike, and on the way back he asked when Murray would like to go again.

"Why not tomorrow?" answered Murray, remembering that there would be no bank open on Sunday.

"Why, that's Sunday, old man," said Warren, laughing.

There was such a look of amusement on Warren's face that

it warned Murray. Sunday! What the dickens difference did that make, he wondered. But he caught himself quickly. It must make some difference or Warren would not look like that, so he responded with a laugh.

"Oh, that's so. Got my dates mixed, didn't I? Well, let's see. What do we do in Marlborough? How is the day laid out on Sunday? Much doing?"

"Well, not much time for idling, of course. We have our Ushers' Association meeting in the morning before church. They'll be sure to elect you to that. They were speaking about it."

"Ushers' Association?" said Murray, puzzled.

"Yes, I s'pose you belonged at home. In fact, they said you did. Well, we meet at quarter to ten. Then the regular morning service is quarter to eleven, and Sunday school is in the afternoon. Have they asked you to take a class yet? Well, they will. Then the Christian Endeavor meets at seven. They're planning to make you president at the next election. Perhaps I oughtn't to tell you that, but it's a foregone conclusion, of course. And the evening service is eight o'clock. Of course, it's short and snappy and gets out by nine fifteen, but it's a full day. Not much time left for your family if you go to everything."

"No, I suppose not," murmured Murray, trying to keep the amazement out of his voice. It was his policy to agree with everybody, as far as possible, until he had further insight, but was it possible that grown men and women went to Sunday school? Some nurse of his childhood had taken him for a few months once when he was quite young, but he had always supposed it was a matter merely for children. Yet Warren spoke as if he went to Sunday school. What was he letting himself in for if he stayed in this strange place? Could he possibly go through with it? And what were these "services" that he spoke of? Just *church*? Well, he could get out of that probably. Say he had a headache.

But when Sunday morning came and he sat down at the little round breakfast table opposite Mrs. Summers and ate the delicate omelet, fresh brown bread, sweet baked apples with cream, and drank the amber coffee that composed the Sunday breakfast and heard her talk, it was not so easy to get out of it.

"There's an article in this week's *Presbyterian* I'd like you to read. It speaks of that very subject we were talking about last night. You'll have plenty of time to read it before we go to church. I left it over on the Morris chair for you," she said. It was very plain she was counting on his going to church. Indeed, he had been made to understand everywhere all the week from many different people that church was where he was expected to be whenever there was service there, and he sighed and wondered how long he would be able to keep up this religious bluff. If he only had thought to profess to be going to spend the weekend with some old friend a few miles away, it would have given him freedom for a few hours, at least, and a start of almost two days on his pursuers, in case he decided not to return.

But then there was the old question again: Where could he go, how would he get another name, and why try to find a better place of hiding when this one seemed fairly crying out for him? Then, too, where would justice be less likely to search for him than in a church?

So he settled into the Morris chair with a sigh and took up the paper to read an article, the like of which he had never read nor heard before, and the meaning of which touched him no more than if it were written in a foreign tongue.

The article was about church unity. He gathered there was a discussion of some sort around, some theological crisis imminent. The article was couched in terms he had never even heard before, so far as he remembered—the Atonement, Calvary, the Authenticity of the Scriptures, the Virgin Birth, the New Birth, the Miracles. What was it all about, anyway? There seemed no sense to it. He read it over again, trying to get a few phrases in case someone began to talk in this strange jargon, and he was evidently expected to be a connoisseur in such things. He must master enough to put him beyond suspicion.

Take, for instance, that phrase "the new birth"; how strangely like the sentence he had seen in the trolley car, "Ye must be born again!" It had come from the Bible. He had discovered that the first night he spent in this house. There must be some slogan like that in all this discussion. He was rather interested to know what it all meant. It fitted so precisely in with his own needs. He was trying so hard to be born again, and he felt so uncertain whether he was going to succeed or not. Perhaps if he read this paper he would discover something more about it. At any rate it would make the good lady with whom he lived feel that he was interested in what she had been saying, and he had taken good care that she did the talking when she got on such topics, too. So he asked if he might take the paper up to his room for further perusal. Mrs. Summers said yes, of course, but it was time to start to church, and he must get his hat and come right down. And in spite of his desire to remain at home, he found himself yielding to her firm but pleasantly expressed wishes.

The sermon that morning was short and direct. The text was, "We must all appear before the judgment seat of Christ to give account of the deeds done in the body," and from the time those firm, mobile lips of the pastor began to repeat the words, and the clear, almost piercing eyes began to look straight down at him from the pulpit, Murray never took his eyes from the preacher's face.

It was, perhaps, the first real sermon he had ever listened to in his life. Oh, he had been to church now and then through the years, of course—mostly to weddings, now and then to a funeral, occasionally a vesper service where something unusual was going on and his mother wished him to escort her, once or twice to a baccalaureate sermon. That was all. Never to hear a direct appeal of the gospel. It was all new to him.

The minister was an unusual man. He knew scripture by heart, chapter after chapter. When he read the lesson he scarcely looked at the page, but repeated the words as if it were something he had seen happen, or had heard spoken, and about which he was merely telling in clear, convincing tones. His sermon was rich in quotations. The quotations clinched every statement that he made. Murray heard for the first time about the great white throne and the books to be opened, and the *other* book that was to be opened, where inside were written names, the Lamb's Book of Life. And whoever's name was not found written there was to go away into everlasting punishment.

Everlasting punishment! That was what he was under now. Life as himself, the Murray Van Rensselaer that he had started out to be, was done with so far as this life was concerned. His punishment could only end with death, and now this that the preacher was saying made it pretty sure that it would not end even then. He had somehow felt all along ever since the accident that if he could only die, all this trouble would be over, and he would have a square deal, as he called it, again, but it seemed not. It seemed things of this life were carried over into the next. If what this preacher said was true, all this about the books and the dead, small and great, being judged out of what was written against them, why, then there was no chance for him. The preacher further stated that those whose names were written in that other book, who were not to be punished, were the "born again ones." That was what that "born again" meant that he had been hearing about so much. Or what was it, after all? Nobody had said. The "born again ones." He had been trying to be born again and had taken a new name, but what were the chances that Allan Murray any more than Murray Van Rensselaer would be a born again one? Well, pretty good, if all they said about him were true, only if he was dead he would be over there himself and would preempt his own name, and besides, Murray had a sudden realization that there would be no chance of deception over there in the other world.

The preacher's words were very clear, very simple, very convincing. The words he repeated from the Bible were still more awe-inspiring. Murray walked silently back to the house beside Mrs. Summers with a deep depression upon him. He felt that he had taken out from that church the heavy burden of an unforgiven sin—that there was no place of repentance, though he might carefully seek it with tears, and that he must bear the consequences of his sin through all eternity.

He could not understand his feeling. It was not at all like himself, and he could not shake it off. He sat in his room for a few minutes looking into the red glow of the coals on his hearth and thinking about it, while Mrs. Summers put the dinner on the table. It somehow did not seem fair. When you came to consider it, he had not meant to be a murderer. There was not anyone he would have protected sooner than Bessie. He was just having a good time. It was not quite fair for him to bear unforgivable punishment the rest of his life for a thing he had not meant to do. Of course the law of the land was that way. It had to be to protect everybody. But the law had no right to you after you were dead. You had satisfied it. But if, after having escaped punishment in this life, he had yet to meet the judgment seat of an angry God, what hope had he?

He dwelt for a moment upon those whose names were written

in the other book, the "born again" ones. Mrs. Summers was likely one of those, if there was any such thing. Yes, and Mrs. Chapparelle. She read the Bible and believed it. He remembered the stories she read them Sunday afternoons. And was Bessie? Yes, she must have been. It must have been that which gave her that look of set-apartness, that sort of peace in her eyes—well, these were odd things he was thinking about. Strange they never came his way before. He had never really taken it in before what it would be to die—to be done with this earth forever! Bessie was gone! And he would be judged for it! Even if he escaped a court of justice, he would be judged. What was the use? Why not go home and take his chances? But no, that would drag his mother and father through all that muck. . . . Bah! He would stay where he was— awhile.

The little tinkling bell broke in upon his thoughts, and he found he was tremendously hungry, in spite of his serious thoughts. Fried chicken and mashed potatoes, and gravy over delicately browned slices of toast! A quivering mold of currant jelly! Little white onions in a cream dressing, a custard pie for desert. It all had a wonderful taste that seemed better than anything he knew, and he really enjoyed sitting there with her eating it. It seemed so cozy and pleasant. Even the blessing at the beginning was rather a pleasant novelty. She had asked him again to take the head of the table and ask the blessing, but he had looked at her with a most engaging smile and said, "Oh, you say it, won't you? I like to hear you." And she had smiled and complied, so now he was not anymore worried about that. If ever he were asked, he had learned what words were used. He could get away with it, though somehow he did not like to be faking a thing like that. It was strange, but he did not. He had never felt so before about anything. He wondered why.

He helped Mrs. Summers carry the dishes out to the kitchen, and while he was doing it the doorbell rang, and Jane presented herself. She announced that she had come as a representative of her class to ask Mr. Murray to be their teacher. She flattered him with her beseeching eyes while she pleaded with him not to say no.

"Class? What class?" he asked blankly, wondering what dog-gone thing he was going to run into now.

"Why, our Sunday school class. There are twelve of us girls. You know our teacher was Miss Phelps, and she's gone away for the winter to California. Perhaps she won't ever come back. Her sister lives out there. She resigned the class before she went away, and we haven't elected anyone else to fill her place. We were sort of waiting to see if you wouldn't take it. I hope nobody else has gotten ahead of us. I tried to see you this morning, but there were so many people speaking to you. Now, you *will* be our teacher, *won't* you?"

Chapter 17

Murray was appalled! He was aghast! He simply could not take this extraordinary request seriously. It seemed as if he must somehow get back to his former companions and tell them the joke. They wanted him to teach a Sunday school class of young ladies! Was ever anything more terribly ludicrous in all the world?

But he managed to keep a perfectly courteous face while he let her talk on for a minute or two, and while he summoned his senses and tried to figure out a line of safe reply that would not be inconsistent with his supposed character, the doorbell rang again. Ah! Now! Perhaps here was deliverance!

The caller proved to be the Sunday school superintendent, Mr. Marlowe.

"Mr. Murray, I hope I'm not too late," he began, after the introductions. "I've been away in New York all the week. I just got back late last night, and I missed you this morning at the service.

Mr. Harrison had some things to talk over, and when I looked around, you were gone. I've come over to see if you won't take a class of boys in our Sunday school. I've sort of been saving them for you. They're bright little chaps about ten years old and up to no good, of course, but they need a young man of your caliber, and I've just eased them along with some of the elders for a few Sundays until you would arrive. I do hope you'll be interested in them. They are one of the most promising classes in the school, and just at an age when they need the touch of a young man."

"Now, Mr. Marlow," pouted Jane, as soon as she could break into the conversation, "Mr. Murray is going to take *our* class, *aren't* you, Mr. Murray? I came over *first*, Mr. Marlowe. We've had it in mind ever since we heard Mr. Murray was coming, and the girls are *just crazy* to have him. . . ."

The superintendent turned a keen, scrutinizing glance on Murray.

"Well, that's up to you, Mr. Murray, of course. Which do you prefer to teach? The young ladies or the kids? Of course I've no wish to bias you if the girls have gotten their request in before me, but I certainly shall be disappointed. It isn't everybody who can teach these boys."

Murray was going to say eagerly that he had never taught young ladies in his life, nor anybody else, till it suddenly occurred to him that he did not know what reports of his exploits in Sunday school teaching had reached Marlborough. He must proceed carefully. He caught his sentence between his teeth and whirled it around.

"With all due apology to the young ladies," he said gracefully, turning a look on Jane that almost made her forgive him for what he was saying, "I think I'd fit better with the kids, if I'm to teach at all. You see—I'm"—he floundered for an explanation—"I'm just crazy about kids, you know!"

"Oh, Mr. Murray!" pouted Jane stormily.

The superintendent brightened.

"Well, I certainly am thankful," he said. "I didn't know what to do with those little devils! They spoiled the whole service last Sunday. They had little tin pickles from some canning factory, and they sent them whizzing all over the room. One hit an old lady's eye and made no end of trouble. I'll be grateful forever if you can see your way clear to taking them right on this afternoon."

"Oh!" gasped Murray. "Really, I—you know—I—"

"Yes, I know what you're going to say. You haven't had any chance this week to study the lesson. They all say that the first time, but it doesn't matter in the least. You can tell them a story, can't you? You can at least keep them from raising a mob or stealing the minister's hat. I'm about at the end of my rope, so far as they are concerned. Perhaps I'm not giving them a very high recommendation, but I heard of you before you came, that you were eager for a hard job, so here it is! Will you come over and get acquainted with them? Let the lesson take care of itself. Anyhow, they will teach it to you, if you ask questions. They are bright little chaps, if they are bad, and they've been well taught."

It was a strange thing, perhaps the strangest of all the strange things that had yet happened to Murray Van Rensselaer, that fifteen minutes later he found himself sitting in front of a class of well-dressed, squirming, whispering lads who eyed him with a challenge and were prepared to "beat him to it," as they phrased it.

What he was going to say to them, how he was going to hold them through the half hour for which he was responsible for their actions, he did not know, but he certainly was not going to let seven kids beat him, and besides, had he not a reputation connected with his new name which he must keep up? He wasn't going to be under suspicion because he could not bluff a good Sunday school teacher's line. That suggestion about letting the boys do the teaching had been a good thing. He would try that out.

During an interval when a hymn was announced, he overheard two of the boys talking about the football scores in the last night's papers, and as soon as the superintendent announced that the classes would turn to the lesson, he collected the attention of his young hopefuls with one amazing offhand question.

"You fellas ever see a big Army and Navy game?"

This, perhaps, was not the most approved method for opening a lesson in Acts, but it got them. The seven young imps altogether dropped the various schemes of torment which they had planned for this first Sunday with their new teacher and leaned forward eagerly.

"Naw! D'jou?"

A moment later and Murray was launched on a vivid and exciting description of the last Army and Navy football game he had seen, and for twenty brisk minutes he had the undivided attention of the most "difficult" class in the Sunday school.

"He'll do," whispered Marlowe to the minister as they stood together on the platform looking toward Murray, with his head and shoulders down and the knot of seven heads gathered around him. "We picked the right man all right. He's got 'em from the word *go*."

The minister nodded with shining eyes.

"It looks that way. It certainly does," he beamed, and the two good men turned to other problems, fully satisfied that the seven worst little devils were well started on the way to heaven, led by this wonderful young Christian, who had not yet stopped at anything he had been asked to do. They began to plan how much more they could get him to do in places where they desperately needed help.

The superintendent's warning bell rang before Murray suddenly came out of that football game and realized that something had been said about a "lesson"—that, in fact, the lesson was supposed to have been the principal thing for which they were here as teacher and pupils. It would not do to ignore that utterly. Some of these young scamps would be sure to go home and tell, and his good name, of which he was beginning to be a little proud, would be damaged if he made no attempt at all to teach something sort of ethical. That was his idea of Sunday school teaching. "Boys, you must grow up to be good citizens," or something of that sort. He supposed there was some kind of a code, or formula, for the thing, and he recalled that he was to ask the boys to tell him, so he straightened back and began: "But we must get at our lesson, kids; the time is almost up."

"Aw shucks!" spoke up the boldest child impudently. "We don't want 'ny lesson. We want you to tell us more about that game."

"I've talked enough; now it's your turn. What's your lesson about? Who can tell me? I'm a stranger here, you know."

"'Bout Paul," said another boy, whom they called "Skid" Jenkins.

"No, 'twas Saul," said "Gid" Porter.

"It was Saul first," explained Jimmy Brower. "He got diffrunt after a while. Then he got a new name."

"I see," said Murray, fencing for time. What a strange lesson. Who was this Paul, he wondered. Not Paul Revere, of riding fame? He searched his scant knowledge of history in vain. Of Bible lore he knew not the slightest shred.

"Well, he was Paul the longest, anyhow," insisted Skid. "Everybody calls him Paul. You don't never hear him called Saul."

"Tell me more about him," said Murray. "What did he do?"

"Why, he was *fierce*!" said Jimmy earnestly. "He *killed* folks!"

The teacher sat up sharply and drew a deep breath. *He* had killed some one.

"Yes," said Skid, "he went right into their houses and took 'em to the magistrates and had 'em whipped and sent to prison, and burned their houses and took their kids'n everything, an' he was the one that held the men's sweaters when they was stoning Stephen, ya know. Gee, I'd like to a been living then! It musta been great! When they didn't like what anybody said, they just stoned 'em dead! We had Stephen last Sunday. And Saul—I mean Paul—but he was Saul then when he held the clothes—he was to blame, ya know. He coulda stopped 'em stoning Stephen ef he'd wanted. He was some kinda officer, ya know. But he didn't, 'cause he didn't wantta. Ya know he thought he's doin' right? That'uz before he was born again." He looked at his new teacher for approval and found a flattering attention. Murray's face was white, and beads of perspiration were standing on his brow, but he summoned a wan smile of approbation and murmured faintly: "Yes? How was that?"

Jerry Pettingill raised a smudgy hand.

"Lemme tell. He's talked long enough. It's my turn."

Murray turned his eyes nervously to this new boy, and he continued with the tale.

"He was on his way t'rest a lotta folks, an' the lightnin' struck him blind, an' the soldiers he had with him didn't see no one, just heard a voice, an' they didn't know whatta think, an' Saul—no, Paul—"

"He *wasn't* Paul yet—"

"Well, he was right away then, 'cause when he heard God he got borned again."

"What is 'born again'?" came from the lips of the unwilling teacher, almost without his own consent. He had no idea that these children could explain, and yet he somehow had to ask that question. He wanted to see what they would say.

"It's givin' yerself up to God!" said Skid cheerfully.

"It's quit doin' whatcher doin' an' doin' the other thing. Sayin' yer sorry an' all that. Only Saul, he said he didn't know. He thought he was doin' good," said another boy.

"Ya can't born yerself," broke in young Gideon. "The teacher said so last Sunday. He said God had to do it. God borned Saul all over and made him a new heart inside him when he said he wouldn't do them things anymore."

"Aw, well, what's that? I didn't say ya could, did I?" broke in Skid. "Saul, he was blind when he got up, an' he had to go on crutches to the city—"

"Aw, git out! Whatcher givin' us? They don't havta go on crutches when they're blind, and God sent a man to pray about him, and then he said, 'Brother Saul, receive thy sight,' an' after that he wasn't blind anymore, an' he was born again. He was a new man then, ya know, an' he didn't kill folks anymore, an' he went and got to be a preacher."

The superintendent's bell brought the narrative to a sharp close, and the new teacher sat back white and exhausted, the strength gone out of him. Even the kids were talking about killing people. What a lesson! How did the little devils learn all about it, anyway? Why had he ever stayed in this awful place? Why had he ever taken this terrible class?

"Well, you certainly are a winner, Murray," said the superintendent, slapping him admiringly on the shoulder. "You had 'em from the word *go*! I never saw the like of you!"

Murray turned a tired face toward Marlowe.

"You didn't need a teacher for this class, man! They can teach circles around any man you'd put on the job. I never saw the like! What you'd better do is give each one of those little devils a class to teach. Then you could all quit. I didn't teach that class; they taught it themselves."

The superintendent grinned at the minister, who was standing just behind Murray, and the minister grinned back knowingly.

"We're glad this young man has come to live among us," he said with a loving hand on Murray's shoulder, and somehow Murray felt suddenly like laying his head down on the minister's shoulder and crying. When he finally got away from them all, he went to his room and buried his face in the pillow and slept. He felt all worn out. He had never taken a nap in the daytime before in his life, but he certainly slept that afternoon.

It was quite dark when he woke up and heard Mrs. Summers calling him to come down to supper.

She had a little tea table drawn up in front of the fire in the living room, with a big easy chair for him and the Morris chair for herself. There were cups of hot bouillon with little squares of toast to eat with it and sandwiches with thin slivers of chicken on a crisp bit of lettuce. There were more sandwiches with nuts and raisins and cream cheese between, and cups of delicious cocoa, and there were little round white frosted cakes to finish off with. Murray thought it was the nicest meal he ever tasted, eaten that way before the fire, with the flickering firelight playing over Mrs. Summers' pretty white hair and the soft light from the deep shaded lamp over the little white-draped table. Cozy and homey. He found himself longing for something like this to have been in his past.

Mrs. Summers talked about the Sunday school lesson, discussed two or three questions that had been brought up in her class of young men concerning Paul's conversion, and Murray was surprised to find that he actually could make intelligent replies on the subject.

But then it all had to be broken up by the entrance of someone coming for him to go to Christian Endeavor. This time it was a stranger, the vice president of the Christian Endeavor, come to ask him to talk a few minutes. He really must do something about this. He was getting in too deep, going beyond his depth. It might be all well enough to pretend to teach a class of kids something he knew nothing about, but make an address in a religious meeting he could not—at least not yet. He had to draw the line somewhere.

So he summoned all his graces and made a most eloquent excuse. He had not been very well lately, had been overworking before he came here, and his physician had warned him he must go a little slower. Added to that had been the nervous strain of the wreck. If they would kindly excuse him from doing any public speaking for a month or so, at least until he had had a chance to pick up a little and get himself in hand. He felt that it was owed to the bank that he put his whole strength there for the present, till he was in the running and felt acquainted with his work, and so on and so on.

The young vice president smiled and regretted this was so, but said of course he understood. They would not bother him until he was ready, though everybody was crazy to hear him—they had heard so much about him. Didn't he even want to lead a prayer meeting? Well, of course. Yes, it was fair to the bank that he give all his strength there at present. Well, he would come over to the meeting anyway, wouldn't he?

And with a wistful glance at the easy chair and the firelight on Mrs. Summers' hair, he allowed himself to be dragged away with the understanding that he would meet his landlady in her pew for the evening church service. Gosh! Four church services, with a prospect of five for the next Sunday if they carried out their suggestion about the Ushers' Association! Could you beat it? He would have to bolt before next Sunday! He must manage it after he got his week's salary next Saturday. That would give him a little more money to start with. He would work his plans with that end in view. It certainly was too bad to leave when his disguise seemed to be working so perfectly, and seemed likely to be permanent, but he could not keep on this way. It might have been all right if he had anything to go on, but one could not jump into new surroundings like this and take on the knowledge that belonged to them. That was out of the question. It was all bosh about being born again. You could not do it. Maybe if you worked at it for years and studied hard you could. But it seemed like a hopeless undertaking.

That evening the sermon was on the Atonement. He recognized the word and sat up eagerly to discover what it meant.

That was a sermon of no uncertain sound. It pointed the way of salvation clearly and plainly, with many more quotations from scripture, so that the wayfaring man, though a fool, need not err in that, and Murray Van Rensselaer was both of those. He learned the meaning of the word *Calvary*, too, and heard the story of the cross for the first time clearly told. Before that it had been more or less a vague fairy tale to him. Of course one could not live in the world of civilization without having heard about Christ and the cross, but it had meant nothing to him. He was as much of a heathen as anyone could be and live in the United States of America.

He heard how all men were sinners. That was made most plain in terms that reminded him of the morning sermon about the judgment. He did not dispute that fact in his mind. He knew that he was a sinner. Since he had run away from the hospital, his sin had loomed large, but he named it by the name of murder and counted it done against a human law. Now he began to see that there was sin behind that. There were worse things in his life than even killing Bessie had been, if one was to believe all that the preacher said. It was an unpleasant sensation, this listening to these keen, convincing sentences, and trying them by his own experiences and finding they were true. He heard for the first time of the love of God in sending a Savior to the world. This thought was pressed home till He became a personal Savior, just for himself, as if he had been the only one who needed Him, or the only one who would have accepted Him. The minister told a story of two sisters, one of whom was stung by a bee, and the other fled away, crying, "Oh, I'm afraid it will sting me, too!" but the first sister called, "You needn't be afraid, Mary; it has left its sting in my cheek! It can't sting you anymore!" And Murray Van Rensselaer learned that his sin had left its sting in Jesus Christ and could hurt him no more. Strange thing! The sin from whose consequences he was fleeing away had left its sting in the body of the Lord Christ when He was nailed to the cross hundreds of years ago, and could harm him no more! Could not have the power to shut him out from eternal life, as it was now shutting him out from earthly life and all that he loved. Strange! Could this thing be true? There was one condition, however. One had to *believe*! How could one believe a thing like that? It was too good to be true. Besides, if it were true, why had no one ever told it to him before?

Murray went home in a dazed state of mind, home to the deep chair by the firelight, to Mrs. Summers' gentle benediction of a prayer before he went up to his room. And then he lay down in his bed to toss and think, and half decided to get up and creep away in the night from this place where such strange things were told and such peculiar living expected of one. What would they ask of him next?

Chapter 18

The next thing they asked him to do was to let them elect him state president of the Christian Endeavor Society.

It meant nothing whatever to him when they told him, because he did not know what Christian Endeavor even stood for at that time, but he smiled and turned it down flat with the excuse that he could not give any more time to outside things. He owed his whole energy to the bank. Mr. Harper would not like it if he accepted other duties here and there.

Then it developed that Mr. Harper *would* like it very much. It was just what Mr. Harper wanted of his bank teller, to be prominent in social and religious matters. A committee had waited upon Mr. Harper, and he came himself to plead with the young man, stressing that he would like him to accept as a personal favor to himself. He felt it would give their bank a good standing to have their employees identified with such organizations.

The young committee pleaded eagerly and promised to do all the work for him. They would prepare all the programs and suggest competent helpers on each committee who understood their work thoroughly. There really would be little left for him to do but preside at the state conventions and attend a county convention now and then. Wouldn't he stretch a point and take the office? They needed him terribly just now, having lost a wonderful president through serious illness.

It sounded easy. He did not imagine it meant much but calling a meeting to order now and then, and as there was a vice president, he could always get out of it on the score of pressing business when he did not want to go. So Murray "stretched a point" and said yes. He was beginning to enjoy the prestige given by these various activities which they had pressed upon him. He had almost forgotten that he was an outlaw. For the time being he seemed to himself to have become Allan Murray. He was quite pleased with himself that he was fitting down into the groove so well. Even the religious part was not so irksome as he had felt at first. He might in time come to enjoy it a little. He had not slipped away that next Saturday night. He had lived very tolerably through three more Sundays. He was even becoming somewhat fond of those seven little devils in his Sunday school class. His popularity as a Sunday school teacher was evidenced by the fact that seven other little devils, seven times worse than the first seven, had joined themselves to the knot that closed around him for a brief half hour every Sunday afternoon. There was even talk of giving him a room by himself next to the Primary room.

Fearing that he never would be able to teach a lesson, he had conceived the idea of offering a prize of a story to the class after they had told him the lesson for the day. This relieved him of any responsibility in the matter of the teaching, and kept excellent order in the class. All he had to do was to have a hairbreadth experience ready to relate during the last ten minutes of the session.

But Mrs. Summers, wise in her day and generation, perhaps wiser than Murray ever suspected, brought to bear her gentle heaven-guided influence upon the young teacher. If she suspected his need, she never told anybody but her heavenly Father, but she quietly hunted out little bits here and there about the lesson— illustrations, an unusual page from the *Sunday School Times*, a magazine article with a tale that covered a point in the lesson, now and then an open Bible dictionary with a marked paragraph—and laid them on his reading table under the lighted lamp.

"I found such a wonderful story today when I was studying for my Sunday school class," she would say while she passed him the puffy little biscuits and honey at the supper table. "I thought you might like to use it for your boys. I took the liberty of laying it up on your table, with the verses marked in the Bible where it fits. You have so little time; it is only right the rest of us should help you in the wonderful work you are doing in that Sunday school class."

He thanked her, and then because he did not like to seem ungrateful, and he was afraid he might be asked what he thought of it, he read what she had left there and was surprised to find himself getting interested. Strange how a dull thing grew fascinating if you just once gave your mind to it. He wondered if that were true of all dull things. He actually grew interested in getting ready for his Sunday school class. There were times when he even preferred it to going out socially, although that was where he naturally shone, it being more his native element.

Yet he often felt a constraint when he went out to dinner or to a social gathering. There were very few invitations to the kind of thing to which he had been accustomed. The whole community seemed to be pretty well affected by the sentiments of that Presbyterian church. They did not seem to know how to play cards, not the ones who were active, and they did not seem to think of dancing when they got together. Not that he missed those things. He was rather more interested in the novelty of their talk and their games, and their music, which was some of it really good. It appeared that the girl Anita was quite a fine musician. She had been away for a number of years studying. Yet he was always a little bit afraid of Anita. Was it because she reminded him of Bessie, or because she seemed to not quite trust him? He could not tell. When he was in the same company with her, he found himself always trying to put his best foot forward. It annoyed him. She seemed to be always looking through him and saying: "You are not what you are trying to seem at all. You are an impostor! You have stolen a dead man's name and character, and you killed a girl once! Someday you will kill the good man's good name, too, and everybody will find out that you are a murderer!" When these thoughts came through his mind, he would turn away from her clear eyes, and a sharp thought of Bessie like an intense pain would go through his soul. At such times he was ready to give it all up and run away. Yet he stayed on.

He was flooded with invitations to dinners and teas and evening gatherings, little musicals and concerts, and always at these gatherings there was the tang of excitement lest he should be found out. He was growing more and more skillful in evading direct questions and bantering gaiety intended to draw him out. He came to be known as a young man of great reserve. He never talked about himself. They began to notice that. All they knew about him they had heard from others before he came. They liked him all the better for this, and perhaps the mystery that this method gradually put about him made him even more fascinating to the girls. All except Anita.

Anita kept her own counsel. She was polite and pleasant, consulting with him when it was necessary, that is, when she could not get someone else to do it for her, but never taking him into the gracious circle of her close acquaintances. Jane often asked her why she had to be so stiff. Jane was more effusive than ever about the young hero of the town. But Anita closed her lips and went about her business, as charming as ever and just as distant. It intrigued Murray. He never had had a girl act like that to him. If it had not been for the fact that she reminded him unpleasantly of Bessie and made him uncomfortable every time he came in her vicinity, he would have set to work in earnest to do something about it, but he really was very busy and almost happy at the bank and was quite content to let her go her way. His work at the bank was growing more and more fascinating to him. He was like a child who is permitted to work over machinery and feel that he is doing real work with it. He fairly beamed when his accounts came out just right, and he loved being a wheel that worked the machinery of this big clean bank. While he was there he forgot all that was past in his life, forgot that any minute a stranger might walk in and announce himself as the real Allan Murray, and he would have to flee. In the sweet wholesomeness of the monotony of work, it seemed impossible that such things as courts of justice could reach a long arm after him and place him in jail and try him for his life.

He liked most of the men with whom he was associated; also he liked Mrs. Summers. The little talks they had at night before he went up to his room gave him something like comfort. It was a new thing, and he enjoyed it. He even let her talk about religious questions and sometimes asked her a shy question now and then, though most of all he was afraid to venture questions lest he reveal his utter ignorance and lay himself open to suspicion. More and more as the days went by he began to cling to the new life he was carving out for himself and to dread to lose it. The respect of men, which he had never cared about in his other days, was sweet to him now. To have lost his first inheritance gave him a great regard for the one into which he had dropped unawares. It was not his, but he had none now, and he must not let them take this one away from him. He flattered himself now and then that he had been born again, as the sign in that trolley car had advised. He was like a little child learning a new world, but he was learning it, and he liked it.

Into the midst of this growing happiness and assurance entered the State Christian Endeavor Convention.

It was to be held in a nearby city. He had not understood that he would have to go away to a strange place when he took the office, but it was too late to refuse now. He must risk it. Still, it worried him some. Here in Marlborough he was known, now, and would not easily be taken for someone else. Practically everybody in town knew him or knew who he was. He would not likely be mistaken or arrested for anyone else, even if his picture were put up in the bank right opposite his own window. He had by this time ventured to look the picture of the advertised man on the wall fully in the face and discovered it did not look in the least like himself, so he had grown more relaxed about such things. If all this time had passed and nothing had come out about him, surely his father had found a way to hush things up. Poor Dad! He wished he dared send him word that he was all right and on the way to being a man. But he must not. It might only precipitate a catastrophe. He was dead and had been born again. He must be dead to all his old life if he hoped to escape its punishment.

He journeyed to the convention in company with a large party from the Marlborough churches, who hovered around him and made him feel almost like a peacock with all their adulation. They pinned badges on him, chattered to him about their committee work, asked his advice about things he had never heard of before, and it amused him wonderfully to see what answers he could give them that would satisfy them, and at the same time would in no way give himself away.

But when they arrived at the strange city and went together to the convention hall, and Murray saw for the first time the great auditorium, with its bunting and streamers and banners and mottoes, his heart began to fail him. A kind of sick feeling came over him. It appalled him that he was to be made conspicuous in a great public assembly like this. He never imagined that it was to be a thing of this sort. He began to realize what a fool he had been to get into a fix like this—what an unutterable fool that he did not clear out entirely. He did not belong among people like this. He could never learn their ways, and inevitably sometime, probably soon, he would be found out. Every day, every hour he remained would only make the outcome more unspeakable. This business of being born again was an impossible proposition from the start. One could not work it. He ought to go. He would go at once! This was as good a time as any. Much better than in Marlborough, for no one around would recognize him, and he could get far away before his absence was discovered.

He cast a quick glance around him, and saw that his delegation were all being seated up near the front of the auditorium. With swift steps he marched down the aisle and out the door and came face-to-face with the man who was to lead the devotional meeting, to whom he had just been introduced.

"I was looking for you, Murray," he said. "You're wanted at once up on the platform. They want to consult you about the appointment of the committees before the meeting opens. Better hurry! It's time to begin."

Baffled again, Murray turned back up the aisle, resolving to find some excuse to slip out the side door, which he could see opening from the platform. There was to be a devotional meeting. He had heard talk about selecting hymns. He would slip out while they were singing. At any rate, there was no escape here just now, for the leader of the devotional meeting was just behind him.

So he went to the platform, bowed, smiled, and tried to conduct himself in an altogether happy and carefree manner, assenting to all the suggestions about committees, listening to reasons for certain appointments as if he knew all about it and was interested, with that flattering deference that was second nature to him. But his eyes kept turning constantly to the door at the left of the platform, and when they were finally through with him and motioned him to a seat in the center of the platform, he sank into the big chair of honor with relief. Now, at last, his release was at hand! When they arose to sing the first hymn, he would look up as if someone beckoned. No matter where that door led to, he would get out of sight somewhere and stay hidden until this infernal convention was over, and he could safely vanish into the world again.

Someone handed him a hymnbook open to the hymn. He

was not acquainted with any hymns, but it struck him as strange that this one should be about hiding. He accepted the book, as he did all things when he was conscious of his predicament, merely as a mask to keep him from suspicion, and he pretended to sing, although he had never heard the tune before.

"Oh, safe to the Rock that is higher than I,
My soul in its sorrow and anguish would fly;
So sinful, so weary, Thine, Thine would I be;
Thou blest 'Rock of Ages,' I'm hiding in Thee!"

Murray Van Rensselaer had never heard of the Rock of Ages except in connection with an insurance company. He did not understand even vaguely the reference, but as his lips formed the words which his eyes conveyed to his brain from the book, his heart seemed to grasp for them and be saying them in earnest. Hiding! Oh, if there were only some hiding for him! Sinful? Yes, he must be sinful! He had never thought he was very bad in the days that were past, but somehow since he had been in this region where everybody talked about Right and Wrong as if they were personified, and where all the standards of living were so different, it had begun to dawn upon him that if these standards were true, then he personally was a sinner. It was not just his having been responsible for Bessie's death. It was not even his running away when he found he had killed her. Nor yet was it his allowing these good people to think he was Allan Murray—a Christian with a long record of good deeds and right living behind him. It was something behind all that—something that had to do with the Power they called God and with that vague Person they called Jesus, who was God's Son. It was dawning upon him that he had something to do with God! He had never expected that he would ever have anything in the remotest way connected with God, and now suddenly it seemed as if God was there all the time, behind everything, and had not been pleased with his relation to life. It seemed that God had been there dealing with him even before he was born into the family of Van Rensselaer. Before being Van Rensselaer's child, he was God's child! His father had bitterly berated him for the way he had misused and been disloyal to the fine old name of Van Rensselaer; how would God speak to him sometime about the way he had treated Him?

"Hiding in Thee! Hiding in Thee!" sang the gathering throng earnestly and joyously, and he shuddered as his lips joined with theirs. Hiding in God! How could he hide in God? It would be like taking refuge in a court of justice and expecting them to protect him from his own sin!

He recalled the first lesson his Sunday school class had taught him about Saul who was Paul, when a light shined round about him and he met the Lord on the way to Damascus. He had heard more of him since, in sermons, and in the Bible readings, and in his talks with Mrs. Summers. One could not hear a story like that referred to again and again without getting the real meaning into his soul, but never before had it come home to him as a thing that really happened, and that might happen again, as it did while he sat there singing. It seemed to him that he was suddenly seeing the Lord—that for the first time he had been halted in his giddy life and made to see that he was fighting against the Lord God, that his whole life had been a rebellion against the Power that had created him, just as his whole former life at home had been a life apart from the parents who had given him life and supported him. It was not the decent thing at all. He had never thought of it so before. He would not have done it if he had ever thought of it that way. Of course his father had told him in a way—a bitter way, cursed at him, but given him the money to pay for his follies just the same. And he had not been honest with his father! He had not been honest with the law of the land either! He had broken it again and again, and counted it something to be proud of when he got away without having to pay a fine. All his life he had run away from fines and punishments. So far as law was concerned, he had been many times guilty. And then when one went further and thought about the laws of God, why, he did not even know what they were. He had never inquired before until a Sunday school session had forced the Ten Commandments to his attention. Of course he had always heard of the Ten Commandments, but they had seemed as archaic as the tomb of some Egyptian pharaoh. He had no notion whatever that anybody connected them with any duties of life today, until Mrs. Summers had discussed the subject briefly one night in that mild impersonal way of hers.

But now as he sat on that platform, singing those words about a hiding place for a soul that was sinful and weary, he knew that he ought to have known those commandments. He ought to have found out God's will for him. He knew that the right name for the state he was in was sin, and he felt an overwhelming burden from the knowledge. He was hearing God's voice speak to him, "It is hard for thee to kick against the pricks," and he did not understand it any better than Saul had done as he lay blinded on the way to Damascus.

The singing had ceased, and he realized that he had not yet slipped away. This was to be a devotional meeting. Perhaps during a prayer he might find a better opportunity.

Startling into his troubled thoughts came the words of the leader: "I am going to ask our new president, Mr. Allan Murray, to lead us in the opening prayer—"

Chapter 19

Never in his life had Murray Van Rensselaer been asked to make a speech or do a stunt that he had been known to refuse or be inadequate to the occasion. It had been his boast that a fellow could always say something if he would just have his wits about him, but the time had come when wits would not serve him. He was suddenly confronted with the Lord God and told to speak to Him before many witnesses! A great swelling horror arose around him like a cloud of enemies about to throttle him. His speech went from him, and his strength, also his self-confidence. A few weeks back he might have jumped to his feet and rattled off a pleasant little prayer, appropriate in its petitions, correct in its address and setting, and felt smart about having risen to the occasion. Not so now. He felt himself to be sitting confused and ashamed before the Lord, and he had nothing to say.

He was in dire straits. He realized fully that if he did not do what he was asked, his mask was off, and before all this assembled multitude he would be discovered and brought to shame. Yet he dared not say off a prayer that he did not mean. So much he had grown in the knowledge of the Holy One. He knew it would be blasphemy.

There was a dead silence in the room, a settling down of awe and waiting, half-bowed heads, trying to glimpse the new president before the prayer began, yet reverently waiting for him to address the great high throne of God for them.

A panic came upon him. He dared not sit still. Old habit of responding to any challenge, no matter how daring, goaded him; fear got him to his unwilling feet, and there he stood.

The silence grew. The heads were bent reverently now. Such a young man to be such a great leader, they thought. Such a deep spiritual look upon his face!

Murray stood there and faced God, his voice all gone!

Then the audience seemed to melt away behind a great misty cloud. A radiance was before his closed eyes, and his voice came back. Unwillingly it had to speak, to recognize the Presence in which he stood.

"Oh, God!—"

A wave of sympathy came up from the audience inaudibly, as incense from an altar. Murray felt the uplift of their spirits, as if they were far away, yet pressing him forward.

"You know I am not worthy to speak for this people—" He paused. His forehead was damp with the mighty physical effort of the words, as if they were drawn forth from his very soul.

"You know I am a sinful man—"

He felt as if he stood in the courtroom at last, confessing himself guilty before the world. Now his mother would know! Now his father would know! Now Bessie's mother and Mrs. Summers, and all of them would know, but he was glad! Already his soul felt lighter! The burden was going!

"You know I am not what they think!" he burst forth. "I am not able to preside at a meeting like this. Won't *You* take my place, oh God? Won't *You* lead these people, and won't *You* help me and tell me what to do? I am willing for You to do what You like with me. I'm *hiding* in You!"

He hesitated. Then he added what he had heard in prayers ever since he came to Marlborough, what Mrs. Summers always closed her evening petition with—"For Jesus Christ's sake. Amen."

Two ministers at the back of the church whispered to one another softly.

"A most remarkable prayer!" said one.

"Yes, and a most remarkable young man, they say!" said the other. "A wonder in this age that his head is not turned with all the praise he is receiving. How humble he is!"

Murray slumped into his seat with a sense of exhaustion upon him and dropped his head upon his shielding hand. The leader in a sweet tenor voice started softly the hymn:

"Have Thine own way, Lord, have Thine own way!
Thou are the potter, I am the clay;

Mold me and make me after Thy will,
While I am waiting, yielded and still."

The many voices took it up and it swept through the room like a prayer, softly, tenderly, the words clear and distinct. Murray had never heard anything like it before.

"Have Thine own way, Lord! Have Thine own way!
Search me and try me, Master, today!
Whiter than snow, Lord, wash me just now,
As in Thy presence humbly I bow."

Murray felt a great longing sweep over him to be washed whiter than snow. He had never heard talk like this, but it filled his need. He felt soiled inside. He did not understand it at all, but he seemed to have been wandering for a long time in filth, and now he realized that what he needed was cleansing. His own soul began to cry out with the spirit of the prayer song that was trembling about him from all these people, who seemed to know the words and by some miracle to all feel the same way that he did. Why! Were they all praying for him?

—"wounded and weary, help me I pray!
Power, all power, surely is Thine!
Touch me and heal me, Savior divine!"

They sang with such assurance, as if they knew He could and would do what they asked. Dared he ask, too? Were there conditions to such assurance? Would God take a man who had killed a girl and then gone on masquerading as a Christian just to save his skin?

"Have Thine own way, Lord! Have Thine own way!" went on the quiet prayer. Ah! That was the condition. Surrender! Well, he was ready. That was what that fellow Saul did, just said, "Lord, what wilt Thou have me to do?" He could ask that.

"Hold o'er my being absolute sway!" went on the song. Yes, he could echo that. He was ready for anything, if there was only a way out of this awful hole he was in. He was sick of himself and his own way. It had never been much but froth. He saw that now. Why had he not seen it before?

"Fill with Thy Spirit till all shall see
Christ only, always, living in me!"

What would that be like? Filled with Christ's Spirit! And men looking at him would see Christ, not Murray Van Rensselaer anymore. He understood. That was just what he had been trying to put across about Allan Murray, and he had almost done it. That was the reason why he had not been able to get away, because men looking at him had seen Allan Murray and taken him for what they expected Allan Murray to be! Ah! But this was to be Jesus Christ! Could he possibly get away with that? Only this was not to be a getaway. It was to be real. He was to surrender and let Jesus Christ live in him. Just cut out the things he wanted as if they were not, and let the Spirit of Christ do with him what He liked. Would that be unbearable? What was there he cared for anyway now? Why! He *wanted* to do this! He *wanted* to be made over! He *wanted* to die to the old life forever and be made new, and this seemed to be the only way to do it: *Could this be the new birth?*

There were other voices praying now, just short sentence prayers, tender and pleading, and all with an assurance as if the Lord to whom they prayed was quite near. They prayed for the young leader, that the Holy Spirit might be poured out upon him, and Murray sat with bowed head in great wonder and humility, and spoke within himself: "Oh God! Hear them! Hear them! *Let me be Your child, too!*" Surely, then, before the Throne, mention was made of Murray Van Rensselaer's name, and it was said of him, "For behold, he prayeth!"

Murray went through the rest of that convention in a daze of joy and wonder. He was not aware that he was doing an amazing thing, really an outrageous thing when one came to think of it. He had not the slightest perception of the gigantic fraud he was perpetrating upon an adoring public. He was absorbed in the thing that had come to pass within his own soul.

Every prayer that ascended to heaven, every song that was sung, every speech that was made, he drank in like the milk of a newborn babe. It all seemed to be happening for him. He was learning great things about this Savior that was his. He was finding out new facts about the indwelling of the Holy Spirit. For before he was like some of the early Christians, who said, "We have not so much as heard whether there be any Holy Ghost." He was but a babe in the truth.

For the rest he did as he was told. They asked him to preside at the meeting, and with gravity and humility he took his place, not realizing at all that it was presumption in him and that he was a false deceiver. His entire mind was engrossed with the wonder that had been wrought in himself. He went through the entire two days as one goes through a fire or an earthquake or any other sudden cataclysm which changes everything normal, and where one has to act for the moment. He had no consciousness for the time being of the past or its consequences, or that he was in the least responsible for them now. Deep in his mind he knew they were to be dealt with sometime, but he seemed to sense as the babe senses its mother's care that he now had a Savior to deal with those things for him. He was a new creature in Christ. Old things were passed away, and all things were become new!

They were wonderfully kind and helpful to him. They had all the matters of business carefully thought out and written up on little cards, with the hours neatly penned, and what he had to say about each item of business. They handed him a new card at the beginning of each session, and they thought him so modest that he kept in the background and did not try to shine when everybody was ready to bow down to him. He asked intelligent questions now and then about matters of business, and he carried them through without a hitch when it came to voting and appointing committees.

Somehow, too, he got through the introductions that were a part of his duty, though none of the speakers were at all known to him. They would say, "Now the next is Scarlett, from Green County. You know, the fellow that made his mark getting hold of the foreigners in his district and forming them into a society, and finally into the nucleus of a church. Great fellow, Scarlett! Give him the best send-off you can! He isn't very prepossessing in appearance, but he's a live wire!"

And Murray would get up and revamp these remarks into the finest kind of a "send-off," in his own peculiarly happy phrasing, and then sit down and wonder as some plain little man with clothes from a cheap department store and an unspeakable necktie would get up and tell in horrendous English of the souls that had been saved and the workers that had developed in his little corner of the vineyard. Murray found his eyes all dewy and his voice husky when the Scarlett man was done, and he turned for his next cue to his mentor.

"Whipple of China. Yes, *the* Whipple! Stuck by his mission when the mob was burning his school and came through. He's back, you know. Got it all built up again. Raised the money himself—but he'll tell about that, of course."

And Murray would get up and say: "It ill befits me to try to say anything in introducing Mr. Whipple, of China. You all know of his thrilling escape and of his wonderful success in rebuilding the work that the enemy had pulled down. I am sure you want to hear him tell his own story, and I will not take one moment of his precious time in anticipating it. Mr. Whipple."

Then he would sit down again to listen to a tale of God's care for His own, more thrilling than any that had ever come his way in story, drama, or life. And this was what men who knew the Lord had been doing with their lives! While he had been driveling his away in childish nonsense, they had been risking their lives for the sake of telling the story of salvation. Salvation! Oh, *salvation*! What a great word! He seemed never to have heard it before. What if someone had shouted that in his ear as he started away in the night from that hospital door? If it had been whispered behind him as he stood by Mrs. Chapparelle's kitchen window and watched her go away to answer the doorbell! If he could have heard it as he lay under the freight car and rode over the tortuous way! That there *was* salvation! Salvation for him! Why, he had not even realized then that he was a sinner. He had only thought of the consequences of his sin if he were found out. He had felt sorry for having hurt Bessie and her mother, of course, but he had no sense of personal sin. And now he had. Now he knew what the burden had been that weighed him down, growing gradually heavier and heavier through the weeks. And now it was gone! He wanted to run and shout that there was such a word as *salvation*, and that it was his! He did not quite know how he got it nor what it was, but he knew it was his, and that he had surrendered himself for life. He was not his own anymore. He belonged to Someone who would undertake for him. His old self was dead, and Christ had promised to see to all that. There would be things for him to do, of course, when this meeting was over. He did not know what they were, but he would be shown. He was like a person blinded now, groping, being led. It came to him that he was like Saul of Tarsus, waiting there in the street called Straight for someone to say, "Brother Saul, receive thy sight!" Strange what an impression that first Bible story of his life had made upon him! It probably would not have been remembered if he had not heard it in such a peculiar way, first taught by his wild little Sunday school class, and then read slowly, with original comments, by Mrs. Summers not many nights later at her evening worship. He realized that he had gotten a great deal of knowledge from Mrs. Summers. He put that away in his mind for future gratitude and absorbed himself in listening to the speakers, who one and all seemed to have the same power and impetus behind their lives, whether they were from China or Oklahoma or Sayres' Corners. Not all of them could speak good grammar. Not all of them knew how to turn a finished phrase, but all knew the Lord Jesus Christ and seemed glad about it. Strange there could have been so many people in the world who knew and loved these things and believed in a life that was invisible and eternal, and he had never come in contact with any of them before! He had known church people, not a few. His mother went to church sometimes, professed to be a member of one of the most fashionable congregations in his home city, but he felt positive his mother knew nothing of surrender to Christ. Why had no one ever told people in his home circle? His father! Did his father know?

It was undoubtedly Murray's absorption in the great new peace that had come to his soul through simple self-surrender that carried him through the services of those days without self-consciousness or fear. His quiet self-effacement made a deep impression on all. He did not seem to realize that he had evaded all attempts to bring him into the limelight. He had been so entirely taken up with his new thoughts that the old situation that had haunted him for weeks was gone for the time.

They came home on the midnight train, and it happened that the man from China was riding on that same train to the city farther on and sat with Murray.

Now Murray had never talked with a man face-to-face who had been through so many hairbreadth escapes as this man from China. Neither had he ever talked with a man or known a man who was so altogether devoted to his cause. So it came about that he sat an entranced listener again to the words of a disciple who had given his life to preaching the gospel in China.

"And how did you feel the night they surrounded the mission with the fire burning all about you, and creeping in the ceiling above?" asked Murray wonderingly. To think that a man had been through that and could sit calmly and talk about it.

"Oh, well, I had to work all the time, of course, stamping out the fire that fell all around, but I kept all the time thinking in the back of my mind that perhaps I'd see the Lord Jesus Himself pretty soon. That was a great thought. There was only one thing held me back. I didn't want to go till I had told a few more people about Him. I couldn't bear to go when there were so few of us telling the story, don't you see? Why, in China, do you know how many thousands of people there are to just one missionary? People I mean who have *never even heard* the name of *Jesus*?"

"No," said Murray, "but I'm beginning to get a sense of how many thousands there are in my own land who don't know Him, and haven't even got one missionary *to the whole bunch of them*! I'm wondering if you could even *get at* some of them to tell them, they're so full of their own matters. Take my own home city, now—"

Murray had forgotten that he was Allan Murray now of Marlborough. He was thinking of his home and father and mother, and the fashionable circle from which he had fled. There is no telling what he might have said had not someone plucked him by the sleeve and called: "Hey, Murray! This is our station! Aren't you going to get out? Not going on to China tonight, are you?" And they hustled him off into the night, with the stars looking down and a strange feeling that all the earth had been made over anew for him.

Murray undressed in a dream. He had not heard any of the nice things they had said about him as they walked down the silent street to Mrs. Summers' door. He had answered only in monosyllables. He had been thinking that when one got to know the news the next thing was to tell it, and how was that going to work out with the life he had left behind him and the mess that he was in? What was the thing for him to do next?

He did not see the pile of mail lying on his bureau. If he had he would probably have paid very little heed to it. He had gotten over the sudden shock that it gave him to see mail addressed to Allan Murray awaiting him. There had been letters several times, most of them circulars, one or two business letters. He had pried them open carefully to discover any possible clue to the situation and then sealed them and put them carefully away in the trunk. Opening the letters even of a dead man was not to his taste, but in this case it seemed almost necessary if he were to remain where he was.

However, the mail lay unnoticed till morning. He turned out the light and knelt awkwardly by his bed. It is a strange thing when a man kneels for the first time before his Maker. Murray dropped down and hid his face in the pillow, as if he were coming to a refuge, yet did not know what to say.

He knelt a moment quietly waiting, and then he said aloud in a low clear voice, as if there were someone else visible in the room: "Lord, what do You want me to do now?"

In the morning he saw the letters. It was Sunday morning. He remembered that at once, for a bell was ringing off in the distance somewhere. And then his glance wandered to the little pile of letters lying on the bureau. They seemed to recall him to himself. He reached out and got them. Several circulars. There had been mail before from the same firms. Two letters bore the names of Christian Endeavor County Secretaries, and the last in the pile said, in a clear hand, written in the upper left-hand corner: "If not called for in five days, please return to Mr. Allan Murray."

Chapter 20

When Mrs. Chapparelle left her kitchen and the white face pressed against the windowpane and hurried to answer the wheezy old doorbell, her only thought was to hurry and get back to her hot griddle. She knew it was almost smoking hot now, and she wanted to try a little batter to see if there was just the right amount of baking soda in it before Bessie came.

She glanced at the clock as she passed through the door. It was late for Bessie already. What could have kept her? But then, she must have lingered longer at the library, for this was her vacation, and books were always such a temptation to her dear girl. How she wished she were able to buy more of them for her very own.

This would be Bessie, of course. She must have forgotten her key. Strange! Bessie never forgot things like that.

But it was not Bessie standing in the dusky street, with the big glaring arc light casting long shadows on the step. It was the same boy with the silver buttons and the mulberry uniform who had been there that afternoon with the two great big suit boxes, and insisted on leaving them there for a Miss Elizabeth Chapparelle. She had told him very decidedly that nothing of the sort belonged there, and that she could not inform him where they should go. She had even looked in the telephone book for another Chapparelle, but had not found any. Then she had told him that he had better go back to the shop and get further information. Now! Here was that boy again! What could be the meaning of it? She wished Bessie would come home while he was here and tell him herself that the packages were not hers. Bessie might know to whom they belonged.

But the boy was under orders this time.

"Lady, they're a present," he announced with a knowing wink. "I knowed I was right the first time. I've lived in this city since I was born, and I get around some every day. You can't kid me about an *ad*-dress! This here delivery belongs here, and don't belong nowheres else."

Mrs. Chapparelle was quite indignant.

"I'm sorry," she said firmly, "but I'm sure there's a mistake. There is no one who would send my daughter a gift from that shop. I cannot receive it. I cannot be responsible for goods kept here that do not belong to us. You must take it back and say the people would not receive it."

"Say, lady, would you want me to lose my job? You don't know Madame! She said I was to leave it, see? And when Madame says leave it, I leave it. You c'n fight it out yerself with Madame, but I ain't risking my job. You'll find the young lady will know all about it, and I'm leaving it. It's all paid for, lady, so don'tcha worry."

He dropped the package swiftly and returned to the street, where he lost no time at all in swinging himself into the mulberry car with the silver script lettering and glided away from the door, leaving the usually capable Mrs. Chapparelle standing annoyed and hesitating in the open door, a spatula in one hand and the two big boxes at her feet. What in the world could have happened to bring about this ridiculous situation? Now here were likely some very valuable garments that would most certainly have cost a great deal of money, landed at her feet for safekeeping. She disliked keeping them even until morning. Something might happen to them. The house might catch on fire and the clothes be destroyed, and she would be responsible. It would not matter so much if they had money to pay for such things, but they had not, and would be in real trouble if anything was damaged. It was likely the freak of the delivery boy, who did not want to bother to take the things back, and thought this an easy way out of it. She would not stand it. She would call up the shop at once and demand that they come for their property. It was not much after six. If she telephoned at once, she might catch them before closing.

She closed the door and, stooping, read the name and address on the boxes. Grevet's. She studied the telephone book and was soon talking with one of the employees in the office.

"No, ma'am. I don't know anything about it, ma'am. The shop

is closed. Madame is gone. You'll have to call again in the morning, ma'am. I'm only one of the service girls. I don't know anything about it."

She hung up and turned annoyed eyes toward the front door, wishing Bessie would come. How late it was! Why should Bessie be so late? It could not be possible that the child had been saving up money and had bought something for her to surprise her. She surely would not be so shortsighted. It would not be like Bessie. Bessie would know that she would not like it. And Bessie would never go and get anything for herself, either, at a shop like that. It would cost a fortune. As for it being a present, as the boy had said, that was all nonsense. Who would ever send Bessie a present from Grevet's? Nobody had any right to send Bessie presents. No, it was a mistake, of course. They would open it before long when Bessie came and find out if there was any clue to its owner. Just now she could smell the griddle burning, so she dropped the boxes on a chair in the front room and fled back to her kitchen.

The griddle was sending up blue smoke, and she quickly turned down the gas and mopped off the burning grease with an old dishcloth, promptly subduing her griddle back to its smooth, steady heat again. The batter hissed and sputtered and flowed out on the black griddle, shaping itself into a smooth round cake and puffing at once into lovely lightness, with even, little bubbles all over its gray-white surface. Her practiced eye watched it rise and knew that the cake was just right, just enough soda, just light enough, and just enough milk to give it a crisp brownness. She slid a deft spatula under its curling edges, flopped it over exactly in its own spot, its surface evenly browned. Then she turned her attention to the amber syrup bubbling slowly to just the right consistency of limpid clearness. She shoved the coffeepot to the back of the stove, lifted the cake to a hot plate on the top of the oven, tore a bit out of it and tasted it to make sure it was perfect, and then looked at the clock. Why, it was a quarter to eight! Was it possible? What had become of Bessie? How could she stay out so late? She knew her mother would worry! What should she do?

Often she had rehearsed in her mind through the years what she would do if anything happened ever that Bessie did not come home some evening. She would go about it in a most systematic way. She would phone the office to see if she was there. She would ask the janitor if he knew when she left the building, and who was she with? She would phone the other girls in the office. She had carefully gleaned their addresses one by one from her unsuspecting daughter to be prepared for such a time of trouble. Failing in getting any help from the girls or their employer, she would phone the nearest police station, and the big radio stations, and ask for help.

All this carefully planned program began to rush before her mind now as if a scroll with it written out had been unfolded. How many mothers have been through such a time of anxiety, and had a similar plan present itself, and say, "Here, now, is the time to use me," and yet the mother hesitates. So this mother waited and hesitated. Bessie was so careful and so sensible. Bessie had so much common sense. Terrible things did not happen in the world very often. There was some little simple explanation to this delay, and Bessie would surely walk in after five minutes more. Bessie would hate so to have her make a fuss, as if she could not take care of herself. Yet she might have telephoned if she had to stay.

So the mother reasoned and shoved back the griddle, turned the gas very low, heated the oven, and put away the rest of the meal to keep hot; finally abandoning clock, griddle, oven, and all, she went into the little dark front room to sit at the window, as mothers will, and look out and watch the passersby, waiting for the loved one.

The clock struck eight, and Bessie did not come. There lay those two strange boxes. They could have no connection, of course, with Bessie's being late, and yet they annoyed her. Bessie would be annoyed, too, when she came and found them. Perhaps she would not talk about them till her daughter had eaten her supper. Of course, she would soon come, and they would be eating pancakes and syrup, and she would take a deep breath again and know that all was well.

Was that the clock striking the half hour? Oh, what could have happened to Bessie? Never had she stayed away like this before without telephoning. Of course it was not late for a grown girl to be out in the bright city streets, but Bessie always let her know where she was. There had not been anything planned for this evening. She had been going to the library. Perhaps somehow she had gotten locked in the library through lingering too long. How could she find out? Would there be a night watchman who would go and search for her? What was the name of the library Bessie went to? She searched her brain for the right name as she strained her eyes to the street, which seemed full of strangers passing, but no sign of her girl. She went to the kitchen, warm and cozy and safe, with the batter waiting in a yellow bowl on the tiny old-fashioned marble-topped table beside the stove. The first buckwheats of the season, and Bessie loved them so! She looked in a panic at the clock, which was nearing a quarter to nine, and went hurriedly for the telephone book to look up a number. She really could not remain inactive any longer. She had set nine o'clock as her limit to wait, but she must be ready with numbers to call when the first stroke rang. Bessie would not let her go later than nine without phoning. There was a kind of pact between them that she would not get anxious nor do anything foolish till after nine.

She had written out the numbers of three libraries and the police station, and it was three minutes to nine when she heard the front door open. She was so frightened she was trembling, and for a moment her voice went down in her throat somehow, and she could not call. She would hear a voice. Was it Bessie?

"I'm quite all right now, thank you—" It sounded weak and tired. She got to her feet and stood as the kitchen door opened and Bessie walked in.

"I'm so sorry, Mother! You were frightened. But I couldn't help it. Have you had supper? I'm nearly famished. Couldn't we have supper first and let me tell you all about it afterward?"

Bessie sat down by the table and began to take off her hat. Her face looked white and tired, whiter than her mother had ever seen her look before, but she was smiling. Her mother rushed over and clasped her in her arms.

"My little girl!" she whispered softly with her face against her soft hair. "You're sure you're all right?"

"All right, Mother dearie, only so hungry—and a little tired," and she put her arm down on the white table and laid her head upon it. "Cakes! I'm so glad there are cakes! It didn't hurt them to wait, did it? I'm sorry I troubled you. I just know you have been all worried up."

Mrs. Chapparelle smiled and poured a foaming glass of milk.

"Drink some of this quick, dearie. It will hearten you up, and I've got the griddle keeping warm. It won't be a second now till I'll have a piping-hot cake for you."

Bessie drank the milk slowly, and the color began to creep into her cheeks faintly, but there was a sad, troubled look around her eyes. Her mother watched her furtively as she went briskly about getting the supper on the table. She knew something unusual had happened.

But she's here, dear Lord, safe and sound! she said in her heart thankfully as she felt the glad tears come into her eyes.

Mrs. Chapparelle did not ask questions. They talked, not much, about the little occurrences of the mother's day. Yes, the man came to take the ashes, and he only charged fifty cents. He was coming every week now, and they were to pay by the month.

And Mrs. Herron called up and wanted some more towels initialed for Lila's hope chest. She wanted the script letters, and they were worth more to embroider. The little girl next door had been taken to the hospital to have her tonsils taken out, and the milkman had left an extra pint of milk by mistake, so there was plenty to drink with the buckwheats. "And there! I meant to shut that window," the mother added as she hurried over to the corner of the kitchen. "Do you know I thought I saw a man's face looking in awhile ago, just before I began to get worried about you."

"Well, I've often told you, Mother, I think you should shut that blind before dark, especially when you're alone."

Bessie's color was better now. She was sitting up and eating cakes with relish. The droop was going out of her slender figure.

"Oh yes, and a very rude boy brought some packages here this afternoon which he insisted belonged to Miss Elizabeth Chapparelle. You didn't buy anything today, did you?"

"Not a thing, Mother dear. I didn't have but fifty cents in my purse when I started. You know it's almost payday," she rippled out with a voice like falling water, as if it were a joke between them.

"Well, I told him they weren't yours, of course, and I packed him off with his packages. But just when you ought to have been coming back, didn't he arrive again with his parcels and insist upon leaving them. He said he would lose his job if he took them back, that Madame told him not to bring them back, they were paid for, and they were a present. The lazy little scamp didn't want to go back tonight, I suppose, and he actually went away and left them with me right while I was telling him he shouldn't, just sailed away in his delivery car and left me standing with the things at my feet. I was all upset about it. They may be valuable things, and somebody fuming now about them. Maybe we ought to call up the Madame and find out where they really belong and telephone the owners so they can come and get them. Very likely somebody wanted them at once to wear tonight or pack up or something. I tried Grevet's, but they didn't answer. They said the shop was closed—"

"Grevet's!" Bessie lifted eyes wide with alarm, and her face grew white again. "You don't mean they came from Grevet's?"

"Why, yes," said her mother, puzzled. "You don't mean you know anything about them?"

"Where are they, Mother? I must see them first. If it's what I think it is, there's a mistake, and I ought to hunt up the right people at once—"

She rose from the chair and swayed slightly, catching at the table to steady herself.

"Bessie, *you are sick*!" cried her mother. "Something has happened. What is it? You must tell me at once, and you must lie right down."

She caught the girl in her arms and drew her toward an old-fashioned bench in the corner of the kitchen.

"What is it, Bessie? Tell me quick! What has happened? You can't hide it from me any longer!"

"Don't get worried, Mother," said Bessie, allowing her mother to draw her down on the bench. "It wasn't much. Just a little accident. I wasn't hurt, not much more than scared, I fancy. They took me to the hospital and looked me over thoroughly, and they insisted on keeping me there until a nurse could come home with me. That's why I was so late. You see—"

"But why didn't you telephone me?"

"Well, I started to, but the nurse wouldn't let me. She wanted to do it herself, and I was afraid she would frighten you, so I concluded it was better to wait a little and come myself."

"But what was the accident? You are hurt. I *know* you are *hurt!*"

"No, truly, Mother dear, I'm all right now, only a little shaken up. I was riding in an automobile with Murray Van Rensselaer, and a big truck came around a corner and ran into us and over-turned us!"

The mother's cheeks were flushed and her eyes bright with anxiety.

"You were riding with *Murray Van Rensselaer*? But *where* is Murray *now*? Was he hurt, too? Did they take him to the hospital?"

"Why, no, I think not, that is—I don't know. The nurse thought he was all right. They said he was very impatient to know how I was, but when I came down they couldn't find him—"

"Oh!" said the mother indignantly. "He probably had some social engagement. One of his mother's dinners. I could see the cars arriving tonight, and the flowers, and things from the caterer's—!"

"Don't, Mother!" The girl sprang away from her. "Don't! He *may* have been hurt. He didn't seem like that kind of man. Perhaps he went away to a doctor himself."

"Well, I hope he did. For the sake of our old regard for him when he was a boy, I sincerely hope he had some good reason for deserting you after he had gotten you smashed up in an accident. How on earth did you come to be riding with him? I thought you would never condescend to do that after the way he has treated you all these years."

"Mother, I must see those packages, please! I'll tell you the whole story as soon as I've got that fixed up, but I must understand what has happened."

"You lie down, and I'll bring them," commanded her mother gently, and went away to get the boxes.

When she returned, Bessie stared at them gravely.

"I'll have to open them, I guess," she said at length. "There ought to be some card inside that will perhaps give the address."

"He said there was a card inside," said the mother as she began to untie the knots carefully.

They turned the soft wrappings of tissue back and discovered lovely gowns inside, sumptuous in their texture, exquisite in their simplicity.

"Oh, Bessie, if your father had lived, you could have had things like that!" wailed the mother's heart as she caught the first glimpse of shimmering silk and deep velvet.

"I'm just as happy without them, Mother," said Bessie serenely, slipping the card from the little white envelope.

There was nothing written on the card except his engraved

name. It told her nothing. She would have to search out Madame Grevet and find the true owner.

"I think she lives somewhere in the city. I'm almost sure someone pointed out her house to me one day. Let's have a look at the telephone book."

She was almost nervously anxious to get those gifts for Murray's dear friend out of the house. She did not want even to tell her story to her anxious mother until the matter was all set right.

But Madame Grevet was not to be found. She must have a private number. An appeal to the janitor of the shop brought no further help. He did not know her number, and anyway, if she had one she would be out. She was always out when she was at home, he said.

Bessie, exhausted, finally gave it up.

"We'll just have to let Murray know, Mother, and I hate that. Won't you call up?"

"No, I *will not!*" said Mrs. Chapparelle crisply. "Let them wait for their things till the shop comes after them again. It's not your fault that they insisted on bringing them here. We're not responsible. If Murray hadn't run away from you, I might feel differently, but as it is, I think it is not necessary for either you or me to run after them. People who have dresses like that can exist for another night without one more."

"But Mother, he was very anxious to have them delivered tonight. I heard him tell the saleswoman."

"That makes no difference, child; you are going to bed. I'll tie those boxes up and take good care of them, and tomorrow I'll telephone Grevet's to come for their property, but you are not to worry another minute about them. Now let me help you upstairs, and I'll give you an arnica rub, and you may tell me very briefly how you came to be riding in Murray Van Rensselaer's automobile. Then we're going to thank the heavenly Father and go to sleep. Now come, darling."

Chapter 21

But the morning brought no solution to the difficulty. Madame Grevet professed to be too busy to come to the telephone and sent a snippy service girl to negotiate.

Mrs. Chapparelle spoke to her gently, as a lady should, taking it as a matter of course that she would wish to set a mistake right. The girl was insolent, and when at last Mrs. Chapparelle's continued protest brought the Madame to the telephone, things were even worse. The Madame declared that it was not for her to meddle in all Mr. Van Rensselaer's many love affairs. The clothes were paid for and the money in the bank. Her responsibility was at an end. They would have to settle their lovers' quarrel themselves. No, she could not on any consideration take back the things. She did not do business in that way. If they wanted money, they must apply to Mr. Van Rensselaer himself for it, not to her. With which insult she hung up the receiver sharply.

Bessie, standing near the telephone, had heard it all. Her face was very white and haughty. Her eyes seemed darker, almost black, with a kind of blue fire in them. She began to dress at once, rapidly, in spite of her mother's protests.

"What are you going to do, Bessie—you mustn't get up! You are not fit to be out of bed."

"I must, Mother. Don't you see I must? I cannot have that woman thinking those things."

"But Bessie, you can't carry those boxes down there yourself. You oughtn't to go out today at all."

"I'll hire a taxi and take them down, Mother. Now, don't you worry about me. I'm quite all right. I only needed this to strengthen me. No, you don't need to go with me," she protested, as her mother began to unfasten her work dress and take down her Sunday crêpe de chine. "I think it is just as well that you shouldn't. I'm not going to make a scene. I'll be a lady, Mother dear. But that woman has got to understand that I am not that kind of a girl!"

Bessie finished dressing hastily and looked every inch a lady herself as she ran downstairs to call a taxi.

She obediently drank the glass of milk her mother handed her and let the driver carry out her boxes, departing in state, with a promise to return immediately.

She walked into Grevet's clad in righteous indignation, quietly, almost haughtily. She was not wearing the bargain coat this time. She had chosen to put on a little matching suit that her mother had made her from a beautiful piece of dark blue silk material, a touch of exquisite embroidery on the tunic where it showed in front, a touch of really fine fur on the collar. In lines and style it might have come from Grevet's itself, so unique and pleasing was the whole effect. The salespersons were puzzled and looked at her with new respect. Madame came forward smiling before she recognized her and halted half perplexed. The driver had set the boxes down inside the door and touched his cap with a smile for the tip she had given him. This girl had an air about her that somehow took the condescension from Madame's manner.

"There has been some mistake," Bessie said gravely. "I came here yesterday with Mr. Van Rensselaer to help him select a gift for a friend. The purchase has been sent to me instead of the lady for whom it was intended. I have brought it back. I am sorry I cannot give you the correct name and address, but Mr. Van Rensselaer did not happen to mention it. I have a kind of dim memory that he called her Gertrude, if that will help you any, but I am not quite sure. It didn't matter to me to remember, you know."

Bessie spoke with a grave air of finality.

Madame regarded the girl with a lenient, knowing smile.

"I think you will find the garments are yours, my dear. Mr. Van Rensselaer distinctly told me they were to be sent to you and wrote out your address himself while you were changing."

Bessie drew herself up with heightened color.

"Then he wrote it absent-mindedly," she said. "Mr. Van Rensselaer does not buy clothes for me. We are just acquaintances, old schoolmates. I haven't seen him in years till I met him on the street yesterday, and he asked me to stop a few minutes and help him select this gift for his friend. You will find he will be very much annoyed about this if he finds out you have sent it to me. I brought it right back so that you might call him up and ask him at once to give you the address again. I would not care to have him know it had been sent to my house."

The madame smiled again that aggravating smile.

"Mademoiselle had better call him up herself, and then she will discover that what I have told her is true."

"I do not wish to call him up," said Bessie haughtily, "and I decline to have anything further to do with the matter!" She turned toward the door.

Madame took one step toward her.

"One moment, mademoiselle! Does mademoiselle realize that if she leaves the goods here the gentleman will know nothing except that she has received them? The goods are paid for, and my responsibility is at an end."

"Your responsibility is not over until you have let him know that the purchase was not accepted at the address to which you sent it."

Bessie looked steadily at her adversary and spoke in a controlled voice. She was almost on the verge of tears, and she felt herself trembling from head to foot, but she managed to open the door and walk steadily out and down the street.

She felt degraded. To think that that woman had dared to place her on a footing with those women of another world than hers, who lived like parasites on what they could get out of their various lovers! It was maddening that she could not succeed in convincing the woman that she had made a mistake. The worst of it was, though, that she was almost convinced herself that it was not a mistake. Deep in her heart had crept a wild fear that it was true that Murray had sent those things as a gift to herself. That he had dared to insult her that way! To set her down as one of the cheap little butterflies with whom rumor said he played around continually. He had thought he could take her for a ride and toss her a costly gift and have her at his feet whenever he wanted her! He had not remembered the days of their childhood, when they played and read together and respected the fine things of life. He had professed to love her mother and to feel a warm comradely friendship for her, and here now he had shown that he did not even respect her. He thought because she lived in a small two-story house at the back of his father's grand mansion that he could treat her as he pleased!

Well, if he had dared to do this thing, of course it had been easy for him to run away from her in the hospital after he had been the cause of her getting all shaken up that way! Her heart felt like lead as she walked along slowly in the sunshine of the bright November morning. She realized that she had been struggling against all evidence to excuse Murray for not having brought her home, or come to tell her mother about the accident, or even calling up on the telephone this morning to find out if she was all right. She could not understand it. Murray! Her old friend, turned yellow like this! Disgusting! Terrible! Why believe in anybody anymore? But then she ought to have known better than to expect anything from a spoiled boy who had had no upbringing and too much money all his life. It was just what was to be expected every time with a mother like that beautiful doll-faced Mrs. Van Rensselaer. After all, she had known for years that Murray would never be anything to her, not even a friend. Why mourn this way, just because for a brief hour he had chosen to revive old acquaintance, amuse himself with his former playmate, and then vanish?

So reasoning, she went toward home, but her mind was by no means at rest. Another spirit kept continually whispering to her:

"But suppose that Murray was hurt himself! Suppose he is lying now in a hospital, unconscious perhaps, while you are enraged at him? This is not a Christian way to look at the matter. And besides, somehow you have got to let him know that you did not keep those dresses. If he really did try to present them to you, he has got to be made to understand that you are not that kind of girl."

When she reached home it was all to be argued over again with her mother, who was as disturbed as she about the matter. That anybody should dare to misunderstand her dear girl! That was more than the mother could bear. For Murray Van Rensselaer the boy she had always had a tender place in her heart, but for Murray Van Rensselaer the young man who had apparently forgotten his old friends for years, and now that he had chanced upon them again for an hour, had insulted them, she had little charity. It was the way of his world, of course, but she resented it. She did not covet his friendship for her girl, for well she knew how far apart they would have grown, and well she knew the follies and temptations of the life that he with his money and his fast friends had in all probability lived. No, if she had known of his proximity she would have hidden her girl, if it had been possible, rather than have had her come into contact with him again, rather than run the risk of Bessie's heart being touched by one who could never be anything more than an acquaintance to her.

But now that they had met, and he had tried to open the friendship once more by asking her to ride with him, the mother resented hotly both the way in which he had left her alone in the hospital and also the gift that he had presumed to send her. For that he had intended it for Bessie she was now well convinced. Did he think to bind her to him by costly gifts, yet toss her aside whenever the fancy took him? Did he consider her so low that he might pay off an obligation of courtesy by one of money? Having decided in her heart that he probably was worse than good for nothing, she proceeded to cast him out of her love, although she had really loved him when he was a little boy. He had seemed so lonesome, so interesting, so manly besides, and he had taken so kindly to her mothering. Well, that was past, and she must protect her precious girl at all costs. He was a child of luxury now. He was spoiled, and that was all there was to it. If he had been born to a different family, or his parents had lost their money and their prestige when he was small, there might have been some hope for him, but of course it was a foregone conclusion that he would be spoiled, and only of the world. What could one expect?

They argued ways and means for a long time, and finally Bessie sat down and wrote a frigid little note:

My dear Mr. Van Rensselaer:

I feel that you ought to know that the purchases you made at Grevet's yesterday were by some strange mistake sent to my address. The delivery man insisted upon leaving them here with my mother before I reached home, though she told him they were not ours. I took them back this morning, and the woman was very disagreeable about it and declared you had given no other address. I advised her to communicate with you at once. I hope your friend has suffered no inconvenience from the delay.

Sincerely,
Elizabeth Chapparelle

After the note was dispatched, Bessie felt better. Surely Murray could not misconstrue such a letter into an invitation to open the friendship again. If he tried that, she could easily show him that she wanted nothing from him. But she had done her duty toward the beautiful clothes, and now she could perhaps adjust her mind to think better of him. If possible, she wanted to think well of him because as an old friend he had figured largely in her childhood days, and she did not like to have anything haloed by her school days turn out to be common clay. He might go his way and forget her forever if he would only let her think well of him. She wanted to respect him with all her heart, but she did not see exactly how she was ever going to do it again. Supposing even that he had not meant to insult her with a costly gift without asking permission—and such a gift—a gift of clothing! There was still the fact that he had deserted her after getting her into an accident. She would not have supposed even a spoiled heartless flirt would do a thing like that to an old friend. Yet he seemed to have done it.

The hours went by, and she lay on the bench in the kitchen and pretended to read, but in reality she was listening for a ring at the door or the telephone. Yet none came. She stayed on the bench for two reasons. First, to satisfy her mother, who persisted in being anxious about her on account of the accident, and second, because she really felt quite weak and shaken up. Tomorrow her employer would be back in the office, and she must go to work again. The precious two days' vacation was going fast, and had all been spoiled. She felt almost bitter about it; there had been so much joy in its anticipation, but she did not want her mother to realize that. Mother was happy in just having her home with her.

So the letter was mailed, and Bessie waited, thinking surely when he got it he would call up or come around with a belated apology. She could not fully rest until she knew he understood that she was not the kind of girl to whom he could send such presents.

Days passed. A week. Two weeks. Three. Nothing was heard of Murray. Bessie and her mother began to wonder whether after all they ought not to have taken the boxes around to the Van Rensselaer house. Finally Bessie settled down to the belief that Murray was angry that she had not accepted his presents and had decided to drop her. Well, so she was content. She wanted no friendship with a man like that. She was glad if he felt that way. She was glad he knew he could not treat her the way he evidently treated other girls.

She settled back into the pleasant routine of her life, with the big ambition ahead to put her mother into more comfort, with opportunity for rest, and she succeeded pretty well in forgetting the one bright day with her old friend that had ended so disastrously. Only far back in her mind was a little crisp disappointment that her only old friend, whom she had so long idealized, had turned out to be such a hopeless failure, and sometimes in the dark at night when she was trying to go to sleep, her cheeks burned at the thought that she had accepted him so readily and jumped into his car at the first bidding. How she would like to go back to that bright twenty-first-birthday afternoon and haughtily decline that invitation to ride! Sometimes her pride fairly cried out for the chance.

Then one morning Mrs. Chapparelle, scanning the paper as was her habit for bits of news to give her child while she ate her breakfast before going to the office, came upon a little article tucked down in the society columns.

It is beginning to be an interesting question, "What has

become of Murray Van Rensselaer?" He isn't at his home,
and he hasn't gone abroad, at least not according to any of
the recent sailing lists of vessels. He is not registered at his
club, and he has not been seen at any of the popular southern
resorts. His family decline to talk. Polo season is coming on,
and Murray Van Rensselaer has disappeared! Everybody is
asking what are we going to do without Murray? Perhaps a
certain lively countess could give information! Who knows?

Bessie looked up, startled, indignant.

"That's disgusting!" she said darkly. "No matter what he is,
they haven't a right to meddle in people's private affairs that way
and print it all out before the public!"

She did not eat any more breakfast. She began hurriedly to
prepare for the office. Her mother watched her anxiously. Could
it be possible that Bessie was still thinking about Murray? If so, she
was glad she had stumbled on the article. She ought to understand
fully just what he was. That detail about the countess, of course,
might not be anything but a bit of venom from a jealous rival. But
she was glad she had read it.

"Bessie," she began anxiously as the girl went to the hall closet
for her overshoes, "are you sure you are dressed warmly enough for
this stormy day?"

"Mother," said the girl crisply, "don't you think it would be a
good thing if you began to call me Elizabeth now?"

There was a grown-up pucker on the white brow as if the child were feeling her years. The wise mother looked up quickly and smiled, sensing the feeling of annoyance that had come upon her since the reading of the article about her old friend. How her mother's heart understood and sympathized. Another mother might have felt hurt, but not this one, who had been a companion to her child all the way and understood every lifting of a lash, every glint in the deep blue of her eyes, every shade of expression on the dear face.

"Well, maybe," she agreed pleasantly. "I used to wonder whether we wouldn't be sorry we had nicknamed you. I don't know if I ever could get used to Elizabeth now. Bessie was a sweet little name when he called you that. It just fitted you!" There was wistfulness in her voice that reached through the clouds over her daughter's spirit.

"You dear little mother, you needn't ever try. So it is a sweet little name, and I don't ever want to change it. I wouldn't like you to say 'Elizabeth' anyway. It would sound as if you were scolding. Now, I'm not cross anymore. Good-bye, Mother dearie, and don't you even dare to *think* Elizabeth while I'm gone."

She kissed her mother tenderly and was gone, but all day the mother turned it over in her mind. Had it been wrong that she took that little lonely boy in years ago and let him be her daughter's playmate for a while? Was it going to blight her bright spirit after all this time? No. Surely it was only a bit of pride that was hurt, not her sweet, strong spirit!

But the girl thought about it all day long. Could not get

away from that bit of news in the society column. Was Murray really missing? What had become of him? Didn't they really know where he was? Could he be in a hospital unconscious somewhere? Oughtn't she perhaps to do something about it? What could she do? By night she had fully decided that she would do something.

Chapter 22

The first thing she did about it was to stop at a public telephone on her way home and call up her mother to tell her she might be delayed a few minutes with some extra work, and not to worry. Then with a heart that beat twice as quickly as it usually did, she turned the pages of the telephone book rapidly and found the Van Rensselaer number.

Ordinarily she would have consulted her mother before taking as decided a step as this, but something told her that her mother's sense of protection toward her would bias her judgment in this matter. She was a girl who prayed a great deal, and had great faith in prayer. She had been quietly praying all day long in her heart for guidance in this matter, and she believed she was doing the right thing. No need to trouble her mother with it yet. She would tell her before long, of course, but Mother might be alarmed and think she was more troubled than she really was, so she decided not to tell her yet. Besides, this was something that must be done at once if it really was necessary to do at all. She was going to find out.

The ring was answered promptly enough, evidently by a house servant.

No, Mr. Murray Van Rensselaer was not in. No, he was not *at home*. No, they could not tell her just when he would be at home, nor where she could reach him by phone.

There was a pause. She found her heart beating very wildly indeed. It seemed as though it would choke her. Then it was true! They really did not know where he was! But this was only a servant. Probably he would not know. She ought to get one of the family. After all, what had she to tell that would do them any good if they really were looking for him? Only that he had had an automobile accident and had disappeared from the hospital. Would that do them any good? Could they trace him from there if he had been injured?

The thought of Murray alone, delirious, perhaps, in a hospital, and his mother worrying, if such mothers ever worried, set her fluttering voice to going again.

"May I speak to Mrs. Van Rensselaer?"

"Mrs. Van Rensselaer will be dressing now," said the impersonal voice of the butler. "We don't disturb her when she's dressing unless it's for something very important."

"This is most important!" said Elizabeth firmly. She had started it; now she would see it through.

"Wait a minute. I'll put you on the other phone, and you can talk to the maid."

She heard a click, and a voice with a French accent answered her.

"Mrs. Van Rensselaer is having a shampoo and a wave now. Could you leave a message?"

"I'm afraid not," said Bessie desperately. "Do you think she could see me if I stopped by in about half an hour? Just for five minutes?"

"She might," said the maid. "You'd have to be very brief; she's giffing a dinner tonight. She'll not haf mooch time."

"I'll be brief," said the girl with relief in her voice.

"Who shall I say called?"

"Oh, Miss Chapparelle. But she won't know me."

~❧~

Bessie was waiting in a small reception room to the right of the front door when the maid came down and eyed her from head to foot appraisingly. She was sorry she had not waited to dress instead of coming straight up from the office.

"Mrs. Van Rensselaer says she don't know you. Who are you?"

Bessie's cheeks were burning. Now that she was here, she felt that she had intruded, and yet her conscience would not let her run away with her errand uncompleted. She stood her ground with her gravest little manner of self-respecting confidence.

"She would not know me." She smiled. "I'm only a neighbor who used to know Murray when we were children. I had something to tell her I felt she perhaps would be glad to know."

"Are you an agent? Because she won't see agents."

"Mercy, no!" said Bessie, smiling. "Tell her I won't keep her a moment. I would send a message if I could—but—I think I ought to speak with her."

The merciless eye of the maid gave her one more searching look and sped away up the stairs again. A slight movement in a great room like a library across the wide, beautiful hall drew the girl's attention, as if someone were over there listening. Perhaps it was Murray. Perhaps she was making a fool of herself. But it was too late now. She must see this thing through. It was always wrong to do a big thing like this on impulse. She ought to have talked it over with her mother first. But she had prayed! And it had seemed so right, so impossible not to do it. Well, the maid was coming back.

"Madame says she can't see you. She says she has no time to listen to complaints from the girls that hang on to her son. She says she remembers you now. You're the girl she sent him away from to boarding school to get rid of years ago!"

"That will do, Marie!" said the stern voice of the master of the house. "You may go back to Mrs. Van Rensselaer!"

The maid gave a frightened glance behind her and sped away up the stairs in a hurry. The occasions were seldom when the master interfered with his wife's servants, but when he did, he did it thoroughly. Marie had no wish to incur his disfavor. Who could know the master was in that room?

Mr. Van Rensselaer came out from the shadow of the dimly lit doorway and approached Bessie, eyeing her keenly.

"You had something to say about my son?" he asked in a courteous tone.

Bessie lifted eyes that were bright with unshed tears of wrath and mortification, but she answered firmly and with a tone of dignity: "Yes, Mr. Van Rensselaer. Will you tell me, is it true that your son is away and you do not know where he is?"

The father gave her a startled look.

"Why should you ask that?"

"Because I happened to read an article in the paper this morning that implied that. If it is not true, just tell me, and I will go about my own affairs. I did not *want* to come here. I thought I ought to."

"But if it were true, why should that interest you?"

"Because I was there at the time of the accident." She spoke in a low clear voice, very haughtily, her manner quite aloof. "I thought perhaps you might not know."

"Accident?" he said sharply. "Step into this room, please, won't you? We shall not be disturbed in here."

He drew a deep, luxurious chair for her before a softly flickering fire and turned on the electric light, looking keenly into her face.

"Now, will you first tell me who you are?"

Bessie was quite herself again. She was resolved to tell her story clearly in every detail as quickly as possible and then leave this dreadful house, forever, she hoped. How awful that she should be mixed up in a thing like this and be so misunderstood.

"I am Elizabeth Chapparelle, from the next street. Our house is just behind yours. I used sometimes to play with Murray when we were little children. We were in the same classes in school for a while."

"I see," said the father, studying her speaking face. "Could that possibly be your kitchen window that I can see from the back of the house?"

"Probably." Bessie was in no mood to discuss the relative position of their houses. "I had not seen your son for several years, until the day of the accident."

The father started sharply now and came to attention.

"Will you tell it to me in detail just as it happened, please?" he asked. "Begin when you met him, and tell me everything."

Bessie noticed that he had not said whether he knew of the accident or not. He wanted to get every detail from her without letting her know anything. Well, that was all she wanted, too.

"I was standing on the corner of the avenue waiting for the trolley at two o'clock, three weeks ago today. I noticed a car coming down the avenue and was admiring it. I did not see who was driving it until Murray stopped the car and spoke to me. I had not seen him for years before then."

An alert movement of the father showed that he was giving all attention.

"The traffic was congested, and the policeman wanted him to move on, so he asked me to get in and let him take me to wherever I was going. There was no time to hesitate, so I got in, not intending to go but a block or two till I could be polite and make him let me out. The car seemed to go pretty fast—" She hesitated and looked troubled, as if she thought she were at fault for being in the car at all.

"It does," said Mr. Van Rensselaer dryly. "It has a habit of going fast."

Elizabeth lifted troubled eyes to find a shadow of a twinkle in the eyes that met hers. She hurried on:

"I told him I was going to the library, but he asked me to take a spin in the park, just a few minutes, to talk over old school days. He did not really wait for me to say whether I would. He just went—"

She was quite the most conscientious girl the father had met in thirty-five years. He wondered where she was brought up. He wondered if it could be genuine.

"Then when I said I must go back, he asked me if I would just stop at a shop and help him pick out a gift for a friend. Of course I consented. It was on our way from Grevet's to the library that the truck ran into us. We were overturned."

"Murray was *hurt*?" There was a sharp ring of pain in the father's tone, the first evidence of anxiety he had shown.

"I don't know," said Elizabeth. "I didn't think so at first, because they said he took me to the hospital. But after I read *that* in the paper, I thought if he had really disappeared perhaps he was hurt, and was somewhere in a hospital unconscious, and I ought to tell somebody. They say he brought me to the hospital in a taxi, so his car must have been wrecked."

The father's jaw hardened.

"What became of him after he brought you to the hospital? Were you hurt?"

"Not much, only shaken up, I guess, but I was some time coming to consciousness, and when they took me downstairs again they couldn't find him. They said he had been very anxious and impatient to know how I was, so I supposed perhaps he had an appointment and had to go. I went home. I thought probably he would call up to know how I was, but when he didn't, I decided he must have found out at the hospital that I was all right and hadn't thought anything more of it."

"H'm! That would have been a very gentlemanly thing to do, of course, get a girl smashed up and then go off without finding out whether she was dead or alive! I'm sure I hope that's not what my son did, but there's no telling!"

"Oh, we were not close at all, you know," explained the girl. "It was seven years since I had seen him. It was just the ordinary acquaintance of schoolmates."

"I can't see that that alters the discourtesy. But go on."

"Why, that's all," said the girl, suddenly feeling as if she had been very foolish indeed to come. "I—just thought—if you didn't know where he was—that perhaps I was the last one who had seen him, and you would want to make some inquiries if you knew there had been an accident. But of course it was foolish. You probably know all about him, and I beg you won't say anything to him about me. I'm sorry I have troubled you. I'm always doing something impulsive! I hope you will pardon my intrusion—" She turned quickly toward the door with an odd little look of sweet dignity. She felt she was almost on the verge of tears and must get away quickly, or she would break down right here before him.

"Wait a minute!" said the man sharply. "What did you say your name was?"

"Oh, please, it doesn't matter," she said with her hand on the doorknob.

"Excuse me, it does matter. I might want to ask some more questions. You've guessed right about Murray; I don't know where he is. I am taking it for granted that he will turn up all right, as he usually does, but at the same time there may be something in what you have suggested, and I'll look around and make sure. In the meantime, may I ask you to keep this just between ourselves?"

"Certainly," said the girl.

"And—I wouldn't try to see Mrs. Van Rensselaer again—she's—rather excitable—"

"I certainly shall not!" said Elizabeth, her cheeks growing very red at the remembrance of the insult.

"And I'm sorry that you had to endure such impudence from that cat of a maid. She's insufferable!"

"That doesn't—matter—" She turned toward the door again, wishing she were out on the sidewalk now in the cool air. Her heart was beating so fast again, and she was sure she was going to cry!

Perhaps the dewy look about her eyes gave warning of this, for the man suddenly changed his tone toward her:

"Look here, young lady, don't take this thing too seriously. You've done an awfully sporty thing, coming here to tell me this, after the way that young rascal of a son of mine treated you. There's just a chance that you may be right, and he is unconscious in a hospital somewhere. I shall leave no stone unturned, of course, to make sure. But in the meanwhile we'll keep this thing quiet. Now please give me your name. I'll keep it to myself, understand, and I won't let the kid know you've been here either, if you don't want me to. Chapparelle, you say, Elizabeth Chapparelle? Your father living? I used to know a man in business by that name, but that's a good many years ago. Fine chap he was, too."

"My father has been dead a good many years," said Elizabeth with a delicate withdrawal in her voice.

"You live on Maplewood Avenue? What number? You won't mind if I drop in perhaps, to ask you a few more questions, in case anything turns up?"

"Of course," said Elizabeth.

"By the way, what was the name of that hospital? And about what time did the accident occur? You understand, you know, that we're going to keep this out of the papers. And by the way, who else knows all this?"

"Nobody but my mother."

"Your mother?" There was speculation in the tone, a rising inflection.

"You needn't be afraid of my mother!" she said haughtily. "She was quite annoyed with me for having gotten into the car at all, and she is terrified at what might have happened."

"Too bad!" said the father with sudden sympathy. "I'm sorry you've had all this trouble. Wait! I'm going to ring for my car and send you around."

"Indeed, no!" said the girl firmly. "I should much prefer to walk. It's only a step anyway."

He opened the door for her himself and thanked her again most cordially, and she gave him a faint fleeting smile in acknowledgment.

He stood for a moment watching her walk away in the darkness. There was a sweet girl! Why couldn't Murray get her for a friend, instead of smashing her up! Just like Murray to lose his head over a countess and a dance-hall favorite and let a peach of a girl blossom at his feet and never notice her! Oh well, life was a disappointment anyway, whichever way you turned. Now here was Murray! What a bitter disappointment he was! Just when he might have been a comfort. Of course there was a slight possibility of his being injured somehow, but if he had been able to take a girl to the hospital, he couldn't have been very badly off. No, he was probably off with the fellows somewhere having a good time, or off with his countess or his latest fancy! What a son! But he must do his duty as a father anyway. So Murray's new car was wrecked! That was probably the reason Murray did not come home. He was waiting till his father's fury should blow over. Of course the car was covered by insurance, but what kind of a thing was that to do, wreck a new car all to bits the first week!

So he called up the Blakely Hospital first, and it being about the same hour as the accident, he got the same stiff-arched nurse with double lenses who had been on duty at the desk that day.

"Yes, sir, I was here when they came in. Yes, I remember him. Kind of a snob he was. Good-looking. They always are lookers when they're that way, but looks aren't everything. He thought he owned the earth. Said his name was Van something, as if that made any difference here! What's that? Yes, I guess it was Van Rensselaer. One of those millionaire families that think they come of a different race from the rest of us. Oh yes, I remember him. He pranced around here and got upset because we couldn't stop the whole hospital for his benefit. And then he got mad and left before his girl came down after all. Yes, she was a pretty little thing. No, I don't know what the doctor said about her. I guess she was pretty bad at first. They mighta thought she was going to die. I don't know. But they took her home, and I guess she's all right. No, I didn't see the young man go out. There was another patient come in to get a wound dressed, and about that time the nurse come down to report on the case, but she had to call the police station first about a drunk they had brought in, and when she went to say the girl was coming round all right, the young fella was gone."

The father thanked her and hung up. He sat thoughtfully for a few minutes in his big chair, trying to work it all out. Then he picked up the telephone again and went the rounds of the hospitals, but found no trace of any patient in any of them who fit the description of his son. After more thought he even called up the countess, and a few of the other various stars and favorites, without giving his name of course, but each of them professed not to have seen Murray. So that was that! Of course, if Murray was in hiding, he wouldn't have let anybody find him, and they would be in league with him. Well!

So he called up a very extra-secret detective, a private one, who frequented fashionable haunts, and was one of the crowd, knew everybody, and was known, but not in his secret capacity except to a few.

"That you, Eddie? Well, I want you to hunt up Murray. He's off somewhere. Just found out he had a wreck with his new car. Guess he's lying low till it blows over. We had a few words about some bills the other day, and he got upset. But something has come up I want him to sign. You just look around and get hold of him. Tell him I won't say anything about the car or the bills. Tell him I'm in need of him. Get me, Eddie? All right. Let me hear from you as early as convenient, even if it's in the night. The business is important and immediate. All right, Eddie. You understand."

He hung up with a tolerable feeling of ease. He had done his best, and Murray would likely turn up tonight or in the morning. Of course his mother would rave again if he didn't come to her bore of a dinner. But then, she always raved about something. It might as well be one thing as another.

He got up and went to the window, looking out into the dark street, and there came to him a vision of the girl as she had walked away, slim and proud. He knew what she was thinking. She was afraid that they thought her one of the girls who ran after Murray. But strange to say, he did not. If he had, he would not have taken the trouble to rebuke Marie when she uttered her impudent remark. Girls who ran after boys were fools. They deserved all they got. But this girl was different. One could see that at a glance; one could tell it by the first word from her gentle lips. She was the kind of a girl who grew up in the country and went to church on Sundays. She had eyes that saw birds and flowers in spring and loved them. He had known such a girl once when he was a boy in the country, and he had been the worst kind of a fool that he did not stay on the farm and marry her and have a big happy home full of loving kindness and children's voices, and a wide hearth with a big log fire and pancakes for supper. Buckwheat pancakes and maple syrup.

Deliberately he turned away from the window and walked upstairs to his own back room, where he switched off the light, drew up the shade, and looked out across the back alley to the bright little kitchen window with the table with the snowy cloth. There was a pie on the table tonight, and it looked like an apple pie, with the crust all dusted over with powdered sugar, the kind his mother used to make. There would be cottage cheese with the pie, perhaps. Oh! Someone had come to the window and was closing the blinds. It was the girl! She had taken her hat off and laid it on the corner of the table, and her bright hair gleamed in the light from the streetlamps as she bent her head to release the fastening of the blind. Then she straightened up, pulled the shutters closed with a slam, and shot the bolt across with a click. As if she knew she was shutting him out, and she wanted to do it!

Chapter 23

Before Murray could quite take in all that that letter might mean to him, Mrs. Summers knocked on his door.

"Mr. Murray, Doctor Harrison wants to speak with you on the phone. He tried to get you twice last night before you came in. I forgot to tell you about it—it was so late. Can you come right down? He seems to be in a good deal of a hurry."

"Sure! I'll be there in half a second!" said Murray, springing out of bed and drawing on some garments hastily.

He hurried down to the telephone.

The minister's voice came anxiously to him:

"Murray, is that you? Well, I've been trying to get you. You know your church letter came while you were away at the convention."

"Letter?" said Murray, quite innocently, and thought sharply of the letter upstairs. Things were closing in around him. The minister probably had one, too.

"Yes, your letter. It ought to have reached here sooner, but it seems to have been misdirected and gone around by the dead letter office. However, it got here in time for the season meeting, and I wanted to tell you that we accepted it, of course, and that we are counting you in with the others this morning. There'll be quite an accession. We would rather have had you present at the session meeting, of course, but it will be all right. There's really no need. Today is our communion service. You know that, of course. All you need to do is to come forward when your name is called. But I didn't want to take you unaware."

Accession! Come forward when your name is called! What the dickens was the man talking about? He could think of nothing but the astounding situation in which he had placed himself, and that letter upstairs. Then the minister hadn't gotten one yet. But he would soon. He must prevent anything more. At least he could confess before the whole thing was brought down around his ears.

"Yes," he was saying to Doctor Harrison, "yes. That'll be quite all right with me, Doctor," and he had not the slightest idea what it was all about. Some collection they were going to take up probably, that they wanted an unusual number of ushers. Well, it would not do any harm for him to do one more thing, but he simply must do something about this right off at once.

"Doctor Harrison!" he shouted, just as the hurried minister was about to hang up. "I want to have a little talk with you. When can I see you?"

"Yes?" said the minister anxiously. "Why, not before services, I'm afraid. Suppose we say after service, or perhaps after dinner would be better. We'll have more time then. Anytime after dinner before Sunday school. I'll be glad to see you. I have two or three schemes I want you to help me carry through."

He turned with a dazed look from the telephone and met Mrs. Summers' pleasant smile.

"Mr. Murray, I've put your breakfast on a tray, so you can eat while you finish dressing. There isn't much time, you know. Suppose you just carry it up with you and take a bite and a sip while you comb your hair."

He obediently took the tray to his room, but he did not eat anything. His mind was filled with confusion and wondering what he ought to do. One thing became plain to him as he glanced at his watch and saw that it was almost time for church to begin. He had just promised the minister he would officiate at some kind of an affair in the church, and he certainly must be there on time to find out what kind of an ordeal he was to be put through now. But this was the last one of those he would ever endure. Truth for him from now on. After he had talked with the minister and made a clean breast of things, he would clear out. Last week if he had been in these same circumstances, he would have cleared out without waiting for the talk with the minister, but today it was different. Something in him had changed, something that affected his whole life, and he could not somehow even think of running away. Some kind of confession and restitution must be made, so far as he was able, before he could be done with the past.

He was all in confusion as to what or how it must be done, but he knew that he must stay by the situation and clear it up. It was a part of the self-surrender of the day before.

He hurried through his shaving and dressing; as he tossed wildly among the collars and neckties that belonged to another man, in the trunk that was not his, he began to wonder about Allan Murray and what he was going to say to him. That he had also to account to him was another settled fact in his mind. The letter that lay facedown on his bed was like the presence of a stranger in the room, something that had to be faced. As a last act before he left the room, he swept his letters into the bureau drawer, took one swallow of coffee, and hurried down to where Mrs. Summers stood waiting for him at the front door.

"We're late!" he said anxiously, and there was a strained look around his eyes.

"The bell is still tolling," she replied. "We'll get there before the doxology. You look tired. Did you have a pleasant convention?"

"It was wonderful!" he said, and then realized that he was not thinking of the convention at all, but of his own experience. It gave him comfort that in the midst of the perplexities that seemed pressing him on every side, he could still thrill to the thought of that experience. It was not just imagination. It was real. It had stayed with him over night! It was his! Whatever came he would have this always, this sense of forgiveness and redemption from the blackness of darkness!

He escorted Mrs. Summers to her seat, as he had been doing ever since his arrival in Marlborough, and after he had settled himself, he realized that perhaps he ought to have inquired what was wanted of him and where he ought to be when needed. Then he remembered that the minister had said he need do nothing but come forward when his name was called, so he settled back once more and gave attention to the thought of that letter at home in his bureau drawer and what he ought to do about it. All through the opening hymn and prayer he was thinking and praying, *Lord, my Lord, my new Lord, show me what to do next!*

Through the anthem and the scripture reading and collection, he kept on with the same prayer. He roused to the consciousness that the collection was being taken without his aid, and without any apparent need of him, and decided that the minister had not had need of him after all. Or perhaps there was to be a circular or something passed around at the close. That was maybe what he had meant by "letter," probably a letter from the pastor to the people, a sort of circular.

Then all at once something took place quite out of the routine of service with which he had come to be familiar since he had been in Marlborough. A white-haired man named McCracken, whose name he had heard spoken with the title of "elder," though he had never understood what it meant, came forward and began to read names. He had been too much absorbed in his own thoughts to have heard what the minister said beforehand about it. But as the names were read he sat up and gave his attention. This likely was where he was supposed to come in. He noticed that the people got up and came forward as their names were called, and he wondered what they were supposed to be going to do. He would just watch the others. Perhaps they were to pass those "letters" around, whatever they were, and probably somebody would tell him which aisle they wanted him to take. He would just have to feel his way once more, as he had been doing all these weeks, and get away with the situation, but he resolved that not another day should pass before this sort of thing ended.

But as the names went on and the people responded, there began to be a strange assortment down there in front of the pulpit. There were young men and maidens, old men, and actually children. Some twenty-five or thirty quite young people came forward; one little boy only ten years old came down the aisle on crutches, with a smiling face and a light in his eyes. Murray wondered why they selected a lame boy to pass things, and such a little fellow! And if they were going to have children do it, why didn't they have them all children? It would be much more uniform. And there were some women, too. Odd! But they did a great many strange things in this church. Probably there would be some logical explanation of this also when he came to understand it.

"And from the First Presbyterian Church of Westervelt, Ohio, Mr. Allan Murray—"

Murray arose with a strange look around the church, a kind of sweeping glance, as if he were in search of somebody. Somehow it seemed to him that perhaps while he sat there the real Allan Murray had entered and might be coming down the aisle, but as his glance came back to the pulpit, Doctor Harrison nodded to his questioning look and seemed to beckon him, and he found himself walking down the aisle and standing with the rest. He did not know what he was about to do, but he had a strange serenity concerning it. He was not going of his own volition. It was as if he were being led. He thought of Saul with scales on his eyes, being led into the street called Straight by his soldiers and companions, and his spirit waited for what was about to happen to him.

The minister came to the front of the platform and looked down upon them with his pleasant smile. It came to Murray that he stood there to represent God. That was a strange feeling. He had never thought about a preacher in that way before. He had had very little ever to do with ministers. And then the minister spoke, in his strong, kind, grave voice:

"Friends, you are here to make a profession of your religious faith and enter into an everlasting covenant. We trust you have well considered what you are about to do, and so are prepared to give yourselves away, a living sacrifice, holy and acceptable to God through Jesus Christ."

Murray stared at the minister in wonder. How did the man know that that was what was in his heart? Was it in the hearts of these others? These men and women—and also these little children? He looked about upon them wonderingly. Had the same Spirit drawn them that had touched his heart? He felt a sudden burgeoning of interest in them, as if they were newfound brothers and sisters. What a strange thing! That little boy with the turned-up nose and freckles, the red hair that needed cutting, and the collar that was not exactly clean, was his brother. He had been born into a new family. He looked at the boy again and saw something in his face, a wistful, earnest look on the rough little, tough little countenance, and all at once he knew that humanity was the next greatest thing to God. Why had he not known that before? Why had he always thought the only thing worthwhile was having a good name and doing the latest thing that had been heard of? Oh, how he had wasted his time!

The minister's voice came into his thoughts just then again.

"Having examined and assented to our Articles of Faith, you will now profess them before these witnesses."

Murray had not examined any Articles of Faith, had not the least idea what they were. He listened intently.

"We believe in the Father, the Son, and the Holy Ghost, the true God.

"We believe that God has revealed the scriptures as our only infallible rule of faith and practice.

"We believe that all mankind are by nature lost sinners.

"We believe that Jesus, the Son, died to atone for sin.

"We believe that whosoever repents and believes in Jesus will be saved."

Ah! thought Murray. *That means me!*

"We believe that repentance and faith are the work of the Holy

Ghost, showing themselves in forsaking sin and in loving God and man."

Oh! thought Murray. *That means me again. Was that who did it all for me? The Holy Ghost! And I have never known what that was before! There is a great deal I need to know!*

"We believe," went on the minister in clear tones, "that the Sabbath is to be kept holy.

"We believe that Baptism and the Lord's Supper are both duties and privileges."

At that moment Murray noticed for the first time that there was a table down before the pulpit, covered over with a fine white cloth of damask. The Lord's Supper! A solemn awe seemed to come over the room. It was something like the Holy Grail that he had had to write an essay on in school once.

"We believe," went on the minister again, "that there will be a resurrection and judgment, when the wicked shall go away into everlasting punishment, and the righteous into life eternal."

Ah! That Judgment Day! Did this change that had come to him mean a difference at the judgment? The born again ones were those whose names were written in that "other book," he remembered. Then he was one of those!

"These things you believe?" The minister seemed to be looking straight at him, and he found himself assenting. In his heart he knew that he accepted these things. They were new to him, but he meant to believe them. They were a part of the new world into which he had been born, and of course he believed them.

"You will now enter into covenant with God and this church."

Still the minister was looking at him. He thrilled with the thought of what had been said to him. Enter into a covenant with God!

"In the presence of God and this assembly, you solemnly embrace the Father, the Son, and the Holy Ghost as your God forever. You humbly and cheerfully consecrate your entire selves to His glory; to walk in all His commandments, assisted by His Spirit; to maintain private and family prayer; to keep holy the Sabbath; to honor your profession by a life of piety toward God and benevolence toward your fellow man—"

The solemn vows unfolded before his mind with a newness that was startling, and yet they all seemed natural to him, these vows that he was asked to take.

He saw the rest of the congregation rise, taking vows to watch over these who had just joined themselves to their number. He wondered how long things like this had been going on, and why he had been so ignorant of them. And then the words of the solemn charge struck deep into his soul:

"You have now entered into perpetual obligation." What tremendous words!

"These vows will abide upon you always. You must now be servants of God. From this day forward the world will take note of your life, to honor or dishonor Christ accordingly."

Murray caught his breath and looked around at the people from a new point of view. Then he was responsible for what they thought of him! He was dishonoring Christ his Savior if he did not walk rightly! Why, it was just a new family whose honor he must regard. His father had berated him often for dishonoring the old name of Van Rensselaer, and bitterly now he knew how he had dishonored it. Strange he had not seen it before, nor cared, nor tried to do differently. He almost trembled at the thought that his life was nothing but dishonor from beginning to end.

The minister was giving the new members the right hand of fellowship, and as he moved from one to another, taking each one's hand in a quick warm clasp, he went repeating the Bible, giving each one a verse. Murray listened to them, recognizing them as words of scripture, because for the last few weeks he had heard Mrs. Summers read the Bible every evening. But now he was hearing them as if they were just new and handed down from the Lord that day, for the minister had a way of making a verse of scripture speak to the soul as he repeated it. And when he came to Murray, he grasped his hand and held it and looked straight into his eyes as he said:

"To him that overcometh will I give to eat of the hidden manna, and will give him a white stone, and in the stone a new name written, which no man knoweth saving he that receiveth it."

Murray stood as one transfixed while he heard these remarkable words. That they were sent direct from heaven for him he never could doubt. A new name! That was what he had been searching for. He had sinned and dishonored the old name with which he was born. There had been no hope for him. Then he had found a

Savior, and he had been born again with a new name! It was all too wonderful to believe! He wanted to shout in his joy.

Every one of those new members had verses given them, as wonderful and perhaps fully as fitted to the needs of the special soul, but Murray heard none of them. He was exulting in his own. To him that overcometh! Ah! Could he overcome, now that he was born again?

Then began that wonderful benediction:

"Now unto Him who is able to keep you from falling—"

Ah! Then He was able. Then he might overcome!

"And to present you faultless—"

Faultless! What miracle was this? Every word was burned brightly into his soul. He didn't have to do anything at all. It was all to be done for him by One who was able!

"—before the presence of His glory with exceeding joy!"

Murray stood with bowed head and a great sense of thanksgiving. He did not notice the little stir around him at first as the new members went back to their seats. Someone found Murray a seat near to the front, and he sat down and looked around him as if his eyes had just been opened to the world. Then he saw that white-covered table again. Four of the elders were lifting off the cloth that covered it. He saw the shining silver of the communion service. Then the minister's voice again:

"The Lord Jesus, the same night in which He was betrayed, took bread; and when He had given thanks He brake it and said, Take, eat, this is My body, broken for you; this do in remembrance of me. After the same manner also, He took the cup when He had supped, saying, This cup is the new testament in My blood; this do ye, as oft as ye drink it in remembrance of Me. For as often as ye eat this bread and drink this cup, ye do show the Lord's death till He come.

"But let a man examine himself, and so let him eat of that bread and drink of that cup. For he that eateth and drinketh unworthily, eateth and drinketh damnation to himself.

"If we confess our sins He is faithful and just to forgive us our sins, and to cleanse us from all unrighteousness. The blood of Jesus Christ, His Son, cleanseth us from all sin."

It was just at this point that Murray rose to his feet. It was as though the scales had fallen from his eyes, and he understood. He saw for the first time what he had been and what Christ was. And now he knew what it was he had to do. He had come to the Lord's table, and he was unworthy!

He took one step forward, and the minister looked up, astonished, yet feeling that there must be something important. He had great respect for this young man who had come to their midst so highly recommended.

The minister stepped to meet him and bent his tall head to listen.

"There is something I must say!" said Murray earnestly in a low tone. "Now!" he added insistently. The minister laid his hand upon the young man's shoulder and was about to suggest that he wait until the close of the service, but he saw something in

Murray's face that made him desist. Perhaps the Spirit gave him a vision of this soul's need. He straightened up and said in his usual voice, quite clearly, so that everybody could hear: "Our brother has a word to tell us. We will hear it just now."

Murray turned and faced the people who had taken him in so openheartedly and let him know that they honored him. There, almost in the center of the church, facing him with admiring interest and not a little pride, sat Mr. Elliot Harper, his superior in the bank, with three or four lesser dignitaries connected with the bank not far behind him. There, a little to the right, was a group of young people who had the day before hung upon his every word and given him all the honor and respect that one human being can give to another. There, a few seats to the left, sat Mrs. Summers, with her kindly eyes upon him, thinking no doubt he was about to tell some touching incident of the convention, in which he had carried so great a part. And there, beside him, with confidence and interest in his eyes, waited the pastor, sure that they were to hear something that would lift their souls nearer to Christ. And he, what had he to tell? For one brief instant he wavered, and then the memory of those quoted words came back, "He that eateth and drinketh unworthily—" He must not begin the new life wrong, no, not if it shattered every beautiful thing that could ever come to him again. Not if it robbed him of friends and livelihood and freedom. No, this was the great moment of his life, the turning point.

But then came those other words, just heard: "If we confess—

He is faithful to *forgive* our sins, and to *cleanse* us." Oh, to be cleansed!

So out of his heart he spoke!

Chapter 24

"I can't let this go on any longer!"

His voice was husky with a kind of anguish. The church grew very still. Everybody stopped thinking idle thoughts and gave attention.

"I'm not the man you think I am. My name is not Allan Murray. I don't know where he is nor what he is. I didn't mean to deceive you. I arrived here when you expected him, and you took it for granted I was he. I tried several times to get away quietly because I was ashamed, but you blocked my way by some new kindness, and because I was a wanderer from home and needed a home and a new name, I finally stayed. Then you made me president of that society, and I wasn't big enough! I knew I couldn't get away with that, and I meant to run away. But the Lord stopped me. He met me right there and showed me what a Savior He was. I guess I was like Saul. My Sunday school class taught me about him—"

Four boys in the back of the church who had been snickering softly over a picture they had drawn in the back of the hymnbook looked wonderingly at one another and got red in the face and watery round the eyes.

"So I gave myself up to the Lord, and He forgave my sin. Will you? I know it's a great deal to ask of you, but I had to ask it before I came down here when Doctor Harrison called my name because he told me to, but I believed all those things he asked us, and I meant it when I took that vow with all my heart." Then he turned to the minister: "I know I'm unworthy, but you said He would forgive if we confessed our sin, and I'm taking you at your word. I'm glad I came here this morning, and I'm glad I took those vows. They are going to be permanent for me. I'd like to have a part in this ceremony you're going to have here. I'd like to be counted in if you think it's all right, Doctor?" He looked at the minister again. "And then I'm going back to face some hard things at home, but I'd like to be counted in with you all this morning if I may. You said the Lord would give me a new name, one that belongs to me this time, and I want it. You took me in because you thought you knew my earthly father; will you forgive me because I want your heavenly Father to be my Father, too? I'm sorry I interrupted the service, but I couldn't go on without letting you know first."

He would have dropped into the front seat, but the minister's arm was around him, and the minister drew him close to his side and said with a joyous voice: "'There is therefore now no condemnation to them that are in Christ Jesus.' 'Beloved, now are we the sons of God, and it doth not yet appear what we shall be: but we know that, when He shall appear, we shall be like Him; for we shall see him as He is.' Let us pray."

And then with his arm still around Murray, standing together as they were, with Murray's head bowed reverently, and such a light of love in that pastor's face, Doctor Harrison prayed as he had never prayed before. Murray felt himself prayed for as Ananias must have prayed for Saul! Ah! if Murray's companions, back in his home city that day killing time in their various frivolities, could have looked into that church and seen their former companion, they would have stared in amazement and perhaps remained to ridicule. But in that audience there was not one who looked critically upon the young man. It was too much like a scene out of the New Testament. One could almost seem to see a flame of Pentecost coming down. Mrs. Summers sat wiping away the happy tears, for she had spent many hours in praying for the dear boy under her roof. There were others weeping and many who were led to look into their own hearts and lives through Murray's words, finding themselves unworthy also.

"And now," said the minister, "let all who will forgive our dear brother and take him into our full fellowship stand with me and join with us in singing 'Blest Be the Tie That Binds,' and then we will partake of the Lord's Supper together."

Such a volume of song went up from the hearts of those

Christian people as must have made the angels rejoice. Murray, looking up in wonder, could not see a single person sitting down. All were on their feet. He was overpowered with the wonder of it.

He knew he would never forget the beautiful communion service that followed. No other could ever be so beautiful. The choir sang softly and reverently bits of hymns that he had never heard before, but that they voiced so sweetly and distinctly that they sank into his soul to be a part of the picture of this day that was to stay with him to the day of his death.

They flocked around him when the service was over, some with tears in their eyes, and wrung his hand, and shyly said they were glad he knew the Lord. Even Elliot Harper, dazed and a bit mortified though he was, that something had been "put over on him" before the world, had the good grace or the Christianity to come over and shake his hand: "Well, sir, you gave us a surprise, but I admire your nerve and your frankness. You did the right thing. Come and talk it over tomorrow. You're a good business-man, whatever your name is, and I'm not sure but we can get together in spite of this."

Elliot Harper was a good man in many ways, but he couldn't help thinking that perhaps it would be a good thing for the bank to have it known that a young man in their employ had been so out-and-out honest as to make public confession at the communion table. That bank was a little idol that he had set up unawares.

But perhaps the greatest surprise of all that he had was to find the girl Anita standing quietly in the aisle up which he had to pass to Mrs. Summers, who was waiting for him.

She put out her hand and said frankly: "I'm glad you did that, and I want you to know I'm very glad you've found Christ."

He looked at her in surprise.

"You are?" he said, amazed. "I wouldn't suppose you'd care. I always felt you didn't trust me."

She gave a quick glance around to see if anyone was listening and then lifted clear eyes to his face.

"I went to school with Allan Murray's sister," she said. "He came down to commencement, and I saw him several times. He has curly red hair and brown eyes, and he is *taller* than you."

Murray gave her clear glance back again, and then his face broke into a radiant grin.

"You certainly had it on me," he said, his eyes twinkling. "I might have known I couldn't get away with a thing like that anywhere on the face of this little globe. But say, why didn't you give me away?"

Anita was nearer liking him then than she had ever been before. She looked at him with a warm, friendly smile.

"I had a notion it might be better to let the Lord work it out," she said.

"He has!" said Murray soberly. "I shall never cease to thank God for bringing me here."

"There's one thing more," said Anita gravely. "I wish you would tell me just how much Allan Murray had to do with this."

"Allan Murray! Why, not one thing, only that I have been

using his name and his things and his position."

"And you don't know where he is? You have no evidence that he was killed in that wreck?" There was an undertone of deep anxiety in her voice.

He gave her a quick, comprehending glance.

"I don't know a thing yet," he said gravely. "I've been wondering that myself every day I've been here, and wishing I knew, but I'm going to make it my next business to find out. Within the next twenty-four hours, if possible. I'll let you know the result if you would like me to."

"I wish you would," said Anita, her eyes cast down. "His sister was very dear to me. She died two years ago, and I've lost trace of him since. But I know there are none of his immediate family living." She was trying to excuse her deep interest, and Murray answered heartily: "I'll lose no time in letting you know when I find him," he promised. "I think he is alive, I have reason—but I can't tell you about that yet."

He noticed a look of relief in her face as he spoke, but several people who had been talking with the minister came down the aisle just then and separated them, and he went on to where Mrs. Summers waited for him.

Half shyly he looked up, suddenly remembering that he must not be too confident. He was no longer Allan Murray, the Christian, whose name brought only honor. Perhaps Mrs. Summers would not feel like taking him back to her house now.

"Are you going to forgive me, too"—he hesitated—"Mother?"

"My dear boy!" she said warmly, slipping her hand into his unobtrusively and squeezing his fingers gently with her warm rose-leaf grasp.

He had a choking sensation in his throat as if he were going to cry like a child. It was so good to be forgiven and loved. This was real mother-love!

"Did you suppose I was going to stop caring for you just because you had a new name? You are not Allan Murray, but you are my boy, and you always will be."

"That is great of you," he said huskily, because somehow his throat seemed choked with tears. "I appreciate that more than you can ever know! I'm not Allan Murray, but you may call me Murray. That's my own first name. That's how it all came about. That girl came out and called me Mr. Murray, and for the first instant I thought someone had recognized me!"

"How strange!" she said. "What a coincidence! The Lord must really have sent you here."

"Well, I rather think He did," said Murray. "I don't know anywhere else I've ever been where I could have gone and met *Him* and been taught about Him the way I have here. It's been a miracle—that's all there is to it."

They were walking across the path to her house now apart from all the other people. There were still groups of people here and there talking with one another about the wonderful service and the astounding revelation concerning the stranger in their midst. Jane had met Anita at the door of the church. There were traces of tears of excitement on her cheeks.

"Oh, don't you just *adore* him, Anita!" she greeted her friend. "Wasn't that simply *great* of him to be willing to come forward like that and tell the truth?"

"Don't be blasphemous, Jane," said Anita crisply. "He's not a god, or he wouldn't have gone around lying for weeks."

"Oh now, Anita! There you go! I think that's unchristian! I thought you stood up to say you were willing to forgive him."

"Forgiving's one thing, and worshipping's another, Jane. Don't be a fool! That's the one thing about you I can't abide, Jane. You will be so awfully silly! Why don't you say you're glad he found out what a sinner he was? Why don't you rejoice a little in the Lord, and worship *Him* for His saving power? We don't have miracles like that every day. It's really something worth talking about and worth giving God a little extra worship and adoration."

"Oh, mercy! Anita! You're always so long-faced! I think you talk a little too intimately about God—I really do! Of course *I* understand you, but some people mightn't think you were a Christian, you are so free talking about religion."

Anita's answer was a hearty, ringing laugh as she turned into her own gate.

"Oh, Jane, you're unspeakable! Well, good-bye! See you at Sunday school!" And Jane went on her gushing way, thinking how handsome the hero of the hour had been that morning, and losing the real significance of the occurrence entirely.

The minister had been detained with a messenger, who asked

him to come at once to the bedside of a dying woman, and Murray had slipped away without a word from him, but later he came back across the lawn to Mrs. Summers' cottage and took the young man by both hands.

"Dear brother," he said, "I want you to know how glad I am that you gave that confession and testimony this morning. Aside from your own part in it, and the joy you have set ringing in heaven over a sinner that repents, you did more in that brief confession to show my people what sin and true repentance means, and what the communion service stands for, than I could have done in a year of sermons. I've come over to congratulate you on your new birth, my boy, and to offer my services in any way I can be a help to you in the further reconstruction of your life, and the hard things you have to meet from your past."

There with the minister and Mrs. Summers, while the dinner waited in the oven, Murray told them his story. Briefly, with very few details of his home, beyond the fact of his name, and that he had been the means of killing a girl in an automobile accident and had run away from justice to protect the family name from being dragged through the criminal courts.

"But I'm going back at once," he said firmly. "It was all as plain as day to me while I sat in the service this morning. I asked God to show me what to do next, and that was what He seemed to tell me. I'm afraid I made a mess of your service, not understanding just what came next and where would be the proper time to interrupt you. But I just couldn't go on and take that communion with that on my soul!"

"You did right, brother. I'm glad you did just what you did," said Doctor Harrison sincerely.

"Well, I've got to make everything clean and clear, and then I don't care what comes to me. I'll have to suffer the penalty of the law, of course—that's right—but now I know I'm not going into it alone. I've got to go to the girl's mother and confess and ask her forgiveness, and then I'm going to give myself up. It's the only right thing, of course. I ought to have seen that before. But first I've got to hunt up that Allan Murray and make things right with him while I'm free. And that reminds me. Mrs. Summers, there's a letter upstairs among those you laid on my bureau that seems to be from him. I'll run up and get it."

He was gone up the stairs with a bound, and the minister sat and smiled at Mrs. Summers indulgently.

"Well, Mrs. Summers, he's a dear boy, isn't he? And our Lord is a wonderful God. He worketh mighty miracles and wonders. Now, I wonder what can have become of that man Murray! I feel responsible for him. I wrote his pastor that he was here, and he was all they had said he was and more. I wonder if we shall like the real man as much as his substitute."

"I wonder!" said Mrs. Summers sadly. She was looking ahead and knowing that this boy, too, she must give up.

Murray came down with the letter, and Mrs. Summers tore it open and read it aloud:

"My dear Mrs. Summers:

"You will have been wondering why I have not written you before, but since the first word that my nurse says she sent you I have been quite seriously ill. There was some kind of a pressure on the brain, and they had to operate.

"But I am getting on finely now, and hope soon to be up and around again. I am writing Mr. Harper tomorrow. They won't let me write but one letter a day yet. Of course he has probably had to fill my place with someone else, and if so, there will likely be no further chance for me in Marlborough. In which case I shall have to ask you to forward my trunk to me, and to send me the bill for whatever I owe you. I hope you have not had to lose rent on my room all this time, and if you have I shall want to pay for whatever you have lost through my illness.

"If, however, it should prove that there is still an opening for me in Marlborough, the doctor says that I may promise to come around the first of the year, if all goes well, and I certainly shall be glad to get into a real home again, if such be the Lord's will.

"I shall be glad to hear from you about the room and my trunk, which I am not sure ever reached you. I am a little puzzled that I have heard nothing from any of you, but I suppose you have been busy, and perhaps there has been some mistake about my address, and my mail has been forwarded to you. If so, will you kindly send it to me, as there may be *something that needs immediate attention.*

"I am taking it for granted that you know all the details of the wreck which changed all my plans, even better than I do, but thank God, I am told that I shall be as good as new again in a few weeks.

"Hoping to hear from you at your earliest convenience, and thanking you for any trouble you may have had with my belongings,

> *"Very sincerely,*
> *"Allan Murray"*

There was silence in the cheery little parlor as she finished reading the letter. Each one was thinking, perhaps the same thoughts. How very strange that this letter should have arrived just at this time!

"But it came several days ago," said Mrs. Summers, looking at the postmark. "I must have taken that up and put it on the bureau with the rest of the letters the morning you left for the convention. Strange I didn't notice his name!"

It was as if she had read their minds and was answering their thoughts.

"Hmm!" said the minister thoughtfully. "The Lord never makes a mistake in His dates. He meant this should all come about for His glory. Where was that written from, Mrs. Summers?"

"Why, it's Wood's Corners! That's not far away! To think he has been there so near, all this time!"

"How far is that?" asked Murray gravely.

"Between twenty and twenty-five miles," said the minister. "He will have thought it strange that none of his father's old friends came over to see him. Did you never get any word from him before, Mrs. Summers? He says his nurse wrote to you."

"Nothing at all," said Mrs. Summers thoughtfully.

"I must go at once!" said Murray, rising hastily. "You will excuse me, I know. There is no time to waste to make this thing right. Something might happen to stop me!"

"You must have your dinner first!" said Mrs. Summers, hurrying toward the kitchen. "Doctor Harrison, you had better stay here and eat dinner with us. Just telephone your wife that I've kept you."

But Murray was at the door already.

"Wait, young brother," said the minister, placing a detaining hand on his arm. "You've a duty here not yet finished, I take it. You've a Sunday school class to teach in a few minutes, and it is a very critical time for those boys. They will have heard of your confession this morning, and their hearts will be very impressionable."

"Doctor Harrison, I can't teach a Sunday school class. I never *did* teach! *They taught me!* You surely would not have me go before them again, now that they know what a fake I am! I have nothing to teach them!"

"You can teach them how to confess their sins, can't you? You can show them the way to Jesus, I'm sure, now that you have found it yourself? You have not finished your confession here until you have met your class and made it right with them, my boy. I'm counting on your testimony to bring those boys to the Lord Jesus."

Murray's face softened.

"Could I do that?" he asked thoughtfully, with a luminous look in his eyes. "Would you trust me to do that when I will in all probability be in jail next Sunday?"

"You could do that, my son, and I will trust you to do it. I want you to do it. It will make the jail bright around you to remember that you had this opportunity to testify before the opportunity passed by forever. You have made an impression on those boys, and you must make sure that it is not spoiled. Tell them the truth. Show them how Jesus forgives. Show them that it is better to confess soon than late."

So Murray taught his Sunday school class, taught it in such a way that every boy in the class felt before it was over that he had been personally brought before the judgment seat of God and tried. Taught it so well that several boys went home and took out personal and private sins that had been hidden deep in their hearts and renounced them in boyish prayers, in dark rooms at night, after the rest of the house was sleeping. Taught it so powerfully that the superintendent nodded toward the class and said in a low tone to the minister, "What are we going to do about that young man? Isn't there some way to keep him here? The real man can't possibly take his place now. Those boys will resent his presence, no matter how fine he is."

A moment later the minister stood behind that class for a

moment and noticed the sober, thoughtful faces of the boys. The usual restless merriment was not present. The boys had been in touch for a half hour with the vital things of the soul and had no time for trifling. He watched them a moment as the closing hymn was announced. Then he laid a hand on the shoulder of the teacher.

"Now, Murray," he said, using his first name familiarly with a fatherly accent, "I'm ready to take you over to Wood's Corners. We'll just slip out this door while they're singing. We'll have plenty of time to get back for the evening service. Mrs. Summers has prepared us a lunch we can eat on the way back, and so we needn't hurry."

Chapter 25

It was very still in the small gloomy room of the little country hospital where the sick man had been taken when it had been determined to operate on him. The woman down the hall who had been having hysterics every two or three days had been moved to the next floor, and her penetrating voice was not so constantly an annoyance. The baby across the hall was too desperately ill to cry, and the other patients had dropped off to sleep. The hall was almost as quiet as night.

The patient lay with his eyes closed and a discouraged droop to his nicely chiseled mouth. His red curls had been clipped close under the bandages, but one could see they were red. He had long, capable fingers, but they lay pallid and transparent on the cheap coverlet, as if they never would work again. His whole attitude revealed utter defeat and discouragement. As he lay there, still as death and almost as rigid, a tear stole slowly out from under the long, dark lashes. A weak, warm tear. He brushed it away impatiently with his long, thin hand and turned over with a quick-drawn sigh. Even the effort of turning over was a difficult and slow performance. He felt so unacquainted with the muscles of his heavy, inert body. He wondered if he ever again would walk around and do things like other people.

As if she had heard him far out in the hall, the nurse opened the door and came in. It annoyed him that he could not even sigh without being watched.

"Did you call, Mr. Murray?"

"No, Nurse."

"Did you want anything, Mr. Murray?"

"Yes, I want a great many things!" he snapped unexpectedly. "I want to get up and walk around and go to my work." He had almost said, "I want to go home," only he remembered in time that he had no home to go to. No one to care where he went.

"I want my mail!" he added suddenly. "I think it's time this monkey business stopped! I suppose the doctor has told you I mustn't have my mail yet. He's afraid there'll be something disturbing in it. But that isn't possible. I haven't any near relatives left. They're all dead. I suppose I've lost my job long ago, so it can't be anything disturbing about business, and I haven't any girl anywhere that cares a cent about me or I about her, so you see there's really no danger in letting me have it. In fact, I *will* have it! I wish you would go and get it right away. Tell the doctor I demand it. There would surely be something to interest me for a few minutes and make me forget this monotonous room and the squeak of your rubber heels on the hall floor!"

He had red hair, but he had not been savage like this before. He had just reached the limit of his nerves, and he was angry at that tear. It had probably left a wide track on his cheek, and that abominable nurse, who knew everything and thought of everything and presumed to manage him, would know he had been crying like a baby. Yes, she was looking hard at him now, as if she saw it. He felt it wet and cold on his cheek where he had not wiped it off thoroughly.

The nurse came a step nearer.

"I'm real sorry about your mail," she said sympathetically, "but your suspicions are all wrong. The doctor asked me this morning if I couldn't find out someone to write to about your mail. There truly hasn't been a bit of mail since you came here. And the head nurse wrote to that address you gave her, I'm sure, for I saw her addressing the letter. Isn't it likely they have made some mistake about the address? I wouldn't fret about it if I were you. You'll forget it all when you get well. Wouldn't you like me to read to you awhile? There's a real good story in the Sunday paper. I'll get it if you want me to."

"No thanks!" he said curtly. "I don't read stories in Sunday papers, and besides, you can't sugarcoat things with a story. And you're mistaken when you say I'll forget it. I'll never forget it, and I'll never get well, either! I can see that plain enough!"

With that he turned his face to the wall and shut his

nice brown eyes again.

The nurse waited a few minutes, fussing around the immaculate room, giving him his medicine, taking his temperature, and writing something on the chart. Then she went away again, and he sighed. All by himself he sighed! And sighed! He tried to pray, but it only turned out in a sigh. But perhaps it reached to heaven, for God heard the sighs and tears of his poor foolish children of Israel, and would He not hear a sigh today, even it if really ought to have been a prayer?

"I'm all alone!" he said, quite like a sobbing child. "I'm all alone! And *what's the use*?"

Then the nurse opened the door softly and looked in. It was growing dusky in the room, and the shadows were thick over where he lay. But there was something electric in the way she turned the knob, like well-suppressed excitement.

"There is someone to see you," she said, in what she meant to make quite a colorless voice. The doctor had said it would not do to excite the patient.

"Someone to see *me*?" glowered the man on the bed. "There *couldn't* be! There *isn't* anybody. Who *is* it?"

"One of them is a minister. He looks very nice."

"Oh!" groaned the patient disappointedly. "Is that all? Who told him to come?"

"Nobody," said the nurse cheerfully. "He's not from the village. They came in a car. There's a young man with him. You'd better let them come up. They look real jolly."

"Did they know my name?" He glared, opening his eyes at this.

"Oh yes, and they said there had been a letter from you or about you or something. They came from a place called Marlborough."

"Well, that's different!" said the patient with a jerk. "Can't you straighten this place up a bit? It looks like an awful hole. Is my face clean? It feels all prickly."

"I'll wash it," said the nurse brightly. She was quite gleeful over these interesting-looking visitors.

"You can show the minister up," said the patient. "I don't know the other one."

"But he's the one that asked after you. He seems real pleasant. He was quite anxious to see you. The minister called him Murray. Perhaps he's some relative."

"I haven't any!" growled the man, "but you can bring him, too, if he's so anxious to come."

He glared out from under his bandages at his visitors with anything but a welcoming smile. It was too late for smiling. They should have come weeks ago.

They stood beside his bed and introduced themselves, the nurse hovering nearby till she should be sure that all was well with her patient.

"My name is Harrison. I'm the preacher from Marlborough you wrote to several months ago. I've just found out today where you were, and I'm mighty sorry I couldn't have been around to help you sooner. I'll just let this young brother explain, and then we'll all talk about it some more."

The minister put a big, kind, brotherly hand on the weak white hand of Allan Murray and then dropped back to the other end of the little room and sat down on the stiff white chair. Murray stepped closer to the bed.

"And I'm a man that stole something from you, and I'm come to bring it back again, and to ask your forgiveness."

"Well, I'm sure I didn't know it, and you're welcome to it, whatever it was. It wouldn't have been much good to me, you see. Keep it if you like, and say no more about it." There was not much welcome nor forgiveness in his glance.

"But you see, I'm to blame for the whole thing," explained Murray gently, "and I want to tell you about it. Are you strong enough to listen today, or ought I to wait?"

"Go on!" growled the patient impatiently.

The nurse was still hovering, openmouthed. This was too unusual a morsel of news to miss. She could not tear herself away.

"You see, I was a renegade anyway—" began Murray.

"What did you steal?" the patient interrupted, raising his voice nervously.

"I stole your name, and I stole your job, and I've been living at your boarding place and using your things!"

"Well, you certainly did a smashing business! As I say, it didn't matter much to me, you see, if you could get away with it."

"But I didn't get away with it—that's it. I was held up."

"Who held you up?"

"God."

The patient eyed his visitor a moment, and a strange softened expression began to melt into his face.

"Sit down," he said. "Now, begin and tell."

"Well, you see, my name's Murray, too, my first name. Murray Van Rensselaer. Son of Charles Van Rensselaer. You've probably heard of him. Well, I broke a law, and then I didn't like the idea of facing the consequences, so I ran away. I don't know why I ran away. I hadn't been used to running away from things. I always faced them outright. But anyhow, that doesn't matter to you. I ran away, and after I got away I couldn't quite see coming back, *ever.* I had some money, and for a few days I kept out of sight and got as far as I could away from home. The day of your wreck I'd been traveling under a freight car because I hadn't any money, and we landed in Marlborough just at dark. Ever try traveling that way? Well, don't. It isn't what it's cracked up to be. When the train stopped at a crossing, I rolled off more dead than alive. I was all in. I hadn't had anything to eat all day, and I kept seeing cops everywhere I turned. So I hid till the train went on, and then I crawled off in the dark up a hill.

"By and by I spotted a light, and came to it through the dark, because I was so sick of going on I couldn't go a step further.

"There was an open window, and down just below me on a table in a basement I saw a row of cakes and bread. There didn't seem to be anybody around, so I put my hand in and took some and began to eat. I didn't call it stealing. I was starved."

The patient's eyes were watching Murray intently, and in the back of the room the minister was watching the patient.

"It turned out to be a church, and they were getting ready a big dinner to welcome *you*!"

A light shot into the eyes of the man on the pillow that seemed to suddenly illuminate his whole face. A surprised, glad light.

"A girl rushed out and called me Mr. Murray, and I tried to beat it, but it was all dark behind me, and my eyes were blinded looking at the lighted room, so I only got deeper in behind the bushes and ran against more church wall, and the girl followed me, laughing, and said she would show me the way, and that they were waiting for me. She said they had been so afraid I was caught in the wreck. She tried to pull me into the church, but I held back and said I was too dirty to go in, that my clothes were all torn and soiled. I said I had lost my baggage in the wreck. It seemed to be providential, that wreck, and I used it for all it was worth, for you see at first I thought I must have met that girl at a dance somewhere, and she recognized me and hadn't heard yet what trouble I was in. So I wanted to get away before she found out.

"But she said my trunk had come, and somebody named Summers was expecting me, and I could go right over to my room and get dressed, but I must hurry, because it was late. I tried to get directions, but she insisted on walking over there with me. I couldn't shake her. She seemed to think she had some special connection with me because her mother, she said, had known my mother.

"When we got to Mrs. Summers' house, she opened the door

herself and pulled me right in before I could slide away in the darkness. Of course I could have broken away, but that would have roused suspicion, and anything I *didn't* want was an outcry and the police on me; so I went in, and she took me up to the room she had gotten ready for you, and she actually smashed the lock on the trunk and went so far as pressing a pair of *your trousers* for me to put on, while I was taking a bath!"

By this time Allan Murray's eyes were dancing, and there was actually a little pucker of a smile in one corner of his mouth.

Murray hurried on with his story.

"There was no alternative but to get into some clothes and pretend to please the lady, for she was so insistent. You better believe I was glad of that hot bath, too, and I was still hungry as a bear. I hadn't eaten much for two days, and there didn't seem any way to get rid of her, so I helped her carry the scalloped oysters to the church, thinking I could slide out easily there. Boy! Those oysters had some delicious odor! I couldn't resist them. I almost took the pan and bolted before I got in, only there were too many people around watching."

The minister was smiling broadly now in the background, and Allan Murray was all attention. He had lost his sinister glare.

"Well, I got in there, and I couldn't get out. They introduced me right and left as Allan Murray, and I didn't dare deny it. I never realized before what a coward I was till I got into that fix, and then the doctor here asked me to 'ask a blessing,' and I didn't know what he meant. I never hailed with a gang like that before, and I hadn't been used to blessings."

The patient suddenly threw his head back and laughed.

"I found out I was a great Christian worker, and that I was the new teller in the Marlborough Bank, and that everybody was grateful that I hadn't been killed in the wreck," went on Murray with a flitting smile, "but I was mighty uncomfortable. There didn't come any good opportunity of getting out of there, however, and so I stuck it out, to my surprise, and got away with it! Even when Mr. Harper, the president of the bank, came to me and began to say how glad he was, I *got away with it*! Am I tiring you?"

"Go on!" shouted Allan Murray eagerly.

"Well, they herded me over to Mrs. Summers' again and sent me up to bed. There wasn't a second's chance to get away all that time without arousing the town, so I decided to wait till my hostess was asleep. But I made the mistake of lying down on the softest bed I ever touched, and boy! I was tired! And the next thing I knew they were calling me down to breakfast, and Mr. Harper was down there in his car waiting to take me to the bank.

"All day long they kept it up—for days. Never left me alone a second. I expected you to turn up every half hour, and I was worn to a thread with trying to keep up my part. At first I thought I'd stay till I got my first week's pay, but afterward I decided that as I had no name of my own I dared use, and as yours didn't seem to be needed by anyone, here was a perfectly good name and job, and I couldn't hide anywhere better than by taking another person's identity. So I settled down to be almost content in a condition like that! I was used to taking chances in anything that came along, and I suppose I just fell into it naturally.

"Then one day they did a dreadful thing. They made me president of the State Society, Christian Endeavor, you know. They say you know all about that."

Allan Murray's eyes lighted with keen appreciation of the situation in which his double was placed.

"I didn't know what it was like from a polo club, so when they made a great fuss about it, I said all right. But when I got to that state convention and saw what I was up against, I decided to beat it while they were singing the first hymn. And brother, I got the door in my sight, and my foot stretched out to take the first step toward it when God met me! Somehow He got it across to me that it was *He*, and I was a poor wretch of a sinner! And He wouldn't let me get out of that building! They were singing a hymn about hiding, and I was trying to hide, and right there, just as God stopped me, they asked me to make the opening prayer! Perhaps you wouldn't realize what that was like, being asked to pray before hundreds of people when you hadn't ever opened your mouth or your soul in prayer in your life! But I had to get up. And there I was facing God! I forgot all about the audience and just talked to God. I told Him what a wretch I was. I knew it then. I'd never known it before, but I knew it then. And when I sat down God talked with me! Sometimes it was in a prayer He spoke, sometimes in a Bible reading, or somebody's speech, but it came right home to me, and I found out I was a lost sinner, and only Jesus Christ could save me. I'd seen something about being born again, before I knew what it meant, and I'd wished I could begin life over with a new name and all, but I didn't know how, see? But somehow I've found out, and everything is different. I made a clean breast of everything this morning in church, and then I found your letter to Mrs. Summers. It got up in my room by mistake while I was away, you see. So as soon as we could we came to hunt you up. Now, Mr. Murray, can you see your way clear to forgive the rotten deal I gave you? I've done my best to square things up, and if there's anything else you'd like me to do, I'm ready. I belong to a new family now, and I hope I'm going to honor it more than I did the first one. I've heard ever since I've been in Marlborough what a great Christian you are, and I'm going to try all my life to be like you, to make up for the rotten way I masqueraded as you before I knew the Lord. *Can* you forgive me?"

Allan Murray reached out a long, thin hand and grasped the warm, firm one of Murray.

"I'll forgive you all right, brother, and from all I can see, you put over a pretty good effort at being me. Now you better try one better. Follow Christ, not me! I've found out the last few weeks that I hadn't as much religion as I thought I had. When everybody seemed to desert me and the good prospect I had was lost, and I seemed to be lying on the very verge of the grave, I lost hope and began to doubt the Lord. It was pretty tough lying here not knowing what was going on anywhere and thinking nobody cared. But I guess you've begun to make me see what it was all for.

It must have been a test, and I didn't stand it so very well either. I can see now. But if it's helped to bring a fellow like you to the light, it's worth all the suffering!"

Murray grasped both the other man's hands and held them.

"You're the right stuff, all right," he said. "Some fellows I know would have been too angry to speak to me for what I had done. But say, you're all wrong about nobody thinking about you. There's one. There's a girl. She wanted to know how you were. Her name is Anita. I don't know the rest of it. She went to school with your sister, and she was interested enough to ask me to find out about you and let her know. She'll be down to see you someday, or I'll miss my guess. And say, she's a good sport! She knew I wasn't you all the time. She remembered you had red hair. And she never told."

"She *is* a good sport," smiled the sick man. "You tell her I remember who she was. She played tennis with the champions and wouldn't take a handicap. And she gave up her place in a crowded hall once that a little lame girl might see! I wish she would come and see me. It would remind me of my little sister, Betty, who used to love her dearly."

"Yes," said the minister, rising and coming to the front, "Anita is a good sport. She's the best girl in the town of Marlborough. I could tell you a whole lot more things about her, but I haven't time now. I've got to get back to my evening service. The question is, how soon can we hope to be able to move you to Marlborough, where we can look after you personally? There's a whole church waiting to welcome you. I know, for look at the way they welcomed the man who came in your place! We love him, and we're going to love you just as much." He put his arm lovingly around Murray's shoulder.

"It looks to me as though I shall have a hard time keeping up with the pace you've set," said the sick man, trying to smile.

"No, you won't. Oh no! Don't you think it for a minute. You were born to it, but I've just been a great big bluff. Well, good-bye. You don't know how much easier you've made the rest for me, now that I know you don't hold this against me. I'll think of you in my room and teaching my class. I'm glad you're the kind of fellow you are. I shan't be jealous of you. I shall like to think about it."

"Nonsense! Man! Don't talk that way. You're coming to see me soon again, and we'll work things out together. I've a fancy you and I are going to be awfully good friends."

"I wish I could," said Murray wistfully, "but I've got an entirely different proposition to face. I'm going back home and give myself up for getting a young woman killed in an automobile accident, and I don't expect to see freedom again this side of heaven. But sometimes you think of me and work a little harder just for my sake, because I can't."

"Look here, brother," said Allan Murray, raising himself on one elbow and looking earnestly at Murray, "don't you talk like that! The Lord never saved you just to see you imprisoned for life. I'm going to get well in a few days now, and I'm going to spend time seeing you through. I'll begin right now by praying, and don't you give up!"

But Murray looked up with a bright smile.

"It's all right, you know, buddy. I belong to the Lord Christ now, and *what He wants is to go, from now on,* with me. I'm ready to face it all if that's what He wants for the honor of His name. That kind of living makes even dying worthwhile."

When they were gone and the nurse came in to turn on the lights and give him his medicine, Allan Murray was lying with wide-open eyes and an eager expression on his face.

"Nurse, how soon can I get up? I've a great deal to do, and it ought to be done soon."

The nurse looked up with a knowing smile.

"I don't know," she said brightly, "but I'll ask the doctor in the morning. I knew the best tonic in the world for you was to get in touch with the world again."

"It isn't the world," said Allan Murray contradictorily. "It's something better this time. *I'm needed.*"

Chapter 26

Murray Van Rensselaer had never held such sweet conversation with a man as he held with the minister on that ride home. Murray had never supposed there could be such a man as that minister, so strong and fearless, yet so tender and gentle, so wise and far-seeing, yet able to laugh and see a joke quicker than most: so wholly given up to the will of God. That was the secret of it all, really. He recognized that, untaught in holy things though he was.

And the minister on his part had conceived a great love for the young man who had come into their church under such peculiar circumstances. Somehow it seemed as though the Lord Himself had sent him and was caring for him in a special way. For it was no one's fault that Murray Van Rensselaer was taken into the church of God without the usual formalities and without knowledge of what he was doing. Not that there are not many thousands of young people swept into the church without any adequate idea of what they are doing, but they at least know enough to know that they are, as they call it, "joining the church." Murray did not know by that name that was what he himself was doing, but in heart he belonged to the Savior, body and soul. The work had been done in preparation wholly by the Holy Spirit Himself. Murray was in every sense begotten of the Spirit. Born anew.

As they rode along in the early dusk of the mid-winter afternoon, the minister marveled at this newborn Christian and the simple, childlike way in which he had grasped great truths and accepted them, which even scholars found difficult to believe. Taught of God, that was what he was. Not with the knowledge of men, but of the Spirit.

They rode into Marlborough five minutes before the evening service and stopped only long enough to pick up Mrs. Summers and move on to the church.

The news of Murray's confession had spread throughout the town that day, and the church was crowded. After the service the minister came down among the audience to speak to one and another, and happening to stand near Murray for a moment, he leaned over and whispered: "What a pity! See, Murray, all these people, and how you might influence them—*if you only hadn't to leave us!*"

"I know," said Murray, and his eyes drooped sadly; then, lifting his gaze anxiously, he said, "Do you suppose that heaven will have any way to make up for all the opportunities I've wasted here?"

Mrs. Summers and Murray sat by the fire a long time that night and talked after Mr. Harper had left.

Mr. Harper had come to say to Murray that he had entire confidence in him and felt that all would still be well in every way for his position in the bank, but he advised him to say no more about his past. One confession was enough. He needn't be telling it all the time. It would soon be forgotten, and everything would be as before.

Murray waited until he was all through, and then he looked him straight in the eye.

"That's all very kind of you, Mr. Harper. I know you're saying that for my sake. But I don't want it to be as it was before. It couldn't be. I've found out I was all wrong, and I'll have to be telling what God has done for me the rest of the time I have to live. As for the bank, I've *got* to leave you. You're very kind to ask me to stay after the way I've treated you and deceived you. I'm sorry to have to go away right off without waiting till you get a temporary person in my place, but you see it's just this way. I'm wanted by the state to answer a criminal charge, and there are some things that I must do to make right a cowardly thing I did, before I'm put where there is no chance for me to make anything right. Now that there are so many people who know who I am, there is no guarantee that I may not be arrested any minute, or else I would wait till you can fill my place. But I was with Allan

Murray this afternoon, and he thinks he will soon be able to come to you, if you still want him. He is a better man than I am. And everything will be all right for you when he comes."

But Mr. Harper was not to be appeased. He had taken a liking to this young man. He fit perfectly in with his schemes for the bank. The other might be all right, but he wanted this one. He was under no obligation to Allan Murray, since he did not come at the time arranged, and besides, there was room in the bank for another person if it came to that, of course. It was with great reluctance that he finally withdrew and left Mrs. Summers and Murray to have their last talk together.

It was then that Murray told her about Bessie and Mrs. Chapparelle. Told of his own home and his lonely childhood, though that was merely seen between the lines, not put into words. Told of the brightness of the little cozy home around the corner, and of the little girl who had been so sweet and cheerful a friend, then of the years between, and finally of his finding her that afternoon and taking her for a ride. He did not tell of their visit to Grevet's. He did not realize himself what part that incident had played in the tragedy of the fateful afternoon. But he told of his long wait in the hospital and finally of the approach of the nurse with the sad news, and his flight.

As he put it all into words, his own disloyalty and cowardice arose before him in their true light, and his shame and sorrow came upon him so powerfully that once he put his head down on the little tea table and groaned aloud. Then the little warm rose-leaf hand of the woman was laid upon his head tenderly, and he felt the comfort of her loving spirit.

They read together for the last time the precious fourteenth chapter of John, which has been the stay and comfort of so many saints in trouble throughout the ages, and then they knelt and prayed together. Mrs. Summers prayed for Murray, and finally Murray lifted a sorrowful voice and prayed, "Oh, God! Bless her—and help me!" Just a whisper of a prayer, but it must have reached the throne.

In the morning he drove away in the minister's car. The minister would only have it so.

"You are not safe in the train, son. They might get you arrested before your work is done."

The minister would have gone along, but Murray said no.

"I must face the music alone, you know. It was I who ran away from it, not you. And I'm not going to take you away from your busy days. But I'll send the car back safely, and I'll let you know how it turns out. I'll let you both know."

So he drove away.

Chapter 27

Mrs. Chapparelle was in the kitchen making pancakes again when Mr. Van Rensselaer came to the front door. She had to push the griddle back just as she had done once before, lest it burn.

The caller said he would like to see Miss Elizabeth, and she showed him into the pretty little living room, with its small upright piano and its few simple furnishings. He sat down and looked around him while he waited for the girl, for her mother said it was almost time for her to arrive home. Mrs. Chapparelle had gone back to her kitchen. She knew who the visitor was, although he had not given his name, and she had no desire to talk with him until Bessie came. She had little patience with Murray's parents. She thought they were to blame for what he was. Also she had not approved of Bessie's visit at the big house. She thought it had been unnecessary. Very likely that aristocrat had come to offer Bessie money or something, for her information, or else to bribe her not to say anything. She shoved the griddle back over the flame with a click and stirred her batter vigorously. The less she had to do with wealthy aristocrats the better!

Then the bell rang again, and she hurried to the door. Bessie must have forgotten her key.

Mr. Van Rensselaer had been looking over everything most carefully and approving of it all. There was taste in every article in the room. The one oriental rug before the couch was a fine old piece, and the couch itself was covered with pretty, comfortable-looking pillows. There was a tall reading lamp gracefully shaded over the chair where he sat, and there were books and magazines and a few fine photographs. It all had a homelike look, as if the room was used and loved.

A frown of annoyance gathered on his brow when the bell rang. He had hoped there would be no other visitor. Perhaps he could get the girl to take him out in the kitchen, where they could talk uninterrupted. He would like to see that kitchen. But then perhaps this was the girl herself.

Mrs. Chapparelle opened the door, and someone stepped in from the shadow of the front porch. She glanced at him, astonished.

"Why, *Murray*! Is it *you*?"

He looked so white and tired she felt sorry for him. But why should he come here after all these weeks? Had he then really been ill somewhere?

"Yes, Mrs. Chapparelle, it's Murray. But I'm afraid you don't want to see me."

"You look so white! Have you been ill?" she evaded.

"No, Mrs. Chapparelle, I've only been a fool and a coward and—a murderer—" he added bitterly.

"Murray!" She spoke in a startled voice.

"Yes, I know that's what you've been calling me, and coward, too, and I deserve it all and more. But thank God, He stopped me and brought me back. I'm going down now to give myself up and confess. But I had to stop here first to tell you and ask you to forgive me. I don't suppose you'll find it easy, and perhaps you won't give me that comfort. But I knew you were a Christian woman, and I thought perhaps— Well, anyway, I wanted you to know that God has forgiven my sins, and I belong to Him now. I thought that might make some difference to you. You were good to me when I was a kid—!"

At the first word from his son's voice, the father stiffened in his chair and grew alert, listening with all his senses strained. As the boy went on, an icy thrill went around his heart. What had Murray done now? A murderer? There had never been a murderer in the Van Rensselaer family to his knowledge. He tried to rise, but his muscles would not obey him. He found himself suddenly weak.

Murray's voice was going on haltingly. He seemed to be struggling with deep emotion.

"I thought I wanted you to know that I loved Bessie! I've always loved her, only she grew out of my life. Of course, I never was good enough for her, and she wouldn't probably have looked at me. I couldn't have hoped to marry her. She was a flower, a saint from heaven! But I loved her, and I shall always love her! If I were free—but there's no use talking of that. I don't want to be free! I want to pay all the penalty I can for what I did. But I do want you to know that I did not do it carelessly. I was not driving fast. My carelessness was in paying more heed to her than to what was going on around me. But I'm not excusing myself, only I didn't want you to think I was careless of her, or that I had been drinking!"

"Murray, what on earth do you mean, child!" broke in Mrs. Chapparelle. "Come into the kitchen, dear, and sit down, and let me give you a cup of tea! Why, your hands are like ice. Come with me!"

Mr. Van Rensselaer had got to his feet somehow and was standing in the doorway by this time, but neither of the two saw him. Mrs. Chapparelle had hold of Murray's hand and was drawing him toward the kitchen door. But just at that moment a key turned in the front door, and Bessie entered, all fresh and rosy from the sharp winter air.

Holding each other's hands, the mother and the young man turned with startled looks and faced her. None of them saw the shaken man standing in the doorway with a hand on a curtain on either side, looking at them all with growing comprehension and apprehension in his eyes.

The young man and the girl saw only each other.

"Bessie!" said Murray with a sudden light of wonder in his

307

eyes. "Bessie? You are not dead!" He dropped the mother's hands and stood an instant watching her to see if she were surely not an apparition.

"Murray!" There was great gladness in the girl's voice. A melting of the wall that had grown up through the years.

And then he had her in his arms. Her face was against his chest. His face was buried in her hair, her sweet bright hair. The others standing by did not exist for them.

The griddle in the kitchen had not been shoved far enough back. There was flame still under it. It sent up a strong odor of burning grease, and suddenly Mrs. Chapparelle, eyes blinded with wondering happy tears, hurried into the kitchen to see to it, mindful that she was not needed in the hall just then. She had forgotten entirely the visitor in the parlor, who was shamelessly happy at what he was witnessing.

He became aware that he ought not to stand there watching those two, at the same moment that Mrs. Chapparelle remembered his existence and hurried back to try to help out the situation. Murray and Bessie came to their senses about the same moment also, and there they all four stood and looked at one another, ashamed and confused, yet happy.

It took the man of the world to recover first.

"Well, my son," he said in a pleased voice, "you seem to have done something worthy of your family name at last!"

"Yes, Father, isn't it great? But everything's going to be different from now on. Oh boy! Mother Chapparelle! I just realized. I haven't got to give myself up after all, have I? I'm not a murderer! She's alive! And she loves me!"

They sobered down after a while, and Murray told them his story.

Mr. Van Rensselaer called up his house and said he was unavoidably detained and could not return until late that evening, and they all sat down in the little white kitchen and ate pancakes and talked. For hours it seemed they were eating and talking. Mrs. Chapparelle had to get more syrup and use the rest of the batter she had saved for the next meal and stir up more cakes. Mr. Van Rensselaer thought he had not been so happy since he was a little boy at home with his own mother.

The father did not talk much. He watched his boy. He listened to the wonderful story that fell from his lips, and in another language his sorrowful, hungry soul kept crying over and over to himself as the father of old, *"This my son was dead, and is alive again; he was lost, and is found!"* He began to rejoice that he would be able to kill the fatted calf for him. Nothing was too good for Murray now.

Then he turned his eyes to the lovely girl who sat with starry eyes and watched her lover who had come back through the years to fulfill the promise of the roses he had given her long ago. Come back a new Murray, with a new Name upon his lips, a Name that was above every name dear to her!

GRACE LIVINGSTON HILL (1865–1947) is known as the pioneer of Christian romance. Grace wrote more than one hundred faith-inspired books during her lifetime. When her first husband died, leaving her with two daughters to raise, writing became a way to make a living, but she always recognized storytelling as a way to share her faith in God. She has touched countless lives through the years and continues to touch lives today. Her books feature moving stories, delightful characters, and love in its purest form.

Love Endures

Grace Livingston Hill Classics

Available in 2012

The Beloved Stranger

The Prodigal Girl

A New Name

Re-Creations

Tomorrow About This Time

Crimson Roses

Blue Ruin

Coming Through the Rye

The Christmas Bride

Ariel Custer

Not Under the Law

Job's Niece